THE CASELLA BROTHERS

THE CASELLA

C.B. FREY

At times, even the strongest among us bear wounds that never fully heal; the pain shadows them throughout their life...until they encounter someone who teaches them that acknowledging the pain is the first step toward genuine healing.

To all who love a broken bad boy who is a hopeless romantic at heart, let me introduce to you Mr. Nicholas Casella...

Author Note

The Casella Ruin is a stand-alone, dark romance book part of an interconnected series. It does contain situations that could be triggering for some readers.

If you are after a steamy, enemies to lovers, slow burn, look no further. This book contains explicit language and explicit sexual content.

It is intended to be for readers 18+.
For a full list of triggers, please visit the author's website at
https://www.cbfreyauthor.com/

Alternatively, you can visit the author's Instagram at
https://www.instagram.com/c.b.freyauthor/

This is your last warning, this book is not for the faint of heart. It contains dark content, which may be triggering for some readers.

Playlist

Misery ❈ MEMPHIS MAY FIRE

Sympathy ❈ TOO CLOSE TO TOUCH

So Called Life ❈ THREE DAYS GRACE

Drowned In Emotion ❈ CASKETS

Bad Habits ❈ NERV

Hold Me Now ❈ CASKETS

Make Hate to Me ❈ CITIZEN SOLDIER

GODDESS ❈ WRITTEN BY WOLVES

Angel ❈ THEORY OF A DEADMAN

Tears Don't Fall ❈ BULLET FOR MY VALENTINE

Take Me First ❈ BAD OMENS

Fire on Fire ❈ SAM SMITH

Elastic Heart (Rock Version) ❈ WRITTEN BY WOLVES

Gone Forever ❈ THREE DAYS GRACE

Time of Dying ❈ THREE DAYS GRACE

Another Life ❈ MOTIONLESS IN WHITE

Hell and Back ❈ SELF DECEPTION

Without Me ❈ WIND WALKERS

Promise Me ❈ WRITTEN BY WOLVES

Sinner ❈ OF VIRTUE

Hopeless ❈ NERV

Masterpiece ❈ MOTIONLESS IN WHITE

Outta My Head ❈ OMIDO, RICK JANSEN, ORDELL

Heartbeat ❈ ISABEL LAROSA

Who Do You Want ❈ EX HABIT

Want Me ❈ EX HABIT

I Found ❈ AMBER RUN

PROLOGUE
Darcy

The musty air hits me in the face the moment the front door swings open, and I'm transported back to a time I worked so hard to remember. Memories I trained my brain not to forget. It's when I step into my bedroom that I realise it's been years since I have stepped foot in this home. A home I once hated. One I thought had high walls and gilded cages, hiding the secrets within it. The events of the last few days play in my head, and a tear trickles down my cheek before I swat it away.

Well, Darcy, you got what you wanted.

I brush the pads of my fingers along the crisp white walls which were once decorated with my family's portraits, but are now empty, just like me.

The faint scent of lavender creeps its way into my nose, and I notice a breeze carrying the scent through the open door. The familiar smell of my childhood—a time when so many things were much simpler. It's no secret that my family was not innocent, but I was.

Not anymore.

The things I've done are not forgivable. They cannot be forgotten, and there will come a time when I will need to accept that. But right now, all I want to do is remember the moments that I took for granted. The ones I imprinted in my brain, forcing myself to never forget.

I never thought the last few years of my life would ever happen to me. I thought I was destined to live like any other person would. The slow life…a life of *normalcy*, but in the Mafia, in the roles we play, our lives are anything but *normal*.

Being back here feels wrong, but I needed to relive what I thought was the cage keeping me out of the real world, but in reality, it was a cage keeping out the nightmares waiting for me.

I grew up believing that one day I would know another world other than the one I'm currently living in, and now that it's within my reach, I hesitate to grasp it. I hesitate because of the things I once believed, the people I once trusted. I want nothing more than to be done with this place, but my bleeding heart wants something else.

It wants him.

In a way, he saved me.

If there was one thing I was sure about, it was the way he looked at me. The way he really saw *me*. Not just some girl who was groomed to be something she wasn't supposed to end up being, but a woman who wore her heart on her sleeve, wanting nothing more than to be loved like she deserved it.

I'm not regretful about what happened, just how they did. I was young, naïve, and stupid for thinking love would be enough to fight the world we live in, the darkness that ensnares us when we sleep, and the lies—the never-ending lies and secrets that surface anytime things would go remotely right.

The rain patters on the roof of my childhood home as I sit on my bed, thinking about all the lies I've told and the secrets I kept hidden for so long only for them to creep up in my dreams, threatening to lay waste to everything I worked so hard to keep. Forgiveness isn't easily given by those who live in our world, but there's one person in particular I know whose heart is as fragile as mine, even if he hates to admit it.

I had spent the last six months living in a lie I forced myself to swallow because of all the things I had done and left unsaid. I lived a life I thought I wanted in a place far from here, but my heart remained in London with the man I swore I would never love. The same one who shares similar memories with me, the same life but in a different body. I never once considered us a possibility, not even when we were forced to marry, forced to be around each other even when we despised one another, but all that changed in such a short amount of time.

All of which…changed *me*.

Part One

CHAPTER ONE
Darcy

What is worse than living a life in the darkness? Marrying into the family who owns it.

The Casellas and the Brayfords have an extended history, spanning over generations. Throughout those generations, the life of a Casella, or a Brayford, has been filled with bloodshed, betrayal, and animosity, until today.

Or so they think.

There is nowhere left for me to go, and no one left for me to call. Throughout my entire life, all I've known is a war between our two families, and all I've seen is the blind hatred the men have harboured for one another and how quickly greed has taken the lives of thousands of people. As a woman born into a Mafia family, your role is simple.

Bear an heir.

I wanted more for myself than this. I even had plans in motion to escape, but then it all came crashing down when the Casella brothers murdered my uncle.

There will be no escape from this world.

No escape from *them*.

The door slams shut as Aries exits the bridal room, leaving me staring at myself in the mirror. If it were actually my wedding, one I did want, I would be ecstatic that I found the one person who was going to vow to love me forever. Instead, my stomach churns at the thought of marrying Nicholas Casella. He's arrogant, selfish, and conceited.

He makes me want to vomit.

As if it couldn't get any worse, he's the younger brother of Ezra Casella, the most notorious murderer and arms dealer in London.

My family's one true enemy.

Not that it matters anymore, now that they're all buried six feet underground. Besides me, the only living, breathing Brayford blood left.

I grit my teeth as my eyes skate over the stunning embellishments of my wedding dress, the gems shimmering in the light streaming through the stained-glass windows of the church. I was asked to pick a dress of my liking by my new mother-in-law, but I refused. Like anything they asked me to do, I refused. Which left Aries to pick one out for me. It's tight satin, hugging all of my curves, with thin spaghetti straps and a short train.

Makes it easier to run.

I hear the voices of guests who are beginning to gather in the church and consider every possible escape. I would do *anything* not to be married into this family. My mind races with thoughts of my freedom, and my heart begins to pound harder beneath my chest. Grabbing the knife that's sitting on the tray beside the scones, I wipe it clean from the jam and slide it inside my corset underneath my dress. This is the only chance I have at an escape, and if I don't try, I will never be free.

Quietly, I open the door to the small hallway, which leads to an exit opening to the back of the church. Luckily for me, there's no one in sight. Slowly, I slide out of the room, gently shutting the door behind me and making my way to the back door. I keep checking over my shoulder, nervous that someone will see, and when I finally reach the door, relief floods my entire body when I close it behind me and swiftly make my way through the trees surrounding the church, heading for the road. Adrenaline pumps through my veins as the air burns my lungs with every stride I make.

I can't worry about what I will do after I escape.

I can't let myself think that far ahead, because right now, I just have to make it out.

An eerie feeling settles in my chest as I see the road peeking through the trees. Turning my head back to glance at the church, I spot *him*, his long legs eating up the distance between us. It's like a fire has been lit beneath me as I pick up speed, my legs burning to outrun him. I purposely chose to wear shoes without a heel because this had been my plan all along, but even that choice didn't benefit me.

I feel a sharp sting on my arm as it scrapes against the tree, and I plummet to the ground, my muscles firing with each cell as I force myself up to keep moving. When I turn my head, I feel his firm hands on me, and the wind is knocked out of my lungs when he pins me to a tree.

"Let me go!" I yell as I struggle in his hold.

He grips me harder, his thick fingers digging into my skin, pulling me back, and shoving me into the tree again. Pain shoots down my spine as I look up into his chocolate eyes.

"You know as well as I do that if I let you go, you'll be dead before you could see another sunrise." His voice permeates the air surrounding me.

"I'd rather fucking *die* than be your wife." I force the words out through my teeth, and he leans forward, close enough for me to smell the alcohol on his breath.

"You have no fucking idea how much I wish you were dead." His fingers dig further into my arms as he looks me dead in the eyes. "If it weren't for my family, I would slit your throat right here." His eyes skate down to my breasts, and a smirk plays on his lips. "What do we have here?"

I glance down and notice the knife I had stashed earlier has ridden up, the handle clearly visible from my corset. His hand comes between us and slowly slides the cool metal out of my dress, holding it in front of my face.

"What were you planning to do with that, *fenice?*"

"Slice that disgusting smile off your smug face." I smile, doing my best to assert dominance back at him, but it's no use.

His temples twitch. "Don't promise me a good time if you can't deliver."

I struggle in his hold once more, moving every muscle I have to somehow overpower him, but it's useless. His six foot five frame is stocked with pounds of pure muscle, and as my eyes skate over his body, it hurts me to admit that if he wasn't my nemesis, I would consider him to be attractive.

"Let go of me," I say more calmly now.

"Are you going to run again?" he asks as he lifts a brow, a strand of dark hair falling onto his face.

"It wouldn't matter if I did, because you wouldn't let me get away."

"And don't you forget it." He leans into my space, his mouth barely brushing my ear as he speaks. "I vow to make it my personal goal in life to make yours a living hell. Until death do us part."

Pulling me off the tree, he shoves me in the direction of the church, and just like that, my one opportunity at escape has been burnt to ashes.

CHAPTER TWO
Nicholas

ONE DAY EARLIER

Music booms through the club as the women on stage sway their hips from side to side in their next-to-nothing outfits. I lift the drink in my hand and polish off the rest in one gulp. It's my tenth drink of the night, and it doesn't even begin to numb the pain clawing at me from within. I ignore the voices in my head as I grab my credit card out of my wallet and begin cutting a line on the table.

"Not again, Nico." Asher's voice is muffled by the buzz in my ears as I inhale the white powder. "You *just* fucking had one."

I shrug, sinking further into the seat. "Doesn't fucking matter, Asher." I lower my voice. "Nothing fucking matters anymore."

My eyes flick to a tall blonde walking over to me. She's been a dancer here for over a year now, that's how long I've been a loyal customer.

"Nico," she drawls as she sits on my lap, wrapping her arms around my neck. If it were another man, I guarantee they would be hard just at the sound of her voice.

I feel nothing.

"Why don't you fuck off, Lee?" Asher gives her a sarcastic smile, and she stands up.

She flicks her blonde strands of hair off her shoulder to her back. "You're always so rude, Asher," she says as she saunters off behind the bar.

"You need to stop this," Asher warns, leaning across the table, but I ignore him.

"I can't fucking watch you do this to yourself anymore." His voice sounds pained, but I don't care. Because what does he know about pain?

Asher has been close to me all my life. Our mothers are friends and have been for years. His older brother is Ezra's close friend, and Asher is mine. We spent our childhood growing up together, learning with each other what it means to be a part of this life. Our families have a long history together as allies, so consequently, we became thicker than thieves. He's seen the worst in me, and I've seen the worst in him.

"I'm not asking you to." I rest my head on the back of the lounge chair, the room now spinning.

"I know what you feel—" he begins to say when I cut in.

"No, you fucking don't." I sit up, gripping the edge of the table to steady myself. "Don't fucking sit there and pretend like you know what I went through when your father was everything mine was not."

"Dominic wasn't a father to you."

"Don't ever say his fucking name again!" I slam my fist on the table, rattling the cups, the painful reminder of my deceased father now in the forefront of my mind.

"I really wish you would just speak to someone about it."

"You sound just like my brother." I stand up out of the

14

chair, and my eyes clash with Lee's, so I nod her over to the private rooms. I lean over the table and stare him straight in the eyes. "Now if you'll excuse me, I'm going to bury myself deep inside Lee's throat until I pass out."

Following behind Lee, we enter the room and I take a seat on the lounge across from the pole. My hand slides inside my jacket pocket, and I pull out a cigarette, lighting it up as she saunters to the pole in the middle of the room, bathed in red lighting. I'll bet whoever saw me walk into this room with Lee thinks they know exactly what I'm after, but they have no idea what it's like to be me or be inside my head.

Music starts, and she begins to sway her hips when I feel my phone vibrate in my pocket, but I ignore it.

To hell with responsibilities.

Tonight is my night to stew in my pain, to accept my reality that no matter what I do, I have no choice when it comes to marriage.

I will be married.

And it will be to my enemy.

Taking a long drag from the cigarette, I feel the burn in my lungs as it travels back up and out of my mouth, a cloud of smoke blurring the air in front of me. The moment I am in right now is the one I seek, the comfortable numbness within my body and my mind as the drugs take effect, silencing the voices in my head.

"How do you want it?" Lee asks as she turns around, her back to me, and bends over, revealing the thin line of her G-string underneath her short skirt.

"I don't want to hear your fucking voice." My tone is harsher than I mean it, but she obliges as she walks over to me and kneels before my widespread knees. Taking another drag of my cigarette, she unbuckles my belt and unzips me, freeing my cock. I have a semi-hard-on, thanks to the drugs, but that doesn't stop her from taking me into her mouth and flicking the bar on my crown. I groan, my hand snaking into her hair and pushing her down until I hit the back of her throat. She gags, and her mouth doesn't even cover half my cock.

But I feel the need for more. More drugs to amplify the numbness as the voices crack through the invisible barrier I've desperately tried to build.

You will never be loved.

I shake my head, willing my eyes to open and focus on Lee, who is working desperately to get me off. I force her head up and down on my cock, taking my pleasure as the pain resurfaces.

"Open your fucking mouth like you mean it," I growl, and she complies, her eyes widening as she looks up at me.

Her hands cling to my thighs as I push her down, the piercings on my cock hitting the back of her throat over and over again. The sounds of her chokes fill the room, but I don't give her a moment to breathe because this is not about her.

It's about me.

"Ah fuck," I groan as the pleasure surges, my cock pulsing inside her mouth, feeling her throat close as she swallows around my cock. I push her to the side, letting go of her hair, zipping myself up, and I watch as she wipes her mouth, wobbling as she stands up off the floor.

"You may leave." I gesture toward the door, and her eyebrows pull in.

This isn't a night I want company, it's a night of mourning.

Walking toward the door, she mutters under her breath, "Dick." And I ignore her comment, not having the energy to fight anything or anyone tonight other than my own demons. My eyes close as I rest my head on the lounge, the voices overcoming me once more.

You're pathetic.

A fucking disgrace to the Casella name.

Why can't you be more like Ezra?

His fist comes flying into my face, and my body lands flush on the concrete floor, pain radiating through my arm as I taste the familiar metallic taste of blood pooling inside my mouth.

"The men in the Casella family do not have trivial goals in life, son." He reaches to touch my face, and I move away. "One day, I will make you into a man, even if I have to mould you into one with my bare hands."

His voice induces a toe-curling shiver through my body as I lay here on the cold floor, cradling my arm. The skin on my skull stings as he grabs the hair at the top of my head and forces me to stand. Before I can stop it, his knee jams into my ribs as I double over once again, my face pressed against the concrete. Tears sting my eyes, and I force them back, holding onto every bit of courage I have left inside me. There is no room for weakness with Dominic. Not from his enemies and certainly not from his own sons.

"Until that day comes, I will beat you black and blue." He kicks me again, and I cough, blood flying out of my mouth and landing on his shoe in front of my face. "No son of mine will have dreams other than remaining on top of the food chain, where we belong!"

I grit my teeth and force myself to breathe through the pain, just like Ezra taught me. In through my nose and out through my mouth.

My eyes spring open, and I watch the fan on the ceiling whirl, circulating the cloud of smoke in the room.

I was thirteen when he started hitting me. No one

knew. Not my mother or my brother. Even if they did know, what could they do?

Nothing.

Dominic wasn't just the king in the Mafia world of London; he was the king in our home.

A mad king.

I swallow down the bile rising in my throat at the memory. Although the bruises and cuts have healed and faded over time, the pain remains, etched into my skin and my bones, branding me, enslaving me to a lifetime of hurt. No amount of drugs I take will be enough to snuff out the memories, but that won't stop me from trying.

CHAPTER THREE
Nicholas

PRESENT DAY

The tingling I feel under my skin is usually there because of the things I do to escape. The decisions I make are questionable on most days, and I'm not an idiot…I can admit that. Tonight, however, those tingles feel like fucking needles against my skin as I watch her staring at her plate with a scowl covering her face.

She should be fucking grateful we spared her life, but instead, she insists on being a spoilt fucking brat about it. I don't want this either, but I'm doing it for my family because I have a duty to them—a duty to the founding families—and it seems she couldn't care less.

I hate it.

I hate everything about her. The way she speaks, the way she eats, the way she fucking breathes. She's an embodiment of the hatred that's plagued our families for generations, and she wears it with pride.

Her green eyes peer up at me from across the room, and I want to slide out the knife in my breast pocket and aim it straight between her eyes. She squints at me, and my teeth ache, the pressure in my jaw building as Asher yaps away.

"Did you do it?" he asks, and I don't respond, staring right back at Darcy, wanting her to break my gaze first.

"Hello?" he continues, then follows my vision and sighs. "Fuck, man, you have to let it go. If it was you, you'd have done the same."

"I don't run away. From anything," I say, still focused on her.

"That's a fat fucking lie." He scoffs, and thankfully, Aries approaches Darcy, forcing her to break the channel of our staring competition.

My gaze turns to Asher in his dark grey suit. "Name one time I ran away from something."

"Physically, maybe not, but you do it every damn day, Nico." He steals a glance in Darcy's direction, then back to me. "You can't keep running. Not from that."

"I'll never hear the end of it, will I?"

"Not until you decide to do something about it."

I don't want to admit it to him, so I won't, but he's never been wrong about me. "I don't want to talk about this." I push past him and head back to the table where Darcy sits. The music stops, and guests are ushered back to their seats as the emcee invites the bride and groom to the dance floor for their first dance. I can visibly see Darcy tense up, her body going rigid beside me. Clearing my throat, I glance around the room to see three hundred pairs of expectant eyes on us.

"Get up," I say under my breath, holding out my hand to her.

She takes her time, slowly rising and reluctantly placing her soft hand in mine. Avoiding eye contact, I guide her to the middle of the dance floor, and when our eyes meet, I want to smother the fire in hers. She steps into me, and I wrap one arm around her waist, feeling the delicate material beneath my fingers. A slow ballad begins as I lean down into her ear and whisper, "Make it look like you fucking enjoy it."

My feet move, but all I can see is the hate in her eyes, and all I feel is the hate in my chest with her perfume gliding around me, surrounding me in a cloud, when a sharp pain stings its way through the top of my foot.

"Oh, did I step on you?" She gives me a fake smile and chuckles. "My bad, I'm enjoying myself way too much."

Fucking bitch.

The engine roars underneath me as I pull out of the wedding reception with Darcy in the passenger seat. I stopped drinking the moment I caught her, knowing I'd have to be somewhat sober for tonight. Not because I want to remember it, but because I know if she's tried to escape once, she'll do it again.

The car ride is silent, as I prefer it to be, anger sizzling in my gut as I think about my life and how I must now spend it with someone who has been my enemy since before I was born into this world. Part of me wanted to run to escape this life and all its responsibilities, but another part of me craved the release that came with the blood and the pain.

I think about Darcy, the Mafia princess of the Brayford family. She no doubt would have had it easy. People would have dropped to her feet at her word if she so pleased it, and my lips curl into a scowl as I think about the stark differences in our upbringing, and it makes me sick to my fucking stomach.

Tonight was all for show, to let the other families in

London know that the last remaining blood of the Brayford family now belongs to us.

Loyal…to *us*.

There was no love, no lust, and no connection prior to this arrangement, but as for hate, there was *plenty* of that. If it were up to me, I would rip her head off, stick it on a pike, and wave it around at our enemies.

"Where are we going?" Her soft voice cuts through the silence as she looks out the window, watching the buildings pass. I don't owe her shit. *She's* the one who owes me and my family for sparing her fucking life, and like a typical spoilt Mafia princess, she demands to know where we're going.

"My apartment," I say curtly, and a silence falls within the car again, swallowing up the words left floating in the air.

She sighs, looking down at her hands, and I keep my eyes firmly on the road, refusing to feel even the slightest bit of guilt for how I'm treating her.

I look into the rearview mirror and spot Jayson in his own car, following us. He's been faithful to our family for years, just like Henry. His father worked for us as a bodyguard, and so did his grandfather. I trust him as much as I trust Ezra. Being the most feared family in London, unfortunately, you cannot go anywhere without a bodyguard.

"I want my own room," she demands, and I chuckle at her pathetic attempt at dominance.

"It's a one-bedroom. Sorry, *fenice*, we don't always get what we want," I say in a sarcastic tone.

"I am *not* sleeping in the same bed with you."

"Fine by me, you can take the floor." I shrug.

"Such a gentleman," she mocks.

"Guess what?" I pause for dramatic effect. "I don't give two fucks where you sleep," I whisper, a sly smile on my lips. "For all I care, you can sleep outside in the cold."

"I fucking hate you," she says through her teeth.

"Feeling's mutual."

God knows how much I cannot fucking stand her. All she is is a byproduct of her cunning family, and I refuse to see her any other way.

Reaching the apartment complex, I pull up into the underground parking lot. I refuse to take her into my actual home, so my investment property will do. She exits the car, slamming the door behind her, as Jayson parks next to me and begins unloading our luggage. Heading toward the elevator, I hear her footsteps following me, and when we enter, I push the penthouse button.

She scoffs. "Of course."

The elevator halts to a stop, causing her to jolt and her hands to fly out to reach the handlebars. I close in on her space, my face now just inches from hers.

"Let's get one thing straight, Darcy." Her perfume snakes its way into my senses again, and I hate that I enjoy it. "If you so much as *think* about betraying me or my family, I will bury you right next to the rest of yours."

She swallows, and her eyes drop to my lips.

"I'd feel nothing but relief in taking your life, but I made a promise to my family that I would do this for them." Her eyes find mine again, and the deep green swirls twirl like a tornado around her irises. "So don't get it twisted, *fenice*, I may be your husband on paper, but I will not treat you as such."

"You're delusional if you think anyone would want to

marry you out of their own free will." Her words leave a sting behind as they cut through me, but I don't let her see it.

"I hope you have more where that came from." I smirk. "Because with the way I'm going to make you suffer, you'll need that fire." I lean in close to her ear. "And fire burns, so be careful where you light it."

I press the button, and the elevator begins moving again as I step away from her. Within a few seconds, the doors open, and we step out into the large lounge space. I walk over to the bar cart in the corner of the room beside the lounge and pour myself a scotch. The alcohol stings my throat as I swallow, a sensation I welcome, but it's not enough. I need more.

Without a word, I leave Darcy standing in the middle of the room and head out onto the balcony overlooking the city. I've had this apartment for years now, but I've never lived in it. I always preferred to be closer to family, just in case they needed me.

Now, I need to be away from them.

I hate that they made me do this.

In their minds, it means nothing—just another contract to sign—but to me, it means everything.

It means giving up on the idea that one day I'd find that woman who would love me in all my misery and all my ugly, but there's no going back now…it's done.

I swore to myself I'd try to stop, but I feel the itch creep into my skin again, reminding me that beneath the cool exterior I try to convince others with, there's a demon lying in wait, ready to feast on my mind. I reach into my jacket pocket, removing the little plastic bag, and stare at it in my hands, fighting with myself, trying to convince myself that I don't need it, but the fight always starts this way—giving myself a reason *not* to do it, to find something to hang on to. Then the realisation comes quickly that there isn't anything worth clinging onto. Our world is filled with darkness and slick with blood, nothing good ever comes from living in it.

Glancing over my shoulder, I notice the lounge room now empty. I ordered Jayson to guard the elevator in case Darcy made the wrong choice, so I assume she's already in bed.

Walking inside, I remove the glass inhaler from my pocket and place them both on the table. I stare at them for a really long time when Asher's words ring inside my head.

You need to stop this.

How can you stop something when it controls you?

When in this reality, it's your only escape and your only salvation.

Dominic's presence smothers me when I shut my eyes and feel his hand tighten around my throat. My eyes snap open, and I'm tearing the bag. Before I know it, my nose stings, and the familiar wave of numbness and detachment crackles its way through my skin.

There's no point in fighting it.

This is who I am, who I will be forever.

I lay on the soft leather lounge, pulling my feet up and resting my head on the armrest, as I pictured what my life could have been like if I had run away like I planned when I was sixteen.

Would I be an addict?

Would I know love?

A calmness rushes over my body when my eyes grow

heavy, and I let it take me into its comfortable embrace, slipping into the familiar darkness.

DARCY

"Fucking jerk," I mutter under my breath as I open the suitcase Jayson had brought up. Everything is new, with tags. Given how I came to the Casella house, I didn't exactly have time to pack. Sifting through the clothes, I find some shorts and a tank top. I take them into the adjoining bathroom and close the door, locking it behind me and staring at myself in the mirror, wondering how it all went horribly wrong.

How did I get here?

Tears sting my eyes, but I fight them back, taking a deep breath through my nose. I can't afford to be weak because that's exactly what he wants.

Unzipping the dress, I remove it along with my corset and panties, then I step into the shower and turn on the water, letting the scalding hot water run down my body and hoping that it's enough to wash this night away. The memories of my uncle and my family resurface, but I can't lie and say it was all bad because there were some good times, but as the days pass, the good memories begin to fade, being replaced by the dark ones.

Every family has secrets, and mine was no different.

One thing I've learnt from them is that everyone wants something from you. In the end, it's all about what they can gain from you, not what they can give.

The secret I hold could either be the Casella family's downfall or their eternal reign over this city, and I'm not ready to give it up just yet...if ever.

Finishing up in the shower, I brush my teeth, get dressed, then walk out into the bedroom expecting Nicholas to be in bed by now, but the sheets are still perfectly made. Slowly, I make my way out of the bedroom and peek into the hallway.

It's quiet.

I tiptoe into the lounge room to find him passed out on the lounge, his jacket thrown over the armchair in the corner, and I stop, my eyes landing on a bag of white powder on the table.

Who the fuck sleeps straight after a line of cocaine?

Confusion rattles my brain as I stand there, watching him sleep, the top buttons of his dress shirt hanging open, revealing the intricate, dark tattoos on his chest travelling up to his jaw. I guessed he'd have more, considering his hands are covered in them too. Inching my way closer to him, I notice his phone on the table, and I move slowly, my hand reaching out to grab it.

"Do you need something, miss?" A voice filters through the room, and my head whips up, landing on Jayson.

I snatch my hand back. "No, uh, I just want a drink."

Jayson raises his eyebrows as if to call me out, and I hastily make my way to the kitchen, opening up all the cupboards, searching for the one with cups.

"Beside the fridge." He nods to the cupboard next to the fridge and watches me as I fill a cup with water.

If I'm going to try to escape, I need to come up with a better plan than winging it. Jayson is always with Nicholas, so I need to find a way for them to leave, together.

There isn't a chance in hell that I will accept that my fate is tied to a Casella.

I would rather die than give up on my freedom.

I nod to Jayson and head back to the bedroom.

Nicholas is still passed out on the lounge as I walk by him, and I wonder how he's asleep with us talking in the room. Closing the bedroom door behind me, I place the cup on the bedside table. My feet ache, and my head pounds as I slip under the cool sheets, and tonight is the first night in years where I feel safer than I have in a while.

CHAPTER FOUR
Darcy

Yawning, I open my eyes to find the adjoining bathroom door slightly ajar, and I stare shamelessly at the ink-covered body before me. His hands are placed on either side of the showerhead facing away from me, and the water cascades down his muscular back. Gulping, I watch as the water ripples over the large skull tattoo covering most of his skin, and it makes me wonder how many gruelling hours it must have taken to complete it. I force myself to peel my eyes away and silently walk out to the kitchen, noticing Jayson standing outside the elevator.

"Do you ever sleep?" I ask mockingly.

He smiles but doesn't respond, keeping his eyes averted from me. I reach into the cupboard and find a mug, then begin making myself a coffee. Technically, a newlywed couple should be on their honeymoon right now, soaking up all the love they have for each other.

Not us.

We're condemned to a world that controls our every move because of the blood that runs in our veins. Heavy footsteps thud into the open-plan living space, and my eyes flick up to find Nicholas in nothing but a white towel wrapped around his lower half.

I've seen my fair share of naked men.

Being the Mafia princess, I couldn't ever marry them, but I did have my fun with them. Only, they don't hold a candle against Nicholas, and it infuriates me that he makes me feel this way. His muscles flex as he leans to grab his phone from the table, his dark hair still wet from the shower. My eyes run over his chest, down to his abs, every ridge of him covered in ink, and down to the deep v that leads to where the towel covers.

I swallow, averting my eyes, and focus on stirring the sugar into my coffee.

"I'll be taking the motorbike today, J," he says, his eyes never leaving his phone, completely ignoring me.

Jayson nods "Of course, sir."

"You can stay and babysit." He directs his words to Jayson, looking up at me.

"I don't need a babysitter," I retort.

He chuckles. "I disagree."

I don't say anything as he turns and walks back into the bedroom, returning after a few minutes, completely dressed. His black distressed jeans hang on his hips, and I watch as he lifts his black shirt, tucking a gun behind his waistband. He grabs the black helmet that rests on the console table near the elevator, and within a moment, the elevator doors close, and I'm left alone with Jayson.

It's not ideal, as I hoped he'd take Jayson with him, but it's not something I can't work with.

I have no phone, no weapon, and no immediate friends or family who I can call for help. My freedom is in my hands and mine alone. I promise myself that I will get out, even if it means I might die in the process.

So be it.

An idea pops into my head, and I smile to myself.

Faking a stomach ache, I run to the bathroom and close the door behind me.

"Is everything okay, miss?" Jayson follows me, just like I hoped he would.

I groan and fake a whimper. "No."

"Is there anything I can do, miss?"

Bingo.

I rummage through the cupboards inside the bathroom and search for sanitary items in case they have already stocked them, and to my luck, they haven't.

"How do you people expect a woman to live here when you don't have everything she needs!?" I yell, forcing frustration into my voice.

"I—" He stops, clearly understanding what I mean. "I can get someone to drop them off for you?"

"I need it now, Jayson."

There's silence behind the door.

"Miss, I can't. Nicholas wouldn't want me to leave you."

Fuck these loyal guards.

"I'm bleeding onto my clothes here, and you're telling me that you won't do me this small favour?" I was so sure that was going to work.

"I'm sorry, miss, but I will get someone to bring you what you need."

I hear his footsteps diminish, leaving me with a disappointed scowl on my face. Ripping the door open, it bangs as it hits the wall behind it, and I crawl back into bed to work my brain down to its last cell to think of another way to escape. I don't know how long I lay here until my stomach growls, and I realise I haven't had breakfast. I throw on a dress after ripping the tag off and walk into the kitchen, opening the fridge.

It's bare.

Aside from a jar of jam, some pickles, and butter.

Scanning the apartment, I notice Jayson isn't at his usual post. My heart slams in my chest as the rush of escaping fills my thoughts. I look over to the elevator and rethink that idea when I realise I'll probably need a key of some sort to get to the private basement. Then my eyes glide over to the safety exit, and I feel my lips curve into a smile.

This is my chance, and I'm going to take it.

I walk cautiously over to the exit door and check the handle, pushing the door slightly ajar. I know some buildings have alarms when the safety doors open from any level of the building, but this one doesn't. I count my lucky stars and slip through the door, closing it softly behind me. Without a single drop of hesitation, I fly down the steps, taking them two at a time and skipping the last four. I look down the middle of the stairwell and groan when I see the endless amount of steps. I'm panting and sweating as I reach halfway, the air cutting into my lungs. I keep going, my thighs now burning from taking this many steps, but I don't dare stop.

Finally, reaching the basement door, I push it open, and in the centre sits a Maserati, a Bugatti, and a retro Yamaha motorbike. I glance around to see if anyone else is here, but the room seems empty, and I pray that I can find the keys stashed somewhere in the cars. Trying my luck, I open the door to the Bugatti, grinning to myself that it's unlocked, and slide into the driver's seat. I search frantically for a key everywhere in the car—the glovebox, the middle compartment, the sides, under the carpet mats —only to be left disappointed.

"Fuck!" My fists bang on the steering wheel as I let out

my frustration, and when I look up, I see Jayson in front of the elevator with his arms crossed.

My hands curl on the steering wheel, and my knuckles turn white from my grip.

If Nicholas thinks I will sit around for the rest of my life, he has another think coming.

It feels like steam bellows through my nostrils as I exit the car and walk toward the bench beside the wall, sporting gear hanging from it, and I find a machete resting just beside a row of motorcycle helmets.

"Miss, I think it's best we return to the apartment now," Jayson says calmly.

He has absolutely no idea who I am and what I'm capable of.

Without saying a word, I grab the machete, making eye contact with Jayson when his eyebrows pull in, slowly registering what I'm about to do. He goes to step forward, but I warn him, holding out the knife, threatening him that if he moves closer, I won't be afraid to hurt him.

The knife screeches against the paint of the Yamaha bike, peeling the black paint and ruining the beauty it once possessed as Jayson slowly creeps up toward me. I grip the handle in my hands and swing it, stabbing it into the top of the fuel tank.

"Shit!" I hear Jayson say as his hands come up into his hair.

My screams echo through the basement as I kick the motorbike again and again, letting my anger bubble to the surface and letting it take over me. My chest heaves as I stand back, the cloud of red now dissipating in front of me, revealing the once beautiful bike a tattered mess, scratched and bruised.

. . .

I spent the rest of my afternoon curled up on the lounge in silence. I had considered turning the telly on but decided against it. I wanted—no, I *needed* to figure out a way out of this mess.

Jayson walks into the lounge room carrying a box and places it gently on the table in front of me.

"This is for you, miss." He stands, placing his hands in his pockets. "It's from Mrs. Casella."

I nod, and he walks back over to his post, guarding the elevator. Sitting up, I turn the white box to face me and rip the card from it, tearing it open.

For tonight. Don't be late.

Opening the box, I stare at the emerald-green satin dress folded neatly inside it, and disgust slithers its way into my chest. They want to parade me around their friends and family like a possession, like some sort of trophy they have won. Tonight is the night Nicholas and I will present ourselves to the Mafia families of London to show them we are unified. It doesn't matter how much I hate the Casella family. I'm not stupid enough not to acknowledge that they have done me kindness. After the passing of my uncle and my father, other families will now claw to be at the top of the food chain, and they're all after one thing.

The knowledge and secrets that are left with the last Brayford blood.

Me.

I can't pretend my father was a good man because he was anything but. My uncle, however, was worse. My father died in a car chase with the police a few years ago, leaving me behind to be raised by my uncle. You would think the worst day of my life would have been when my father passed, but it wasn't. It was only the beginning of the horror waiting to unfold right in front of me.

I always thought love was nothing but a fragment of people's imaginations, but the love my mother and father shared was earth-shattering and soul-shaking. She couldn't stand to be apart from him, and so, after he passed, she took her own life. I had been out of the house the entire day, with my friends blowing off some steam, when I returned home and found the house eerily quiet. I called out to her, thinking she was in her room, but there was no answer. So I walked up the stairs and went to sleep. It wasn't until I woke up in the middle of the night that I heard the sound of water running from her room. I snuck in to see if she was okay.

Water seeped out of the bottom of her bathroom door and onto the carpet, and my throat closed up as I realised what I was about to walk into. As I took a few steps closer and opened the door, my eyes landed on my mother in the bathtub. Red streaks of blood tainted the water as it flowed from her wrists down onto the floor.

I froze, not knowing what to do.

What do you do when you find someone you love after they have taken their own life?

How do you react?

CHAPTER FIVE
Nicholas

My nails dig into the skin of my palms as I stare at my bike, the fury inside me multiplying with every second that passes. It's not about the money, I have plenty of that. I can replace that bike ten times over. It's the blatant disrespect she has for me for allowing her to stay with me under my protection that does it. Fury is unleashed within me as I make my way up into the penthouse.

"Sir?" Jayson stands guard at the elevator, quickly following behind me as I stride over to the bedroom.

I try the handle, and it's locked.

My fist pounds into the door. "I swear on my life, if you don't open this fucking door—"

The wood separating us opens, and my eyes fall to her moss green ones, then down to her body, the emerald-green dress hugging her sensual curves. I clench my jaw, swallowing my words at the sight of her, and I don't like it.

I fucking hate it.

My hand comes between us, closing around her throat in a flash, and her eyes widen as her hands come up to meet my wrist. Walking her back, I slam her against the wall, uncaring if it hurts. "This is how it's going to be, huh?" I step closer to her. "I leave you for five seconds and you act out?"

My eyes move down to her arms, and I notice the scars on them. I don't remember seeing them on our wedding night, but then again, I hardly wanted to look at her. My brows pull in, and she notices, taking her hands off my wrist and lowering them beside her.

"You're forgetting I don't *want* to be here." Her eyes pierce through my soul as she lifts her chin in defiance. "So do whatever you must. Kick me, push me, make my life my own personal hell, but you will never break me."

That fire.

She infuriates me so much that I can't see the line. The line is becoming a small dot in the distance, getting smaller and smaller as I fight with myself to stay calm.

"You're so fucking spoilt." Releasing my hand from her throat, she pushes me, but I don't budge in the slightest.

"You know nothing about me!" she yells, tears brimming in her eyes as her fists repeatedly pound on my chest. "You think you know everything about me and my family, but you have no fucking idea!"

I grab her wrists and pin her body to the wall with mine, getting frustrated at her outburst. She breathes heavily, her chest rising and falling against me, and I can't help but lower my eyes to them. Her porcelain skin contrasted with the deep emerald of her dress. A silence falls between us as I stare into her eyes again, hers dropping to my lips.

"Are you done?" My voice is calm, she nods, and I let her go.

We stand there for a minute, both silent, as Jayson interrupts.

"Sir, we're going to be late."

Right. The event in honour of the "happy couple."

"I'll be down in a few minutes," I say, and she nods, exiting the room without looking at me.

She's right. Technically, I *don't* know her. The only knowledge I have is of her family and all their malice towards mine, but I can't stop thinking about the marks on her arms. Some were raised, which looked like deep tissue scarring, and I can't help but wonder how that happened to her.

The car ride is silent, neither one of us wanting to rehash whatever it was that happened between us, and just as we reach the event, I see Ezra waiting for me. They call him the Casella King, and rightfully so. My brother is currently the most feared person in London, and sometimes he can even scare me. The difference between us is that Dominic made him into his prodigy and me into his punching bag. Ezra could do no wrong in Dominic's eyes. He was always beating me in everything, but he was older and faster than me. As the years went on, I started to catch up and even won against him several times in our sparring sessions.

Those days are long behind us now, though. These days, we're a lot more like brothers than rivals.

"Miss me already, brother?" I smirk, exiting the car and walking over to him. I watch as Darcy walks into the hall, her fiery red hair swaying as the train of her dress disappears through the double doors.

"You're not going to like this," he starts, and I sigh, waiting for the next thing that threatens to tip our world upside down. "I have information on our half brother in Italy."

I raise my eyebrows, intrigued by what he found out.

Something within me tells me that the Brayford family

was the tip of the iceberg. When we put them six feet under, we thought we would breathe a sigh of relief, but the joke was on us. All we wanted was for them to bend the knee and acknowledge the Casella family as their superiors, but their pride refused. Consequently, they met the force known as Ezra, but what we *didn't* anticipate was the volatile secret they hid for so many years.

Our half brother.

They took him straight after our mother endured hours of labour, only to be told he was stillborn. She had no idea what they did—how they betrayed her, stole him from her, and raised him as their soldier.

Now it's up to us to find out if he's on our side or if he will start a rebellion on behalf of the Brayford name. We can't afford more lives lost, but I know Ezra will do what he needs to ensure the succession of the Casella bloodline, even if it means an all-out war. Our men are loyal to us and will dive into anything at his whim, but the truth behind the fact is more lives will be lost in yet another bloodbath in pursuit of power. Generations have witnessed violence and malice in search of such, why would it change now?

"You found out where he's living?" I ask.

"Not exactly." He reaches into his pocket and pulls out his phone with the footage. "But we have this video of him entering a bar in Sicily."

I watch as this man, built like a fucking truck, enters a bar, pulling out guns in each hand and shooting five men in the space of a couple of seconds. The footage isn't too clear, so I have trouble seeing his face.

"Fuck."

"He's likely mixed up in some organised crime." He sighs. "Or he's gearing up for something bigger."

"Like revenge." I shake my head. "How fucking ironic."

That's the reality of our world, everything ends up coming full circle.

An eye for an eye, until we're all fucking blind.

"We need to find him, and soon," Ezra says, and I nod in agreement.

"When do we leave?" My thoughts race, and my adrenaline spikes at the promise of a fight, the promise of pain.

"Soon. I'll make the arrangements." He pauses, staring at me. "Darcy will need to come with us."

I grit my teeth. "No."

"You can't leave her here. The Dixons will fucking pounce the minute we're gone."

I hate that he's right.

The Dixons have been allies with the Brayfords for generations, since before we were born, so it makes sense that they would begin making moves against us. Their last act was fucking cowardly, kidnapping Aries's nephew and holding him ransom.

I nod at him, not wanting to admit he's right.

"How are you doing, Nico?" he asks with a softer tone than I am used to.

I shrug. "Fine."

He raises his eyebrows, calling me out on my lie.

"Are you using?" he questions.

"No." I lie through my teeth because it's easier than admitting how pathetic I have become, relying on ketamine to silence my mind. There's a sickness living and breathing inside me, clawing at me from within every day, and no matter what I do, it won't stop. It haunts me until I give in.

"You know I'd do anything for you, brother." He places his hand on my shoulder. "But I won't stand by and watch you dig your own grave."

I shrug out of his hold, turning to walk into the hall. "You don't have to worry about me, Ezra. Spare me your sympathy."

I step into the hall, and my eyes immediately search for her. It doesn't take me long to locate her fiery red hair, and I watch as she plasters a fake smile on her face, taking a sip from her champagne glass.

I don't believe her for a second…I know she knows more than she's letting on.

Grabbing a glass of scotch from the waiter, I make my way over to her when she excuses herself and walks out the door on the opposite side of the hall we entered from. I follow her, keeping my distance, intrigued if she'll try another escape. I watch as she walks out into the garden, toward the fountain in the middle. She pauses, her arms coming across her chest, hugging herself as she crouches down. I look around, noticing we're alone, and I step toward her.

"Darcy." My voice pierces the silence, and she gasps, standing and whirling around, wiping the tears from her cheeks with the back of her hand. My chest does something at the sight of her like this, but I ignore it and shove it back down into the abyss because, as far as I know, this could all be a game to her, one her family were experts at playing.

"What do you want?" she asks bluntly.

"Tell me what you know about my half brother."

"I told you, I don't know anything other than the fact that he lives in Italy." She crosses her arms across her chest, and my eyes fall to her bare arms again, covered with scars. I let my gaze linger on her raised skin, which looked like burn marks.

"Bullshit." My eyes meet hers again. "I don't believe you."

She rolls her eyes. "I have nothing else to say to you, so believe me or not, Nicholas, I don't give a fuck."

Stepping closer to her, I close the distance between us. "Be very, *very* careful how you talk to me, *fenice.*"

"You don't scare me." She tips her chin up, and my hand twitches with the need to close around her throat, our bodies almost touching.

"I haven't given you a reason to fear me." I lean into her ear and whisper, "Yet."

She steps into me, her body now touching mine, sending electricity rushing through me. She leans in, her lips almost touching mine. "There is *nothing* you can do to me that I haven't endured already," she whispers, and we stare at each other, the air crackling with tension between us.

It takes every ounce of self-control I have to keep my hands at my sides as she challenges me, but I still don't believe her. No matter how much she denies it, I know she's hiding something, and I'm determined to find out what.

She shoulders me as she walks back in the direction of the hall, leaving me to wonder about her past and who she was before she became my wife.

CHAPTER SIX
Nicholas

My heart pumps beneath my chest as I ride through the cold air of the night. I have no destination in mind tonight. My plan is to just ride until I can't anymore. Until the adrenaline runs out and I either die in a crash or run out of fuel.

The past couple of days have been the same, filled with tedious planning in our search mission to find our half brother and coming home to find Darcy locking herself in the bathroom until I'm asleep. Then I always wake to her soft snores in the early hours of the morning. She hasn't said a word to me since the event, which makes me furious that she can be as cold as I can.

My bike swerves around the corner, the headlights of the car slowly inching closer and closer. I veer to the left, our two vehicles now approaching head-on. The loud horn of the car vibrates through me, warning me to move out of their lane, but I rev the throttle a little more, inching closer, playing chase with death.

My breath stills, and just as we almost collide, I pull my bike to the right, back into my lane, and my heart thumps angrily, shaking my chest from within. It's absurd the amount of shit we put our bodies through, and yet it never gives up, autonomously pumping the blood through our system to keep us alive, oblivious to some of the cancerous thoughts our minds are able to conjure.

I enter the apartment through the elevator and place my helmet on the dining table. It's late, and I assume Darcy is already asleep, leaving me alone once again.

Jayson emerges from the fire escape and nods to me. "Safety check," he says as he resumes his position by the elevator.

I move into the lounge room and reach into my pocket, pulling out the poison that will one day kill me, but I'm too far gone to care. I'm not afraid of the hurt or the pain because it's something that lives with me, and like a pet, my mind feeds it consistently every day, causing it to thrive.

I placed it on the table and cut a line with a card that was already there. It's becoming harder and harder to drown out the noise, to have peace within my own mind without this, and it's come to a point where I think maybe my family and the world would be better off without another killer in it.

Would it ever be possible to be free of this?

Free of the pain?

I pick up the glass inhaler as an unexpected soft voice filters through the room.

"Why do you do that to yourself?"

I look up at Darcy, now standing by the fireplace in front of me. Her skin was completely covered, masking the pain or hurt she endured in her past life, and I wish it could do the same for me, but my scars run deeper.

"Why do you care?" I ask, my voice void of emotion.

She ignores my question. "You have a family." She pauses, looking to the floor. "Is that not enough?"

I chuckle, leaning back into the lounge. "A Mafia princess like you wouldn't know the first thing about responsibility and how much it weighs to carry with you every. Fucking. Day."

"You don't know me," she whispers.

"And *you* don't know *me*," I retort.

She looks down at the drugs on the table and back at me, but there isn't judgment in her eyes, it's something else. Something familiar.

The night always brings up the worst in us. During the day, it's easy to squash the trauma into yourself as you're surrounded by people and the sun. When the night comes, that's when it gets hard. That's when the voices in your head come out to play, and that's when you thirst for an escape.

Darcy walks slowly and sits beside me, bringing her knees up to her chest, still staring at the line on the table.

"I know more than I let you believe." Her stormy green eyes drift to mine, swallowing me up in them, and for a second, I forget where I am.

"I don't need your sympathy." I look away, not wanting her to see my weakness.

She sighs, and I look back at her.

"Do you ever think about how different our lives might have been had we been born into a different family?" she asks, and my brows pull in at her words. Not once have I considered what she thought about our families or our world, because I didn't care.

"That's called being delusional."

She scoffs. "As opposed to getting so fucking high that you pass out?"

I grit my teeth at her words, feeling like the walls are closing in around me. I stand and walk to the other side of the table, turning to face her. "You will never understand, because your life was so fucking perfect," I seethe.

Her breathing accelerates as she stares at me, her eyes tightening. "Are you so fucking dense to think that just because I grew up as the daughter of a Mafia boss that I had everything I ever wanted?" she questions, standing up.

My jaw aches from how hard I'm clenching.

"You're so self-absorbed that you don't even see what's right in front of you." Her fists close as she practically vibrates from anger. "You don't see that your actions have consequences, and those consequences hurt the people around you."

"Self-absorbed?" I chuckle. "Says the Mafia princess now left with the entire treasure of her traitorous family." I step into her, and she doesn't move, our bodies now flush with one another. I glance down and notice her hard nipples poking through her white shirt. "You *wanted* them to die, didn't you?" I whisper.

Hurt flashes across her face as her hand flies through the air, landing on my cheek with a sting. "Fuck you!" she spits and turns to walk away.

I grip her by her upper arm, yanking her back into me. "What's wrong? Did I hit a nerve?" Her hand rises again, but I catch her wrist this time.

"If you're going to hit me, at least make it hurt." I give her a twisted smile and lean into her, my lips brushing her ear. "You have no idea what it's like to want freedom from the pain I carry in my chest every fucking day of my life."

Her eyes find mine, and she looks away. "I guess that's one thing we have in common," she says softly, her eyes returning to mine.

"What pain could you have possibly endured within the high walls of the Brayford mansion?" I question, and she pulls out of my hold, pushing me away to stare at me with tears pooling in her eyes.

"We both know what grief feels like, Nicholas, but what you don't know is how that grief morphs into hate because of the vile, disgusting acts of the people who you thought loved you." Her words send a knife twisting inside my gut as I realise we might have more in common than we think.

She leaves, slamming the bedroom door behind her, leaving me to fight with myself once again, alone with the echoing voice of Dominic Casella in my head.

You're a worthless piece of shit.

You might as well get it over with…what are you waiting for?

I feel the anger surge beneath my skin, lighting up the flame beneath my chest, and in a flash, I'm snorting the line I just cut, desperately needing to stop feeling. I keep my eyes on the bedroom door, thinking about everything that has been said between us, and I hate that I'm starting to wonder about her past. I hate that it's beginning to affect me more than it should.

My head spins, forcing me to lean back into the lounge, the comfortable numbness now spreading its angelic wings and taking me into its warm embrace. My eyelids grow heavier with each passing minute, forcing themselves shut, and eventually, my mind settles, releasing me of the trauma chained around my neck…for the next hour at least.

CHAPTER SEVEN
Darcy

After what seems like hours pass by, I close my eyes, ready for this night to be over and for a new day to begin, when I hear the bedroom door open. I open my eyes slowly, watching as Nicholas walks into the room, removing his clothes, and I quickly shut my eyes again, hoping he didn't see me. It's dark, and shadows coat the walls, so I assume he thinks I'm asleep. I strain my ears to hear him shuffle toward the bed as it dips on the other side. He sighs as he lays down, and I feel his aura surround me, it sucks me into its vortex, draining any hope I had stashed away in my heart. We may not know a thing about each other, but our families had been at war for so long that it left no part of us to humanise the Casella family, and I'm sure it was the same for them.

This is the first night since we signed the marriage papers that he's been in this bed, and I know it's not because he's a gentleman. I battle with my self-restraint to stop myself from turning around when the image of him in the shower returns, and it stirs something in me I wish it didn't.

I try to focus on something else, forcing myself to give in to sleep, but my body doesn't want it. After a long, long time, what felt like days, I give in, and when I wake, I find myself alone, as I expected.

Sighing, I get ready for the day, remembering that Aries had invited herself over and would be here soon. When I met her, I knew her priorities from day one.

Ezra.

I saw it in her eyes—how much she wanted to please him, how much she just wanted to belong in our world— that she was desperate enough to turn herself over to us to prove a stupid point. Ultimately, they won. My entire family has been eradicated, and Aries was the one who convinced them to spare me, but I'm starting to think death would have been the easier way to gain my freedom.

The elevator dings, and I walk out into the lounge room to greet her. I can't help the smile that covers my face at the sight of her. She's practically the only person I would consider a friend in this fucked-up world. A genuine soul who wants the best for everyone. Too bad she's married to a psychopath.

"There you are." She smiles, placing a tray of food on the table. "I thought Nicholas might have scared you off."

"It takes more than a wounded little puppy to scare me."

She laughs, taking a seat on the lounge, when her eyes land on the glass inhaler still there from last night and immediately rise to meet mine, sadness replacing her smile.

"How often?" she asks.

I shrug. "Probably every night."

Her frown deepens, and it's clear this has been a longtime issue with Nicholas.

A moment passes as I sit next to her. "Do you know why he does it?"

She sighs, unsure if she should tell me. "Nico has a lot of trauma," she begins, then stops herself. "It's really not my place." She shakes her head.

"Have you packed?" she asks, and I nod. After the event, Ezra explained to me why I had to be with them in Italy, and although I wasn't thrilled about being with Nicholas in another country, I had hope that this would be my chance at freedom.

"When do we leave?"

"Tomorrow," she answers. "But I'll be staying in London."

Silence falls between us again, and I know she's here for a reason. Aries and I aren't close, but I thought we had some sort of connection when she was held captive by my uncle. I tried to help her, to get her out, but she was too fucking stubborn to listen to anything I had to say.

"Is everything okay?" I ask.

I'm not good at this, talking about emotions, and wearing my heart on my sleeve. At a young age, we were taught to bottle it up until it overflowed.

She sighs and frowns. "It's my sister, Giselle. I don't think she will ever speak to me again."

Her sister's son was kidnapped by the Dixon family only a few months ago, and I think that's all the family she has. Luckily, Ezra and Nicholas found him, and I feel for her, it's not that I don't, but I have my own priorities to worry about.

"I'm sorry," I say as she wipes away her tears with the back of her hand.

She excuses herself and walks toward the bathroom, closing the door behind her. My eyes drift to her handbag on the lounge, and without thinking, I rummage through it, finding her phone. I try every single passcode I can think of, but none of them work. Getting frustrated, I shove the phone back into her bag and wait for her to come out.

I have a plan, but I guess I just need to wait for the right moment to execute it.

She emerges from the hall with a grin plastered on her face. "I have good news." She beams.

"Unless the news is that I'm finally free, I don't particularly think it's good news *for me,*" I counter, and her smile falls. I feel a little guilty for being this way with her sometimes, but I can't let myself get close, especially not to someone who's married to Ezra.

"Ezra approved for us to go shopping together." She raises her hands just as I'm about to protest. "Now I know what you're going to say, but it'll be good for you to get out of these walls."

I fucking *hate* shopping, but it would give me a chance to escape, or at least find a phone and call my *friend.*

"Fine." I give in, hoping I can formulate a plan that I have been stuck on figuring out.

The guards stand by us like we are royalty, and in a sense, I guess we are. Just not the same royalty as a lot of people would think. There are only two guards, Henry and Jayson, which makes things a little easier. Not that this is going to be easy, but it's better than having four guards watching your every move.

"Aw, this is so beautiful, don't you think?" Aries asks as she holds up an obnoxious fluffy pink little girl's tutu, and my heart sinks.

I try to hold back the anger as I swallow my words. "Sure, if you're into that."

I pretend to browse the rack filled with tops when I notice an older woman beside me has her handbag left open. I take my chance, and as she holds up a shirt to view it, I slide my hand into her purse, and by luck, the first thing I touch is her phone. I hide it under my shirt in between my skin and the waistband of my pants, my eyes skating to the door where Henry and Jayson wait. They didn't see me, and I need to make sure we get out of here before this woman realises what I've done and creates a scene.

"I'm not feeling too well, I think I need to head to the restroom." I don't wait for Aries to respond when I walk out the door and head to find a restroom with Jayson on my tail.

Once I'm in the cubicle, I hastily remove the phone from my waistband and begin dialling the number I've had memorised since I was twelve. I'm lucky the old woman had an older phone and not a new one which almost always requires a passcode. Holding the phone to my ear, I wait as the dial tone begins.

Please pick up.

Please pick up.

Please pick up.

He answers on the second ring but stays silent.

"It's me," I say in a hushed voice, hoping Jayson is still standing by outside the restrooms.

"I thought you were dead." His gruff voice echoes through me, but I sigh in relief.

"Cheated death, once again."

"Where are you?"

"The Casella brothers have me, they forced me to marry Nicholas to show solidarity between us."

"Are you okay?" he asks, and tears brim my eyes, but I fight them back, not wanting to sound weak.

"Fine, but I need your help."

"Name it."

"I'm going to Italy with Ezra and Nicholas, and I need you to get a message to the Dixon family."

"Are you sure you know what you're doing, Darcy?" he questions, and my confidence in myself to pull this off wavers slightly.

"Positive."

"What's the message?"

CHAPTER EIGHT
Nicholas

The clouds above grow darker as we stand out there, waiting. We leave for Italy tomorrow, and although I'm glad to be leaving London for a bit, I'm also hesitant about what this journey is going to bring for our family. Ezra is convinced everything is going to work out in our favour, but that's him. If things don't, he will force them to in his own sick, twisted way. One question that I can't get out of my head is if this man knew who he was, why would he not make contact years ago?

I lean against the car and watch Ezra type away on his phone. For as long as I can remember, it's always just been us, and now that we could possibly have another brother, it just seems bizarre to me.

"How's Mama?" I ask.

She took it the hardest when we found out. They made her believe that our half brother died at birth, and there was never any mention of him again. Why would there be? He was a bastard. Born out of wedlock. The worst part is that our mother stood accused of having an affair prior to her wedding to Dominic.

"She's working through it," he says without looking up from his phone. "But she did ask me not to kill him."

"We're not going to, right?"

He shrugs. "I will if I need to."

A young man comes out of the bar and hands me a duffel. "It's all there, boss, I swear. I counted it myself."

Placing the bag on the hood of the car, I unzip the duffel and make sure he's telling the truth. To my surprise, he was. The bag is filled to the brim with bundles of one-hundred-pound notes. "Great, now make sure the rest of your establishments know about the new cost of running a business with the Casellas."

He nods and walks back into the bar.

Usually, this sort of job would be done by some of our collectors, but tonight, we made it a point to collect ourselves. After the death of the Brayfords, you don't know who will be turning on you now that one of the founding families has been sent to meet their makers.

There were four founding families, including ours. The Brayfords, the Dixons, and the Guerras. Throughout generations, the space between our families continued to grow as the financial climate in London grew, the piece of the pie beginning to get larger and larger. People got greedy and wanted a lot more than they were given. Now, as it stands today, our family and the Guerra family stand strong together where the Dixons had always favoured the losing side, the Brayfords.

"I need you to be straight with me," Ezra speaks, and I turn to him, his eyes locked on mine.

I clench my jaw, already knowing what he's going to ask me.

"If you're using again—"

Opening the car door, I throw the bag into the back seat. "I already told you. I'm not."

"Don't lie to me, Nico."

"Fuck, Ezra, why does it fucking matter as long as I show up?" I slam the door shut.

"It matters because I need you, brother. It matters because I can't fucking do this without you."

"Spare me the older brother lecture." I throw him the car keys and begin walking away.

"Where are you going?"

"Somewhere you're not, my king." I turn to bow sarcastically and continue to walk.

It's late, and although I drove here with Ezra, I can't stand to be with him any longer because I can sense the judgement from his voice alone.

The sky darkens further, and droplets of rain patter against my face as I continue walking home. Ezra has it good, married to the love of his life, the king of London's crime lords, but I wonder if he wasn't so lucky if he'd be telling me to pull myself together or joining me in snorting lines. I bet it'd be the latter. After all, who are we without someone to love and give all of ourselves to? What the fuck is the point of all this shit if you have no one to share it with?

I can't help but feel jealous of what my brother and Aries have.

After a good hour of walking, I finally make it to the penthouse, completely drenched. There's something cleansing about taking a walk in the rain, and whilst others hide from the thunder and lightning, I embrace it.

Scanning my card, I press the button to the penthouse and lean against the wall, water dripping from my clothes onto the floor. I remove my jacket, and just as I remove my shirt, the door opens. Soft music floats into the hallway as I make my way to the kitchen to see Darcy mixing something in a bowl.

"What are you doing?" I question, and I watch her eyes

find mine, but I don't miss the way they scan my chest, down to my abs.

"Baking." She continues mixing the contents in the bowl, chocolate powder smeared across her forehead.

"Why?"

She slams the bowl on the counter in a huff and washes her hands without replying to me. Glaring, she tries to speed past me, but I grab her by the arm.

"I asked you a question." I speak through gritted teeth.

She looks up at me, and the hate in her eyes would be enough to melt metal.

"What else is there to do between these four fucking walls!?" she yells, trying to push me away. "Let go of me!"

I hold on to her tighter, almost bruising her as her body presses against mine, reveling in the fact that being here is causing her pain. She fucking deserves every bit of it.

"This is nothing compared to what your family did to mine, *fenice.*"

She stops for a moment, staring at me and her eyes drop to my lips.

"Your uncle shot mine, stole a baby, who happens to be my half brother, and the worst part is he convinced another founding family to betray us." Her perfume engulfs my senses, and I instinctively want to bury my face into her neck. "So I think keeping you prisoner in these four walls is considered *mercy.*"

"Are you saying I should be grateful?" she asks, astonished.

"You should be praying to whatever or whoever you believe in that I don't change my mind about killing you." I let her go, and she stands there, chin up, staring at me with defiance, and it makes me so fucking mad. It makes me want to throw her against the wall and make it hurt.

"Go pack your stuff. We leave for Italy in the morning."

She crosses her arms, the outline of her nipples clearly visible through her tank top, and it takes everything in me not to stare, so I reluctantly tear my eyes away and head to the bathroom for a hot shower.

Darcy follows me into the bedroom, and I watch from the mirror in the bathroom through the door ajar. She places a suitcase on the bed and begins packing some of her clothes.

Placing my hands on the sink, I lean forward, slumping my head down, and take a breath. I feel the itch consume me again, and I try so fucking hard to hold it back. The thing about drugs is it starts off slow, maybe one hit a week, then it turns into something more. Before you know it, you're sitting on the couch, snorting lines until you can't feel your fucking face.

After removing my belt, I take off my pants and briefs and turn the shower on. My eyes catch Darcy's in the mirror, and something foreign places itself inside my chest. She quickly averts her eyes, and an involuntary smile plays on my lips.

Once I've showered, I wrap my bottom half in a towel and turn the light off, entering the bedroom to find Darcy already underneath the covers. The urge to use again is still there, nagging at me, calling my name so fucking loud, it's almost deafening.

"I can't fucking do this without you."

My brother's words ring in my ear, merging with the echoes of my demons, chewing away at me. I know he's right, and yet, I know what I'll feel if I stop. I know what I'll go through because I tried to stop once.

I was sober for an entire month, and it was fucking

hell. The rage, the insomnia, the fatigue, and the nausea alone are enough to cause anyone aggrievement, but couple that with Dominic's voice inside your fucking head, and you have your own personal asylum.

I chew the inside of my mouth, fighting with myself again as I watch Darcy stir beneath the sheets.

Giving in, I walk myself out to the lounge room and cut a line, then another, and another. I feel it all hit me at once, and I lean back into the couch, the numbness overpowering my will to keep my eyes open. I give in, succumbing to the darkness once again, sitting here with the familiar feeling of shame and guilt swirling around in my gut. I want to be better, it's not that I don't, but I can't. I will never live up to the expectations of others because of the sickness that breeds inside me every fucking day, licking at my wounds with a razor-sharp tongue.

It hurt.

I was too fucking young to experience what I did.

No child should ever be abused by the hands of their parents, the only people whose only goal on this earth is to protect their children from pain. Unfortunately for me, Dominic Casella only cared about his status and reputation.

CHAPTER NINE
Darcy

Something has changed between us since last night, and I don't know what. I want to believe that I'm doing the right thing for myself and seeking my freedom. Even if it means he might catch me and kill me, I can't give up. I can't give in, not when I'm still living and breathing. I will never again put my faith in the wrong people.

Only in myself.

I sit across Asher and Jackson, brothers from the Guerra family, in the Casella private jet. They're both staring at me, trying to read my mind from where they sit. They obviously don't trust me, and I don't blame them. Our families have been at war for a long time.

Nicholas sits on the other side of the jet with Ezra, away from me. We haven't said a word to each other since last night, and I can't help but wonder what he's thinking. We've been in the air for about an hour now, so there's not much left of the flight.

"I hear you ruined Nico's bike." Asher smirks at me.

I shrug. "Not like he doesn't have the money to replace it."

He chuckles, and my eyes skate to Jackson, whose expression is comparable to a stone.

Leaning forward, he rests his elbows on his knees as he

clasps his hands. "Let's clear the air before we land." His rough voice vibrates through the air. "I don't trust you."

As you shouldn't.

I lean forward, mimicking his posture. "I. Don't. Care." I give him a sarcastic smile.

They both look similar, both have brunette hair, Asher's slightly shorter than Jackson's. Both have blue eyes that are dark, like a gyre. Jackson's hair is slightly lighter, with grey speckled throughout.

He scowls at me, leaning back into his seat, his eyes never leaving mine. I get it, he doesn't like me or trust me. The feeling is mutual. Fuck these guys, I don't need their approval any more than I need them to like me.

We finally make it to Sicily. Ezra, Asher, and Jackson have taken off somewhere, leaving Nicholas and me to travel together to wherever the hell we'll be staying. He doesn't say a word to me. Static silence cracks loudly between us.

We pull up to an enormous white villa that looks like something out of a movie. It's ridiculously large and definitely doesn't look like a rental property. I wouldn't be surprised if this was a holiday home of some sort for them. Nicholas kills the engine and, without a word, steps out of the car, grabbing his bag from the back seat, leaving mine behind as I watch him walk off toward the villa.

Fucking jerk.

I slam the car door after I've grabbed my bag and reluctantly follow him. The double entry doors open into a wide, open-plan living area. There is a lounge on the left and a huge white kitchen on the right with all the latest appliances. The floor-to-ceiling glass doors extend throughout the entire back of the house, revealing a scenery I have never seen before in my life. The exquisite blue of the beach sparkles in the sun beneath the cascading mountains, and I instantly feel lighter. I guess being here wouldn't be so bad with a view like this to wake up to every day. Even so, I know I need to continue with my plan.

Nicholas drops his bag and answers his phone. "We just got here." He walks over to the fridge, opening it. "What?" He looks at me, and my heart flutters at the way his large hand squeezes the door of the fridge. "You're fucking joking, right? You said we'd all be staying together." He slams the door shut and walks outside.

Together? I guess that makes sense then as to why we were in such a huge villa. My mouth goes dry thinking about being in this place alone with Nicholas, but then I remember there must be more than one bedroom. A smile creeps onto my lips as I make my way up the staircase and pad toward the double doors at the end of the hall. Opening them, my mouth almost drops to the floor. A huge king bed sits on the right with floor-to-ceiling windows opposite me, overlooking the ocean.

It's beautiful here.

Placing my suitcase on the bed, I walk over to the set of drawers and notice a bunch of picture frames stacked together. Picking them up, I realise they're of a family, and the two boys look very familiar. It takes me a little to put two and two together that the photos I'm staring at are of the Casella brothers, and the innocence in their childish faces makes me smile. Ezra has his arm around Nicholas, who has ice cream smeared all over his mouth, smiling so wide, you can see almost all of his teeth. He's a completely different person from the child in this photo. In fact, I couldn't even recognise the similarities between them when I first picked up this frame.

My chest tightens as Nicholas's voice startles me.

"I was eight."

He leans on the doorframe, the top buttons of his black shirt hanging open, offering a view of his dark, intricate tattoos. My eyes scan over his tall figure, his black eyes on mine, and I hate the way he looks at me.

"You were cute," I say as I set the frame down. "Shame, you're just a dick now."

He chuckles, and I turn away from him, feeling my cheeks heat at the sound of his deep voice. I curse myself for thinking of him in any other way besides as my enemy, but I can't deny the physical attraction between us, as much as I desperately want to. I will, however, ignore it and shove it down into the darkness where it belongs.

"We'll be staying here for a while."

Damn. That doesn't help me in any way.

"How long?"

"Not sure," he says as I turn around, watching him step into the room. "This is the last time I will ask you if you know anything else about our half brother, because after this, if I find out that you do—"

"I don't." I purse my lips, hoping he won't see through my lie.

He stares at me, deciding if he should trust me, and if I were him, I wouldn't. Someone who has been held captive for so long in her own home will always seek freedom. Especially in the home of her enemy. I will never give him what I know. Not unless it secures my freedom from this family and the rest of them.

He nods. "You may take this room." He begins to walk out and looks over his shoulder at me. "You'll be right at home, being a Mafia princess and all."

I scowl at his back as he leaves and open my suitcase.

I'm going to enjoy what time I have here in this house.

Getting dressed in my swimmers that cover most of my body, I grab myself a towel and head downstairs. I couldn't give a fuck if Nicholas was around, I want to enjoy myself before I either escape or get myself killed.

Placing the towel on the chair beside the pool, I walk over and slowly dip my toe in, and it's not as cold as I thought it would be. Standing on the edge, I curl my toes over the coping and push off into a dive, the cool water meeting my fingers first, then surrounding me, drowning out all the noise inside my head.

CHAPTER TEN
Nicholas

The sun sets on the horizon, providing an angelic, soft orange glow throughout the room. Ezra, Asher, and Jackson are all meeting with our allies in Sicily, and I'm stuck here babysitting Darcy. I take another swig of the scotch I have in my hand, thinking about where I can get my next hit from. It's been a while since I've been back here.

Years, in fact.

We used to come here all the time with family, back when we were one. I think the last time I was here was when I was sixteen, but I never really did the hardcore drugs back when I was a teen. It was always the depressive drugs I was into, weed being at the top of the list when I used to smoke with the Italian boys in our neighbourhood, and in a way, I wish I could go back to those days, when I never knew about all the other vile depressants out there. Before I became this shameful excuse of a walking shell.

My phone rings, and I answer on the first one. "Yes, brother?"

"Tomorrow night, I need you to go to the waterfront and give our *friend* a little visit."

Finally, some fucking action.

"Does he know something?" I ask.

"That's why I'm sending you."

"Done."

"I'll be sending Asher to meet you there. Take Darcy with you and don't let her out of your sight."

I clench my jaw at her name.

"Fine."

"See you soon, Nico." He hangs up, and I toss my phone onto the lounge.

Heading up into my bedroom, I stop in front of the main bedroom and see the door left ajar. My curiosity gets the better of me, and I peek through to see Darcy lying on the mattress with a book in her hand. She's only wearing shorts and a tank, her porcelain skin looking bronze under the soft glow of the sunset burning through the window. I tear my gaze away and continue walking to my bedroom.

I didn't know what it could feel like to have another person beside me as I slept. That when I wake alone, it feels odd. These days, the most I can get is probably five hours of sleep because my body repels rest like it's been trained to sustain itself on the very minimum. Usually in the mornings, the voices in my head aren't as loud as they are in the evenings, but this morning, my head feels like it's about to implode. I make my way downstairs and crack open a couple of painkillers. I've abused my body so much that I doubt they will work, but I gulp them down with some water anyway and head for the shower in my room. Turning the knob, I stop. Nothing comes out. I try the cold-water knob and nothing.

For fuck's sake.

Something was bound to break since we've been gone. Since there are only two showers in this place, I make my way to the other one in the master suite. I walk in, noticing the room is empty, and I hear the water running inside the room, so I remove my clothes before I open the door and step in. The glass is fogged up, blurring her silhouette behind it. I consider waiting until she's done, but I quickly dismiss the idea since I did promise to make her life a living hell. Opening the shower screen, I make a note to myself not to look at her, because if I do, I know it'll be over for me.

She screams, covering herself up with her arms as I step in. "What the fuck, Nicholas!?"

Fuck, my name sounds good coming out of her mouth.

"I need to take a shower."

"Can't you wait!?"

I lose the battle, and my eyes fall to her green ones, fury and embarrassment mixed in her stare. They then move south to her arm, covering her chest, and instead of feeling what I thought I would, rage simmers beneath the surface of my skin as I notice scars covering her entire body. The ones on her arms are nothing compared to the ones on her torso. Further down, I see what looks like a large gash just on top of her pubic region, and my heart drops into my stomach as my eyes clash with hers.

"Darcy—"

The energy shifts as she pushes past me, stepping out of the shower, grabbing her towel, and covering herself. I follow her out, stark naked, as she walks out into the bedroom.

"You have no fucking boundaries!" she yells, turning to face me.

"Who did that to you?"

She huffs as she shoulders past me, but I catch her wrist in my hand, pulling her back into me.

"Let me go!"

"Who fucking did that to you?" My tone hardens, the pressure in my jaw increasing the harder I clench.

"Why do you even care?" Tears brim her eyes, and my heart pounds at the sight of her hurting.

"Tell me."

"Someone who I thought would never hurt me." She sniffs, and it takes everything in me not to forget she's the daughter of our enemy.

"Did you—"

"No." She cuts me off. "I didn't have a baby."

"But—"

She rips her wrist out of my hold and wipes a tear from her cheek as she holds up the towel in her other hand. "I will *never* have a baby." Her bottom lip wobbles as she shakes before me, fighting so fucking hard to hold her tears back, and I see myself in her. A person who spent her life dealing with a trauma she never should have been destined to live.

I step toward her, and she breaks, the tears streaming down her face, and I pull her into me, cradling all her broken pieces as if they were my own. She buries her face into my chest as her cries grow louder, and my hand moves up to her wet hair as I lower my chin down to rest on top of her head.

"Shhh." I hold her close to me as her body continues to shake, her cries piercing the air around me.

Who would do this to her?

Eventually, her cries subside until we're both standing here, comfortable in the silence. She lifts her head to look up at me, and as her bloodshot eyes find mine, she wipes the tears from her face. Then her hands land on my chest, sending an electric current straight through me.

"It happened when my parents died," she admits, and I

wait for more, hoping she'll give me some of the answers I've been seeking about her past.

"It was Leo." Her lip wobbles again.

"Your uncle?" Disbelief rushes over me at the information, and I wish I had made him suffer a lot more than he did before he died. She turns away from me, but I place my finger beneath her chin and force her to look up at me.

"Why?"

"They drugged me, and when I woke up, I had this ugly scar and an enormous amount of pain to live with. When I saw him, he said he made sure I would never bear any children for the other Mafia families of London. If he couldn't have the kingdom, he wasn't going to let anyone else further their bloodline." She sniffs. "He forced a hysterectomy on me without my knowledge in pursuit of power."

"Fuck." My heart shatters in my chest for her. "Darcy, I—"

"I know what you think of me, Nicholas. I don't need your pity." She steps away from me, and her eyes land on my cock. Surprise or shock? I can't be too sure which one is plastered all over her features, so I cover myself with my hands as her eyes meet mine again.

She ignores whatever it was that passed between us, so I do the same.

"What do you think it means to be strong, Nicholas?" she asks, both hands now at the front of her towel, holding it up. Her question floors me. Did she think I was weak?

"Those who live through unimaginable pain day in and day out think they're weak because of how much their emotions dictate their actions in life, but when they finally find that reason to heal, even they don't realise how much strength it took to make it through a single day with all that pain."

"What are you trying to say?" I ask.

"You and I have something in common. We live through similar emotions every day, but one of us tries to bury them. Pain is there to be felt, Nicholas. Without pain, how would we be able to appreciate all the rest?" She pads out the door, leaving her last words lingering in the air around me.

It took absolutely no effort to convince Darcy she had to come out with me tonight, and if I'm being honest with myself, I'm craving the chaos that will soon unfold.

The Waterfront is owned by allies of the Guerra family, consequently reporting to us. The owner, Antonio, recently inherited the business from his father, so I know he'd be eager to make an impression on us, which I'm counting on. He's also one of the biggest fish in Italy, meaning nothing happens here without him sniffing it out.

"You stay in my sight the entire night, understood?" I look over to Darcy, who's dressed in a tight black dress that covers most of her skin. The material hangs onto her every curve, and I have to remind myself that she's the last person on this planet who could give me what I want. Why does that not seem so important when she's so close to me that I can smell her lavender-scented shampoo?

"Do you need to cuff me to you?" She grins sarcastically whilst holding out her wrists to me.

My mind flashes to images of her bound before me, but before I can say anything, I'm interrupted by Asher's voice.

"Here's the happy couple." He slaps his hand on my shoulder. "Shall we?"

He motions for us to head into the outdoor bar, and my eyes meet hers. Defiance is written all over them. Reluctantly, I hold my hand out for her to take, and she hesitates for a moment before sliding her hand into mine.

The entire place smells like cigarettes and cheap alcohol, and the further we head into the bar, the more crowded it becomes. I hold on to Darcy's hand tighter, pulling her through the bodies, and finally we make it to the corner booth, which is reserved for us. I motion for her to go first, and she does, my eyes plastered on the thin material barrier covering her breasts as she scoots into the booth.

I sit beside her, eyeing out the room full of people, trying to locate Antonio, when I spot a woman wearing a bikini strutting over to our table, holding a tray of shots. As she bends down to place the glasses on the table, she smiles at me. I'm used to the women, the bars, the clubs, all of it. I did it for such a long time that it became just like any other boring Saturday night. It wasn't fun anymore. Not when no amount of pussy or ketamine is enough to fight the plague within me.

I turn to Darcy, who glares at the woman as she walks back to the bar, and if I didn't know better, I'd think she was jealous.

"Ah, Nico!" Antonio walks over, and I shake his hand. "So good to have you back in the country," he says with a thick Italian accent.

"Antonio, congratulations are in order." I smile. "You must be happy." I motion at the club full of people.

"Thank you, my friend. It's been years that I've been waiting for this moment." His eyes move to Darcy and roam her chest and I clench my fists on the table as he looks back at me.

"But tell me, Mr. Casella. What can I do for you?" He takes a seat opposite me.

Wasting no time, I pull out my phone and show him the video footage Ezra showed me. "We're looking for *him*."

The colour drains from his face as he watches the footage. "No, sorry, I do not know this man." He pulls out a cigar and places it in his mouth. Antonio is your typical Italian, with short, dark curly hair and a moustache.

Leaning over the table between us, I snatch the cigar from between his lips before he can light it and place it in mine. "Now, Antonio, you know what happens to people who lie." He shifts in his seat, looking uncomfortable, then glances at Darcy.

"Is it true?" he asks. "Are they all dead?"

"All besides one." I look at Darcy, arms crossed, anger evident in her stare.

He looks back at me, and I know he's about to tell me the truth. "Nico, you cannot find him. So many have tried, but everywhere we look, it's like he vanishes into thin air."

My brows pull in as I consider his words. No one can just vanish. I know I will find him. It's just a matter of when.

"You won't find him unless he wants to be found."

"Do you know his name?" I ask, hoping I can gain a small sliver of information.

"Only the one he goes by in the streets." He leans over and passes me his lighter. "*Il uccisore.*"

"Killer?"

"Yes." He nods, and I get the sense that he's afraid. Either of him or of me.

"There is someone I know who has spoken to him and lived to tell the story." He hesitates.

"Spit it out, Antonio, I don't have all night."

"But he's no friend to us, *mio amico.*"

"There's more than one way to skin a cat. I'm not leaving Italy until he's either dead or pledges his allegiance to my family."

CHAPTER ELEVEN
Darcy

Asher follows me through the crowd as I head to the ladies' room. I look back and see Nicholas through the crowd, hunched over the table, talking with Antonio. I can always count on someone being in the ladies' room because the line is always so fucking long to wait for your turn in exclusive clubs like these.

Asher nods to me as he takes his stance, waiting outside, and I enter the bathroom to notice two women, one leaning in front of the mirror, touching up her makeup, and the other on her phone. Both look a little younger than me, and I hope for my sake that they speak English.

"Hi." The one on her phone looks up. "Can I please borrow your phone? I dropped mine, and it cracked. Now the screen is completely black." She looks at the other woman, who I'm assuming is her friend.

Nodding, she hands me her phone, and immediate relief rushes over my entire body. Smiling, I impatiently dial the number and place the phone to my ear.

"It's me," I say as soon as they pick up. "I'm in Italy."

"Where?"

"In Sicily."

"Do they know?"

"They know nothing."

"What deal did you make with the Dixons?"

"One that'll bring me death if I fail."

"In exchange for?"

"My freedom."

"And you're sure they will give you that?"

"I have to try."

"Do you need me?"

"I'll let you know when the time comes, I can't risk it right now."

There's a pause on the other line.

"Watch your back, Darcy. These men don't play games."

Taking a deep breath, I hang up, hand the phone back to the woman and wash my hands.

I hope you know what you're doing, Darcy.

Making my way out, I head to the bar with Asher on my tail as sweat rolls down my back. Ordering a shot, I throw it back, itching for another. Nicholas is still in the booth, watching the crowd.

The music pounds within the club as sweaty bodies writhe with one another. It's been so long since I've been out, so long since I've felt like myself, that I want to give in. I want to let go, and I want to try to enjoy what tonight could be if I were truly free. I push all the other thoughts from my mind and focus on the house music coursing through my body. I let it control me, move me as I close my eyes and dance, feeling the alcohol buzzing through my mind, creating a comfortable silence within me. A smile creeps across my face as lights flash around me in the darkness.

I feel an arm slide around my waist, and my instinct is

to pull away. As I open my eyes, I look into green ones, staring back at me hungrily. Before I can pull away, gunfire echoes within the club, and the music stops as screams erupt and people scurry to the exits. I take cover behind the DJ booth and watch everyone exit the club, and as the room empties, I see Nicholas with his hand around a man's throat. The same man who had his hands on me.

The lights come on, and I step toward them. "Nicholas."

"Shut up, Darcy," he says, his eyes never leaving the man in front of him.

"He didn't do anything."

His head snaps to me, a darkness whirling around inside his eyes, almost as black as the night, and a stab of fear shudders through me.

"Go wait outside," he demands, and I clench my fists beside me.

"No."

"Damn it, Darcy. Don't argue with me." He raises his voice, and it takes everything in me not to slap him.

"He didn't fucking do anything!"

"I gave you a chance to go. Now you'll have to watch," Nicholas seethes as his hand closes on the man's throat, his eyes popping out as he struggles in Nicholas's hold. At this moment, I know I should just listen and not draw any more attention to myself than I already have, but that's never been who I am.

Asher and Antonio stand, watching the scene unfolding, and neither of them make a move to stop him.

"Let him go." I straighten my spine, and his eyes slowly rise to mine at my challenge.

"Are you challenging me, *fenice*?" A sinister grin spreads across his face as he lets go of the man, and just when I think I won this one...horror descends on me as he walks across the now-empty club.

The man stumbles to his feet as Nicholas breaks the safety glass housing an axe displayed on the wall, and my eyes widen as his gaze clashes with mine before hurling the axe at the man, impaling him in the back. Blood splatters as he barrels over, falling to his knees, then flat on his front, his eyes still open.

I step back, unable to look away from the innocent man now dead on the floor as Nicholas strides toward me, but I refuse to become the dainty woman, afraid of everything and anything in this world. I have endured too much to be afraid of anyone, especially Nicholas Casella. Death doesn't bother me anymore, not since I have been around it my entire life, so watching Nicholas kill a man right in front of me doesn't affect me like it should. It shouldn't if you come from a family like mine.

"Why won't you just fucking listen to me?" His masculine scent invades my personal space, and I swallow, his tall frame towering over me.

I plant my feet firmly on the ground, refusing to back down from this fight. "Like a good Mafia wife would, right?" I ask sarcastically, "It's like you've never been told *no* in your life, Mr. Casella."

He grabs me with both hands, his fingers pressing into my upper arms. "Don't fucking mock me, *fenice*."

"Stop calling me *fenice!*" I try to fight his hold, then he presses his large body against mine and grabs my wrists as I try to punch him.

"Or what?" He lowers his face to mine, and it's the first time I notice the gold specks surrounding the irises in his eyes.

I stop, unable to move or speak, as his aura surrounds

me, pulling me into his hypnotic charm. It kills me to admit that Nicholas has charisma, and it's so obvious why he is the playboy everyone can't get enough of.

His breath fans my neck when he speaks into my ear. "Next time you want to fight, I can't promise I'll hold back." He releases my arms, and his eyes darken as they land on mine again. "So unless you want to admit you enjoy fighting with me because it turns you on, I suggest you listen." He tucks a stray hair behind my ear as I purse my lips, hating the way he makes me squeeze my thighs together.

I would rather die before I admit that I'm attracted to him.

Huffing, I shoulder past him and out the door of the club as he follows. The waves crash in the background as I look around for Asher. At this point, I'd rather sit in the same car with a Guerra than a Casella.

My eyes land on a motorcycle as Nicholas walks up to it, grabbing the helmet that hangs from the handlebars. It's black, with a smoke design on the sides. He reaches across the other side and holds out a second helmet to me. Rolling my eyes, I walk to him and grab the helmet, placing it on my head. Nicholas has an ease about him where he makes everything look effortless as he throws one leg over the bike, starting the engine. Bracing myself on his shoulders, I lift one leg over the bike until I'm pressed up against his back.

"You're going to need to hold tight. We're not in London anymore." His voice echoes through my helmet as I reluctantly do what he says. My arms reach around his muscular frame, pulling myself into him.

We pull out onto the road, making our way through the town until we hit a highway. I have no idea where we are, so as far as I know, he could be taking me anywhere. My arms tighten around him as he throttles down the highway, flying past passengers in cars. My heart thumps loudly beneath my chest as the adrenaline peaks, and I notice a small smile spread across my face at the rush. I've never been on a motorcycle before, but this feeling is the closest to freedom I have ever experienced. Almost like soaring in the clouds above everyone else.

After riding through the mountains in silence, we come to a stop on a cliff. The only sound in the air is the crashing of waves beneath and the low rumble of the motorcycle. Taking my helmet off, I get off the bike and walk toward the edge, watching the waves thrust upon the shores angrily beneath me. Turning around, I notice Nicholas standing there, watching me with his helmet in one hand.

"Tell me who you spoke to on the phone tonight," he demands, his eyes growing darker as he steps closer to me, and panic flurries inside my chest as I realise I've been caught. My brain scurries to come up with an answer fast enough to make it believable, but I fail, and he steps closer to me, forcing me to take a step back, my heels now inches from the edge of the cliff.

"I—"

His hand closes around my throat like a vice, and I grip his wrists with both hands as I rise to my toes, scrambling to stabilize myself and breathe through his grip, terror rippling through me.

"I told you if you lied to me, I would kill you." His voice is menacing as he dangles me over the edge until I'm gripping his arm like my life depends on it.

My brain works to come up with something—anything—as fear digs its claws deep into my skin. I try to talk, but the only thing I can seem to focus on is to breathe.

"P-please." My voice is barely a whisper as I peer over the edge, the only thing between me and the sea are rocks, and a lot of them.

"I could easily just let you go and watch you fall to your death. You'll be so carved up by the rocks that even those who perform your autopsy won't be able to identify you."

For whatever reason, he doesn't. Instead, he whirls me around, throwing me to the ground, but I waste no time before I rise to my feet.

"You're fucking insane." I cough, my breathing returning to normal.

"Don't confuse my clarity for insanity, *fenice*." He stands in front of me, his tall frame intimidating.

"It was my friend."

"You don't have friends."

Dick.

"I *had* friends before I was married off to you." I scowl at him.

It's the truth, I did. Before my parents died, I had a whole group of friends I could confide in about the world of the Mafia because they, too, were involved in the same world. My closest friend Lila knew about every part of my life, and I knew of hers. We shared everything until the death of my uncle and my marriage into the Casella family.

"You can't just expect me to live my life without friends or *someone* to talk to."

He gives me a wicked smile, moving closer to me, and I tip my chin up.

"That's the beauty of your captivity. I get to decide how to make your life a living hell, and if I don't want you talking to anyone…" He cocks his head to the side. "I mean it."

"That's fucking cruel."

He turns and walks to the bike, completely unfazed, and a part of me is relieved he didn't press me further, but the other part of me struggles to accept my reality.

"Cry me a fucking river."

CHAPTER TWELVE
Nicholas

After my meeting with Antonio, I did some digging and found out that our half-brother is known for his violent tendencies. That's probably putting it lightly, considering he slaughtered an entire organisation in the countryside. The reasons, I don't know yet.

Everything here is a lot more convoluted than in London. It took years to build an empire that people have come to fear so much that they wouldn't dream of rising against us because their chances of death are a lot higher than their chances of overthrowing us. Here, there are no loyalties. All it could take for someone to betray you could be as simple as an exchange of something they want.

My bike is still running as I contemplate if I want to go ahead with what I'm about to do. I haven't been here in years, and just the thought of stepping into this place makes my skin crawl. I look up at the dark house buried deep within the trees, the only thing visible are the lights twinkling through the thick greenery. It sits behind high walls, the only access through the front gate. I have no other choice. If I want what my body is craving, I need to do it now.

I switch the bike off and hold my helmet in my hand as I press the buzzer, and a few moments later, the automated gate opens. The pebbles crunch beneath my feet until I'm met with two burly men at the front door. I take a deep breath and nod for them to open it. Walking inside, I notice a few things have changed. There's no more carpet. It's been ripped up and replaced with luxurious wooden floors all throughout the first floor. The walls are no longer dark and instead have been painted a crisp white, showcasing a few artworks.

I hear the click-clack of a woman's heels walking toward me, and I close my eyes.

"Nico!" Her voice penetrates my ears, and I cringe. "You made it back to me."

I open my eyes and see her standing in front of me, her white robe hanging open, exhibiting her breasts being held up by a black bra and lace panties. If I were me a few years ago, I wouldn't mind spending a night with her again, but something has changed within me, and I despise being this close to her.

"Sara."

"It's so nice to have you back. Come…sit." She motions to the chair in the living room, and I take a seat, placing my helmet beside me.

Sara used to be the person I came to when I wanted something I couldn't get anywhere else.

"What brings you back to Sicily?" she asks, placing a cigarette between her lips as she sits, crossing her legs in front of me.

"Let's not bother with pleasantries, Sara. I'm only here for one thing."

She looks at me and shakes her head. "I thought you stopped that years ago."

"Do you have some or not?" I don't want to be here any longer than I have to.

She clicks her fingers, and one of the burly men walks in and hands her a plastic Ziploc bag. She offers it to me, and as I reach out to take it from her, she holds it tighter in her grasp.

"Don't do it all at once, okay?"

A shiver rolls down my spine as memories flood my vision. Some of her sprawled out on the floor next to me after we had taken one too many pills or smoked until we couldn't anymore. She was the one person who had never judged me for my addictions, and although it felt like a safe space all those years ago, right now, all I want to do is get out of here.

I pull out a wad of cash and throw it on the table. "You don't have to worry about me." I don't give her the chance to speak as I grab my helmet and head straight out the door and down the path, back to my bike.

The ride back to the house is filled with voices in my head. The line between hate and attraction is growing thinner with each day that goes by, and the pressure to find our brother is becoming overwhelming. Every time I think we have a great lead, it turns into complete fucking shit. I promised myself I wouldn't take anything besides ketamine, but tonight, my demons have come out and they want to play.

Specifically with me.

As soon as I get back, I notice the light in Darcy's room is off. She's probably asleep, considering it's late. One of the guards we had with us nods as he makes his way back to Ezra, and I find myself heading to the back of the house.

Stepping out onto the balcony, I take a seat on one of the sun chairs and rip open the plastic bag. Throwing the pill into my mouth, I swallow, anxiously waiting for the effects to overcome me. The last time I had this drug was after the first time I killed a man. I remember every second, from the moment I pulled the trigger to when he fell onto his knees as I watched his soul leave his body. After the first time, I swore I wouldn't ever touch it again, until it became a weekly recurrence. That's the thing about drugs, you swear that you will never try others and stick to the "harmless" ones, but the sad truth is that it never remains this way. There is always a constant itch beneath your skin, craving the comfortable numbness that comes with substance abuse. The familiar, soothing silence that brings relief from the constant battle within your mind.

"Shoot him," Dominic demands as I hold his gun in my shaking hands.

"I can't." My voice wavers as my heart beats frantically inside my chest, watching the man stare at me in horror as I point my father's gun between his eyes.

"Do it!" Dominic yells, standing next to me. "Do it, you fucking pussy!"

I clench my jaw as my finger hovers over the trigger, and my eyes clash with Ezra's beside me. He nods, encouraging me to shoot him, but everything inside me screams to drop the gun and run.

"I'm not raising boys, Nicholas. I'm raising men who will one day run this empire. Now shoot the fucking cunt!"

I pull the trigger, and I could swear I heard the bullet singe through his flesh. He falls to his knees with a thud, his mouth hanging open as his pupils dilate. His body falls forward, his face now firmly planted on the ground as I stare in shock at the thick crimson blood pooling around the man.

Dominic's hand lands on my shoulder, making me flinch at the contact. "Congratulations, son, you are now a true-blooded Casella."

His words ring in my ears as the blood trails slowly to my boots, marking me.

My phone buzzes in my pocket, but my body feels numb, and as much as I try to move, my arms remain still, paralysed by the poison coursing throughout my veins. I struggle to open my eyes, and I can't remember how long I've been out here. The voices in my head are muffled, almost like a distant echo.

"Nicholas…"

"Open your eyes."

I'm trying.

"Stay with me."

What the hell is going on?

"Fuck."

CHAPTER THIRTEEN
Darcy

It's late. Really late. I roll around in bed to check the time, my eyes still refusing to focus as I wake from sleep.

One in the morning.

The moment I stepped foot into the house after our argument last night, I headed straight for my room and slammed the door shut. I forced myself to sleep, because if I did anything else, the fire-fuelled rage that Nicholas continues to light inside me would have made me do some very stupid things, and I'm not reckless. Far from it. I'm calculated and consider each action before I do anything.

Rolling out of bed, I head toward Nicholas's room to check if he's home, but when I reach his door, I notice his perfectly made bed, untouched.

My heart rate soars at the thought of an opportunity to escape when I notice the foyer empty, until I spot Nicholas laying outside on a deck chair. Curiosity gets the better of me, and I shuffle toward the balcony to see if he's fallen asleep. Stepping out onto the deck, I immediately notice the empty plastic bag beside him, his arm hanging off the chair.

A terrible thought enters my mind, and I curse myself for thinking it.

Turning his head to face me, I notice his skin getting

paler by the second I watch him, and I hurriedly search the floor for his glass inhaler to confirm my suspicions, but I can't find it anywhere.

What did he take?

"Nicholas?" My gaze is firmly trained on him, waiting for him to wake, and when he doesn't, panic settles in the centre of my chest.

"Nicholas?" I say a little louder this time, the beat of my heart growing louder in my ears.

No response.

I place my fingers below his nose to check if he's breathing, and I feel a small trickle of air brush them.

Fuck.

My hands latch onto his shirt, fisting it as I shake him. "Nicholas…"

His eyes remain closed, and the panic now vibrates everywhere within me.

"You need to wake up!" I yell frantically, not knowing what else to do.

His phone begins to ring, and I hastily reach into his pocket to answer, fumbling the phone in my hands.

"Ezra."

There's a pause before he speaks. "Darcy…where's my brother?"

"He's barely breathing." Tears sting my eyes, and I slowly back away from Nicholas's slack body, squeezing my eyes shut.

No, no, no.

You can't do this.

I try to shake the vision of my mother in the tub as my heart beats louder and louder, threatening to crack open my chest and run away.

"Where are you?" Ezra's deep voice cuts through the

panic, and I open my eyes, my throat dry, slowly closing up as the night grows darker above me.

"Darcy!" he yells.

"At the house."

"Stay there. I'm a couple minutes away."

I force myself to breathe as I recompose myself and pull him up.

"Nicholas, open your eyes!" I pry one of his eyes open to see his pupils constricted completely.

Fuck.

I do the only thing I can think of and stick two fingers down his throat.

"Come on…" I plead as I force them further down. My tears trickle down my cheek before an immediate rush of calmness washes over me when he gags.

"Oh, thank god," I whisper, falling onto the chair beside him, holding his body up with my own.

"Nicholas!" Ezra frantically races through the house until he stands in front of us.

"He needs a hospital."

Ezra nods and without another word, he grabs one of Nicholas's arms as I grab the other, both of us carrying him down the stairs and into Ezra's car.

I'm slumped against a hospital chair, waiting outside Nicholas's room, biting my nails, when I see Ezra exit his room. The tightness in my chest constricts the air that my body desperately pumps into my lungs and, I sit up.

"How is he?" I ask, the concern in my voice surprising me.

"The doctor said he took fentanyl." He takes a seat

beside me and sighs, running his hands over his face. "I don't know what I'm going to do with him."

Something inside me breaks at the sight of his brother like this. I would give anything to have a family who cares for me, and Nicholas has a brother who would literally give his life for him, but all he does is search for comfort in other places besides the people who mean the most to him.

"He promised me he wasn't using," Ezra declares. "But I guess I should've known better."

"Has he ever stopped?"

"Once." He looks at me. "But I think it was the hardest time in his life."

"What happened to him?" I ask the question that's been on my mind ever since the first night I saw him using.

There's a silence that lingers in the air before he speaks. "It's not mine to share, Darcy. If you want to know, you'll have to ask him."

"Mr. Casella." The attending doctor walks in. "He's awake."

He nods and meets my gaze. "Maybe you should go in."

"No." I shake my head. "He needs his family."

"I've spent years trying to convince him to stop using. He won't want to see me."

I consider his words before hesitantly making my way to Nicholas's room, and when I enter, his eyes clash with mine immediately. Something passes between us, but I can't be too sure as to what.

Mutual respect?

"Why did you do it?"

His question takes me off guard. "Do what?"

"Why did you save my life?"

"Was I supposed to watch you die?"

"Isn't that what you want?"

I notice the needles penetrating through the ink-covered skin on his hands and arms, and I'm taken back to the moment I woke up in the hospital alone.

"Believe it or not, Nicholas, I'm not the monster you paint me to be inside your mind."

We're interrupted as the same doctor walks in to check his vitals.

"Mrs. Casella, I assume?" He looks at me, speaking with a heavy Italian accent, and I nod. "He'll need constant supervision for the next few days as the drugs leave his system completely."

I nod, unsure of what else to say.

"Mr. Casella, your heart rhythms should return to normal by tomorrow morning, but I suggest you consider a path of sobriety." He gives Nicholas a pat on the shoulder. "I've seen many men fall prey to the allure of substance abuse to avoid whatever they are battling, but I can tell you that all their roads lead to one."

He leaves the room, and Nicholas sighs.

"Are you okay?" My question lingers in the air before he chuckles, leaning back into the bed and beginning to remove the needles from his arms.

"Just fucking peachy."

"What are you doing?"

"What does it look like? I'm going home."

I grab hold of his hand, stopping him, and almost regret it when his dark eyes meet mine. I can almost feel the crackle of energy between us as I take note of his strong masculine features, his sharp jawbone, and the way the skin around his eyebrows creases when he narrows his eyes at me.

My hands move on their own as they press onto his

hard chest, feeling the thump of his heart beneath his skin, forcing me to take a deep breath as his gaze falls to my lips.

"You're not going anywhere."

"Is that a fact?" He cocks his brow and slowly removes my hand from his chest, his eyes returning to mine. "I won't stay in here a second longer and feel the judgement of people who know absolutely nothing about me."

I move back, watching him remove the leads on his hard chest, and yank the needles from his skin. When he stands, I stare shamelessly at his bare skin, completely covered in ink from head to toe, the only place hidden being underneath his black boxer briefs. I'm reminded of the other night, when he held me as I cried, and it makes me wonder why he comforted me instead of leaving me to deal with my emotions alone. I watch as he slides his pants on, the machines beeping loudly in the background before he pulls his shirt over his head. The nurses burst through the door, urging him to get back into the bed, but he ignores them, shrugging them off. Then he walks out the door, and I follow.

"Get back in there, Nico." Ezra's voice is hard, and even I know he's fucking pissed.

Nicholas doesn't spare him a glance as he shoulders past him, swinging his jacket over his shoulder. "I'd like to see you make me. I've got work to do."

I speed up and halt, facing him, blocking his exit, and he pauses, waiting for my next move.

"You're not leaving."

"Give me one good reason why I should stay." His eyes trail over me, like he's assessing me.

"Because you almost fucking died!?" I say incredulously.

"It'll take a lot more than a couple of pills to kill me, *fenice.*" He smirks. "Now get out of my way."

"No."

"Fine, have it your way." He strides over to me, and I yelp as he grabs me with one arm behind my knees, flinging me over his shoulder.

"Nicholas!" Ezra shouts as I watch him become smaller in the distance.

"Put me down!" I pound my fists on his back, but it's no use, he's determined to have his way.

Pulling the covers over my shoulders, I stare at Nicholas when he takes a deep breath and closes his eyes. As soon as we got back to the house, I made him shower and get into bed and convinced Ezra that he would be okay in my care, but *why* I did this, I'm still unsure. Seeing him in that state, strewn across the chair reminded me of my mother and how alone she must have felt without my father in this world.

Is this what Nicholas felt?

Alone?

Did he *want* to die?

"I don't need a babysitter."

His proximity shouldn't affect me this much, but it does, and it has been for days.

"I promised your brother."

"Since when do you give a fuck about a Casella?"

"I don't…" I pause as he faces me, his dark eyes burning into mine, and a lazy smile sneaks onto his face.

"You're in my bed, *fenice.*"

The heat rises to my cheeks, and my eyes fall to his ink-covered hand resting on his pillow.

"Well, that should tell you how much you can't be trusted to be alone."

"Dodging questions tonight?"

I try to hide my smile but fail miserably, his charisma too powerful for me to ignore.

"Go to sleep."

"There will be no sleep for me tonight..." He sighs, rolling over to his back, and it makes me wonder what he's thinking, but I hesitate to ask what I desperately want to know.

Biting my lip, I do it anyway. "What happened to you, Nicholas?" I whisper, my voice barely audible.

He stares at the ceiling, and his temples flicker. A silence lingers and I think he won't answer me, but then he speaks. "My father was a monster."

His confession doesn't surprise me because I know growing up the way we did, there would be a lot of pressure on the children of every family. It's almost impossible to come out of it without some sort of trauma, but eventually, some of us learn to accept it for what it is. Like Ezra, I can just see that even if it wasn't something he didn't want, he's the type of person to take it for what it is and use it to his advantage. People like me and Nicholas, however, don't have that within us.

"Ezra keeps telling me I should speak to someone about it, but I can never bring myself to tell a shrink about all the fucked-up shit I lived through at the hands of someone who was meant to protect me."

I move closer to him, trying to give him the same comfort he showed me. "I know it's ha——"

"No, you have no idea." He turns his head to look at me, my arm just inches away from his. "Dominic Casella will always remain a monster in my mind."

I carefully slide my hand into his to show him I want to understand, and when I think he's going to pull back, his fingers intertwine with mine, and my stomach does a flip.

"One night, I was in his study, snooping through his desk. I shouldn't have been in there. We weren't allowed in there unless he was with us. It was his rule." His hand closes tighter around mine. "He walked in to check on something before going upstairs and caught me rummaging through his top drawer. I knew I was in trouble just by the look on his face, but how much trouble I was about to be in would have never ever occurred to me." He pauses, closing his eyes as if he's fighting the memory. "He didn't say a word to me, just grabbed me by the hand and put me in the car. We drove one hour and thirty minutes in silence out into the woods. I know because I counted every fucking minute." His eyes land on mine again, and I see the pain he hides in them from the world. "We came to a stop in the middle of nowhere, and I walked with him deep into the woods until we approached a bunker. He opened the latch, and before I knew what was happening, he pushed me in."

"Oh my god." The shock is evident on my face. I'm sure of it. "I'm so sorry."

"That's not the worst part. He locked me in there for three days, no food or water."

My heart breaks for him that his own father was so cruel. Not knowing what to say, I hold his hand tighter, hoping that somehow he'll feel my sympathy through my touch and that it might encourage him to open up to me further.

I now understand the depth of Nicholas's trauma. I understand why he'd rather not feel...why he wants to escape, and a part of me wishes I didn't because now, Nicholas Casella is no longer my enemy but just another victim of the unsympathetic, monstrous world we live in.

CHAPTER FOURTEEN
Nicholas

My brain rattles inside its cage as soon as I open my eyes. The rays of the sun are like laser beams cutting through my eyes, and all I want to do is pluck them out of their sockets to stop the searing pain. Groaning, I roll over to see two ibuprofen tablets and a glass of water waiting for me beside my bed. Last night was the first time I've ever shared that story with anyone. I don't know why I did, but in the moment, it felt right. The way Darcy listened without judgement with her hand in mine made me realise just how much I may have misjudged her.

Closing my eyes, I try to ignore the churning in my stomach, the sweat on my skin, and the thumping behind my eyes, to no avail. Nausea rolls its way through from my stomach up to my throat, and I gag.

Fuck.

This is the worst part of an addiction, the day after an overdose.

My legs are like lead as I push myself to stand, and I barely make it to the bathroom before hurling everything I have left in my stomach into the bowl. I can't even begin to count how many times I've been through this, and if it wasn't Ezra picking up after me, it would be Asher. Those two have been through the wringer with me for a long time.

I gargle some mouthwash to get the taste of vomit out of my mouth, and when I look up, I see Darcy's reflection in the mirror, watching me.

"They said it'll be like this for days." She leans against the door, dressed in her little black shorts and tee.

"I'll be fine. Like I said, I don't need a babysitter." I feel a pang of guilt with how harsh my voice sounded, but I don't want her sympathy because I don't need it.

"So that's it then?" She crosses her arms, displeased with my response. "As soon as the sun comes up, what happened last night doesn't matter?"

Her words slice through me, but before I can answer, she rolls her eyes and walks out the door.

A shiver passes down my spine when I rouse from sleep. Pulling the blanket up to my neck, I desperately try to warm myself up, the sweat trickling down my temples and my back, sending my teeth chattering as I feel the heat flush through to my face. The only thing that will stop this is another hit. Just one will be enough to rid me of this pathetic fever.

I try to open my eyes, but everything looks black, and as soon as I attempt to lift my head, the entire room begins to spin, forcing me back onto my pillow. I toss and turn for what seems like an hour, trying to soothe the ache in my bones, fighting for my pathetic fucking life through this hell.

I spent the whole day in bed as Darcy brought me food and water, keeping an eye on me from a distance. Silence is the only thing that was exchanged between us the entire day, which is probably why she chose to stay in her room tonight. I would rather she didn't see me like this anyway —pathetic and weak.

Light footsteps approach my room, but when I open my eyes, I see nothing.

Am I imagining it?

Could I be dreaming?

I roll onto my side and reach for the glass of water on my bed, downing it all.

My throat feels like it's on fire, my mouth like cotton when the bed dips beside me, and I turn my head to see Darcy's worried face staring back at me. She reaches up, the back of her fingers pressing onto my forehead.

"You're burning up," she whispers, her beautiful green eyes sparkling in the moonlight flowing through the window. It doesn't take long until the need to close my eyes falls on me like a ton of bricks, and she places an arm behind me, supporting me as my body leans into hers. "Can you stand?"

I think I nod, but I can't be too sure.

My body is ten times heavier than usual, swaying as I walk with Darcy holding me up as best she can, and I know we've entered the bathroom when I my feet touch the cool tiled floor.

"Wait here." She places my hands on the edge of the basin, and I use it to stabilise myself.

The sound of the water hitting the floor echoes through the bathroom, and I feel her hands on me again. She helps me out of my briefs and walks me into the shower, the warm water rushing down from my head to my feet, giving me instant relief. After a moment, I open my eyes to find Darcy in the shower with me, and my eyes fall to hers, her body barely an inch from mine as we stand under the water, her white shirt now sticking to her delicate skin.

Lifting my hand, I gently cup her face, and she leans into it, closing her eyes. Before her, the nights brought me darkness and loud voices that echoed and rattled through my skull, but now…tonight, it's brought me comfort with someone who I would not expect to find it with. The more she does for me, the more it makes me realise how wrong I was about her.

"What are you thinking?" she asks, opening her eyes.

I sigh, dropping my hand from her skin. "I'm craving it."

"You can't." She moves in closer to me, our bodies now touching, and it takes everything in me not to lean down and take her mouth with mine, to taste her on my tongue.

"The sickness that lives within me wants to see my demise, no matter how many times I try to fight it, it always wins."

"Not anymore." She places her hands on my chest. "You can fight it."

I look away, ashamed of how much help she's given me and continues to give me like I fucking deserve any of it. "I don't deserve it."

"What?" She forces me to look at her. "To live?"

My jaw tenses at her words, and I hate how easily she can read me.

"Nicholas…were you *trying* to die?" Her brows pull in as her eyes fill with tears, and I hate it. I hate that she feels sorry for me.

I think about her question because I know at times I've wanted it to end. Maybe subconsciously, I thought the amount I took wouldn't matter because I've used it before.

I've done it so many times that it couldn't possibly be any different this time around, but it was.

I look at her as my heart thumps loudly in my ears, wanting to escape and dodge her questions because I don't want to face that part of myself.

"Oh my god." She throws her arms around me, mine coming around to pull her into me. "I'm so fucking sorry."

I bury my face into her neck as the water continues to run, holding her tighter as my misery binds with hers, and I don't know if it's the shower or her that makes the fever subside.

She pulls back to face me, water running down her nose as we stare at one another, unsure of where this night is heading. I reach over to turn off the water, my eyes never leaving hers, and the air feels tense again, almost like there's been a shift.

"Stay with me tonight?" she whispers. "I don't want to be alone."

"Not if you wear that." I point to her see-through shirt, her pink nipples poking through the material, and my mouth salivates at the thought of having them between my teeth.

A rosy hue appears on her cheeks when I press myself into her, my cock now hard at the sight of her wet body, and what she does next surprises me. Lifting her shirt, she removes it, exposing her bare breasts, and I groan as my cock continues to grow harder.

Her eyes fall to my cock. "Did that hurt?"

"What? My piercing?" I chuckle at her question, and she nods. "Not even close to how much pain the voices in my head cause, *fenice.*"

She bites her bottom lip, and all I want to do is suck it as I grasp her full breasts in both hands. Before I can get the chance, she steps out of the shower, covering herself in a towel, leaving me standing there naked before her.

"Nothing can happen between us, remember?" It's evident she tries to convince herself with her words, facing away from me.

"Is that why you're running away from the way you truly feel?" I follow her out and walk into her bedroom.

"You don't know how I truly feel." She steps into the walk-in wardrobe, coming out a moment later dressed in one of my shirts, which sits like a dress on her frame.

"Why are you helping me then?" I press her further.

"Because I'm a decent human being."

"No, I think it's because you feel something other than hate for me."

"I will never feel anything but hate for you." She bares her teeth, and I step in closer.

"Is that why your body reacts to mine whenever I'm near you?"

"Y-you have no idea what you're saying." She stumbles on her words.

Grabbing her wrists, I place her palms on my chest. "Is that why each time you look at me, I can almost hear your heart beating beneath your chest?"

"Nicholas…" She tries to pull her hands away, but I don't let her. Instead, I guide them down my torso and over my abs.

"Every time I look at you, I just want to take you right there and then on the fucking floor like a heathen. Especially when you directly disobey me."

"But you hate me."

"It doesn't change the fact that you affect me."

"You're only saying this because I'm helping me."

"Are you sure?" I guide her hands down until she wraps

them around my cock. "Do you think I would be this hard up for you if that was the case?"

"We're enemies," she reiterates like I've forgotten and whips her hands away. "We can't."

"It's okay to want something you believe is wrong, Darcy."

"I'm done talking about this." She crawls into her bed, so I do the same, getting in beside her when she turns to face me, and I drink in her beauty.

"Promise me something," she whispers.

"I'm not good with promises, *fenice,*" I confess.

She takes in a shaky breath. "Promise me that you will fight."

I move closer to her, and she wraps herself around me when I roll onto my back. "I will do my best." I close my eyes and focus on the feeling of her hand resting on my chest instead of the itch beneath my skin begging for more poison. It's still there, calling my name like a siren.

Before her, there was never a time I would be caught like this with a woman in bed, but I covet her closeness because she is the only thing other than narcotics that silences the voices that continue to scream within me.

CHAPTER FIFTEEN
Darcy

Thunder cracks in the sky as I run through the darkness. The rising fear inside my chest is almost crippling. He told me if I ever had a chance to run, that I should take it and never look back, because if he caught me, he'd make sure I could never attempt to escape again. My thighs burn as I heave air into my lungs, desperately trying to make my way through the thick foliage.

Please, God, save me.

A twig snaps behind me, causing me to yelp, as I turn around and walk backwards.

There's no one here.

There is no way he will be here. He told me he would be out all night and to stay put in my room until he returned.

The whistle of the wind grows as the night gets darker, the cracks of light disappearing slowly. Tears sting my eyes as they fall from my cheeks, and I brace my lower stomach with my hands and wince, frantically urging myself to keep going.

Fuck, it hurts.

Keep going.

Don't fucking stop.

I look over my shoulder and glance at the streetlights peering in from the tall black gates of the mansion.

If I can make it to the road, I can get help.

Just a little further, Darcy.

I squeeze my eyes shut, taking a shaky breath, and when I open them, a shadowy figure reveals itself behind a tree stump, watching me, and as it surfaces into the moonlight, I scream.

A muffled voice echoes through my head, and I look around, but it's just me and Leo.

"Wake up!"

A scream rips through my throat as I tear my eyes open, sweat rolling down my back.

Nicholas's concerned eyes find mine as he cups my chin. "It was just a dream."

Relief rushes over me, and I release the bunched-up bed sheets in my hand to pull them up to my chest, tears threatening to fall down my cheeks. The dream always starts like this, with my uncle terrorizing me before he gets what he wants. Except the other times, Nicholas isn't there to wake me, and I'm left suffering at the hands of a monster. Even in his death, he still haunts me.

I wipe the tears from my eyes, wanting to fight the rest of them, except there's no point because I'm now crying for the second time in front of the one person who should've never seen me in tears.

"Shhh." He scoots closer to me and pulls me into his arms like I'm fragile, and it makes me feel the safest I've ever felt.

He holds me tight to his chest as his calming voice soothes me. "It's okay. You're safe, *fenice*."

After a while, my tears subside, and I look up at him, wondering if he is just consoling me to berate or embarrass me about it later, but when my eyes meet his, I know it's nothing like that.

"Tell me what I can do," he whispers, and his empathy floors me.

"Do you really want to know?"

"Yes."

"I want my freedom."

Something in his eyes clouds with blackness, and he cups my face gently, not breaking eye contact. "The only time you'll ever be free is when I'm buried six feet deep."

Soft jazz music filters through the old radio as I mindlessly stir the pancake mix in the ridiculously large kitchen. I couldn't sleep after my nightmare, especially not after Nicholas's confession on my freedom, which reconfirmed my plans. I'm doing the right thing by wanting my freedom, everyone is entitled to it, and it shouldn't be different for me.

"Morning." He struts down the stairs in his grey sweats, and I refuse to give him any more ammunition to accuse me of being attracted to him, so I avert my eyes and continue stirring.

"Morning," I mutter, focusing on getting the batter smooth.

I notice him lean against the counter right beside me, purposely toying with me. "Not going to look at me?" he asks.

"Nope."

"Why not?"

"Because I'm your prisoner, remember?" My voice drips with contempt.

I gasp when his hand clasps my wrist, causing the bowl

to wobble on the counter. He pries the whisk from my hand, placing it down on the counter, and reluctantly, I stare into his eyes as we perform this useless dance of dominance again.

"You know as well as I do, that without me, they would be after you."

He means the Dixons. They know the secrets I hold and they want it for themselves, but what he doesn't know is that I haven't shared them all with him.

"I know how to take care of myself."

"I doubt it." He chuckles, and I rip my wrist out of his hold.

"Do you think I grew up in this life and I don't know how to hold a gun?" I question, and before I know it, the front of his body is pressed against my back.

"What if you don't have a gun?" He grabs my wrists with both hands, holding me in place. "What if they attack you from behind?" His hot breath fans my neck when he whispers into my ear and wetness pools between my legs at the deep timbre of his voice.

I press my ass into him, lightly tugging my wrists, and he holds me tighter, pushing me against the bench. My arms ache when he pulls them both behind me, and I feel him growing against my back as I struggle in his hold. "What if they corner you?"

I stifle a moan that was about to slip out of my mouth, and in one swift motion, I throw my head back into his chin harder than I meant to. His grip on my wrists loosen, and without wasting any time, I take my chance to position one leg behind him and use all the force from my hips and upper body to knock him over. His body hits the ground with a loud thud, and I smile at him in triumph, turning to see him grinning up at me as he licks the blood from his bottom lip.

"Not bad." He smiles slyly.

Grabbing the knife I had on the counter, I climb on top, straddling him as I lean over and place a hand on his throat, pointing the tip of my knife under his chin, and his eyes twinkle in the light, smiling back at me.

"If you have certain kinks, all you have to do is tell me." He smirks.

"You wouldn't be able to handle it," I counter.

"Is that a promise, *fenice?*" His hand curls over mine that holds the knife. "Because if you're promising me a good time, you're going to have to make it hurt." My eyes widen when he forces the knife until it breaks his skin.

"Stop." I try to pull the knife back, but his grip is too strong. He glides it down from the side of his chin to his collarbone, droplets of red breaking through his skin.

"I'm not scared of blood, but are you?" he torments, continuing to run the blade over his chest.

"Nicholas!"

He lets go, and I stumble off him, standing to lean on the bench behind me when he stands to full height and crowds me.

"I don't care how much pain I'm going through, *fenice*, but when it comes to your touch, I will gladly suffer through it all if it means you'll admit your true feelings for me." He leans forward, his nose grazing the side of my neck, and I squeeze my legs together to alleviate some pressure, but just as I do, his knee comes between them, forcing them apart. "If you don't want to admit it, then you don't get to reap the benefits."

His presence suffocates me, and all I want to do is wrap

my legs around him and let him hate fuck me. Reaching up, I place my hands on his pecs, feeling the solid muscle beneath them as his mouth hovers over mine. It would be so easy to give in right now, with the way he's pressed up against me, the temptation stronger than ever before.

"I know you don't want to cross this line..." he whispers, licking the little droplets of blood from his bottom lip. "But I would fall to my knees right now if you would just say the fucking words."

My heart fumbles, and I let a moan slip, his words coating every inch of me. He knows exactly what to say and what to do to get a woman into his bed.

"Is this what you say to every other woman?" I question.

His eyes bore into mine, not a hint of a smile on his lips as he stares at me. "I'm not about to stand here and tell you there weren't women before you, *fenice,* but since I married you, I haven't been able to even *think* of anyone else. Ever since you ruined my bike, all I could think about was throwing you against a wall and making you pay for it." His fingers brush the hair from my neck, pushing the strands over my shoulder. "With my tongue."

Fuck.

It would be so easy to give in, to let the curtains drop, but I won't.

I can't, because I have one goal, and one goal only.

To escape.

To gain my freedom.

"You deserved it." I focus on steadying my breathing. "For the way you treated me."

"Fenice..." he drawls.

"What does that even mean?"

He's called me this for so long, and the Italian I had learnt in my younger years, I began to forget because I didn't have to use it much. Only now do I have the confidence to ask and know he'll tell me the truth.

"Phoenix," he whispers against my lips, and I teeter on the edge of submission.

"Everything about you reminds me of a phoenix. From your blazing hair to your stubborn ability to continue to respawn new hope and faith each time it's snuffed out right in front of you."

I stare at him, lost for words.

"If only I was immortal like one." I sigh.

"Man's immortality is not to live forever; for that wish is born of fear…"

"…Each moment free from fear makes a man immortal," I whisper, my brows pulling in as I take in his words. "You read Mary Renault?" I ask in shock.

"More by force than entertainment." He chuckles. "Dominic had a thing for historical novels."

The more I find out about Nicholas, the more confused he makes me, and I detest that the hatred within me is gradually fizzling out the more I discover about him.

I let out a sigh and push past him, my lungs seizing with every step I take, and the only thing I can think about is how my body wants one thing but my mind wants another. Logic tells me it's wrong, that I shouldn't want it. We've been taught our entire lives to breathe hate into our enemies until they've consumed every single part of us, but what if it wasn't meant to be like this?

"I can see your mind working from here, what is it?" he asks, and I turn around, unable to speak. Unable to see clearly. Guilt rises in the pit of my stomach, rumbling through every bit of hate I had toward this man that stands before me.

The truth is, no matter what happens, one of us will end up hurt.

CHAPTER SIXTEEN
Nicholas

She looks at me with fear, but from what, I cannot place. Something haunts her. I can see it in the way she holds herself.

What is she hiding?

"You don't *actually* want me, Nicholas." Her voice is small when she looks away.

I step closer to her and grab the back of her neck, forcing her to look at me. "No one tells me what I want, *fenice*. I would've thought you'd learnt that by now."

"You hate me, and I hate you. Tell me, in what world would this work?" She places her hands on my chest, and her touch makes me want to bend her right over this counter and fuck her senseless.

"In ours, if you want it." It takes every ounce of self-control I have left to not lay my lips on hers, taking what's legally mine, but I feel her hands slip away, and they slowly rise to reach mine.

"I can't be the person you need." Her words hurt me more than they should, and she turns away, leaving me to wonder why she keeps denying herself of what she truly wants.

. . .

A week of hell, just like I imagined. One week stuck in this house with Darcy breathing down my neck, worrying if I'll sneak off and use again. I can't help but think she's only worried about herself and not so much anyone else because without me, she'd be on the streets, begging for her life on her knees, and even then, no one would step in to save her.

Besides me.

I lean along a thick column, my hands shaking as I reach into my pocket, pulling out a cigarette and a lighter, and I curse under my breath for the effects I'm still suffering with, wondering how long it's going to take for my body to recover.

Asher and I wait under the shadow of the night. We're an hour or so away from the city, amongst the ancient ruins they wanted to meet. I've heard of the men Antonio spoke about that night at his club. They're ruthless thugs who take more than what they want. Some don't even live to tell their story. From what I've been told, they've been in Sicily since the Renaissance, and their bloodline goes back to their royal family.

The Petruccis.

Dominic talked about them enough for me to know they're dangerous, which is why my great grandfather had to make the move from Sicily to London. He hated it here, always under the thumb of the Petruccis, and eventually, after paying off his debts to them, he made it out.

How anyone makes it out of this life is a miracle.

But the Petrucci family isn't your typical Mafia family. Once they have you on their list, you're there to stay for life, there are no reconciliations with them. All they know is blood and violence.

"We've been waiting for forty minutes," I say, looking

over to where my car is parked, our two bodyguards leaning against it, and I wonder if leaving Darcy at home with Jackson was the right thing to do.

"They should've been here by now." Asher checks his phone, and just as he slips it back into his pocket, the rumble of motorbikes sound, through the empty air, getting louder as they approach. The man on the largest bike climbs off and removes his helmet, revealing a scar on the right side of his face that spreads from his jaw to the inner corner of his eye. He looks to be about Ezra's age, with a buzz cut and dark tattoos inching their way up to his jaw. As he steps closer to me, I notice the small skull and bones tattoo on the left side of his face near the bottom corner of his eye.

"You're late."

His posse of men laugh at my remark, and he smirks. "You're simply early." Removing his leather jacket, his dark tattoos are revealed, with one of his arms completely blacked out.

Not wanting to be here any longer than necessary, I pull out my phone and bring up the video footage to show him. "Do you know this man?"

His face drops to a sour expression, and his green eyes find mine. "Do you?"

"I don't have time for twenty questions. Antonio said you'd know where to find him."

"Antonio can suck my dick."

My head pounds the more frustrated I get.

"I need to know where I can find him."

He steps closer to me, and without breaking eye contact, he points to my phone. "This *bastardo* stole from me."

"Whatever amount he stole, I can pay it, and in exchange, you will tell me where he is."

"Do you really think I would let him live after what he did?" he asks.

"I don't care if he's dead or alive, but I need proof."

He chuckles as he pulls out a packet of cigarettes, offering me one. I take it, and he lights it for me, then lights his own. "I buried him."

"Where?"

"What is this information worth to you?"

I grit my teeth, acknowledging the power his family holds over Sicily. One wrong move or word, and I could die today, right here. They don't care about our rule over London because we're on their turf.

"If you want him." He smirks, blowing out a puff of smoke. "You'll need to give me something in exchange."

"What's your price?"

"I don't want money."

His smile sends a shiver down my spine when Asher cuts in. "Antonio said you'd accept cash, is one hundred thousand pounds enough?" The duffel bag thuds as it hits the floor.

He ignores Asher and stares at me. "What I want is to play a little game."

Asher nudges me as if to say, "*I don't like this.*"

"I don't have time for games."

"You will. You will show me how far you're willing to go for this information." He waves over one of his goons and takes a clear bag into his hands, "I just received this shipment in," He waves the bag in my face, no doubt cocaine or some sort of narcotic, "It's from a new supplier, so I need to know it's clean."

Fuck.

I know what's coming.

"Nico, let's go. He's not going to tell us anything, we can find him another way," Asher pleads.

"You think I'm afraid of drugs?" I laugh, snatching the bag from him. "Hold this."

I push my phone into Asher's hands, and he holds it flat as I pour some of the powder onto it and pull out my credit card from my wallet to form two lines. The cigarette hangs from my mouth as I roll up a note and pause, considering my actions and how they may affect the hell I've been through in the last few days, but I have no choice. If I want to get any closer to finding our half brother, I need to prove it. The burn in my nostril used to take me back to the moments I felt relief from everything I was hiding, but today, it reminds me just how stuck in this world I am and how all my efforts the past few days have disintegrated into nothing.

"If it's clean, it shouldn't take as long to drop." I hand the bag back to him.

"I must admit, when I heard of the Casella brothers coming into Sicily, I didn't think I'd get the chance to meet them."

"Dreams do come true for some." Sarcasm laces my voice as I start to taste the chemicals in my throat.

Definitely cocaine.

"It's clean, now tell me where he is."

"Oh, that's right," He turns around, tapping his forehead like he forgot something. "I do need something else from you."

My fists clench at my sides, and my focus zeros in on him.

He turns to face me, grinning from ear to ear. "I want you to kill Sara."

"What?"

It's not that I care about her, it's that if I do what he's asking of me, there isn't a chance Ezra and I walk out of this alive, and he knows this. Sara's father was Dominic's right hand. He worked with us for years and pledged his allegiance to our family before I was even born.

"You heard me." He places his jacket back on. "Kill her without anyone knowing it was you. You have three days." Without another word, he places his helmet back on, and they all speed off in the direction in which they came.

"Why Sara?" Asher questions, trying to make the puzzle pieces fit.

I'm already three steps ahead, knowing exactly why he wants her dead, because if I do what he wants, there will be an all-out war between the strongest families in Italy, and he wouldn't have to lift a finger to do any of the dirty work.

There's a loud commotion once we pull up to the house, and I see Jackson slamming the door behind him and walking out to the front, spotting us rolling to a stop.

I step out, and Jackson steps into the driver's seat. "Don't ever ask me to do that again, Nico, because if I spend another moment with her, I will shoot her." A smile creeps up on my lips, but I force it away.

"What did you find out?"

"We'll talk tomorrow, when Ezra's here too." I tap the roof of the car, and he nods.

"Enjoy your handful, she's in a fucking mood tonight."

They speed off, and I walk back into the house, making

my way into the kitchen to see Darcy pouring herself a glass of wine.

"Where did you find that?"

She smiles. "I found your cellar that you were not inclined to share with me." She takes two big gulps and sets the glass down on the counter.

I point at the now half-empty bottle sitting next to the glass. "That's a 1998 Petrus."

"Oh, I know." She cocks her head to the side. "Consider it as payment for holding me captive."

I chuckle as I watch her take another gulp.

"What did you do to Jackson? He was very adamant on not spending another second with you."

"He's the one who didn't listen to me when I told him I would own him in rummy." She shrugs.

"This was all over a card game?"

"He's a sore loser." She takes another gulp, finishing the entire glass in a few seconds.

"Slow down on the wine," I warn.

She doesn't listen and continues to pour herself another generous glass with her stare focused on me. "Or what?"

"Or you might regret your actions a little later tonight." I give her a smug smile.

"You wouldn't dare take advantage of me in a drunk state."

I crowd her, forcing her to walk backwards until her back hits the fridge. "Are you willing to gamble on that?"

"Nicholas…"

Resting my hands above her head, I lean down so our faces are only inches apart. "My name sounds like sex dripping down the corners of your mouth." The mere thought of sex with Darcy is enough to get me hard. "If you continue, I can't be held responsible for what happens between us."

"Since when do you take accountability for your actions in general?" she bites back.

"Careful…"

"The truth hurts when it's spoken, doesn't it?" I feel the venom in her voice and realise she's trying to get a rise out of me. It's working, but I won't let her see it.

My tongue darts out to sweep her bottom lip, tasting the bitter wine lingering on them. "No matter what you say to me, the words you speak will always taste sweet coming from your lips, *fenice.*"

CHAPTER SEVENTEEN
Darcy

I can almost feel my ribs shattering from the thumping of my heart beneath my chest at his proximity. I taste him when I lick my lips and begin to wonder what his tongue would feel like on mine…what his skin would feel like pressed up against me. Dangerous thoughts bounce around in my head as his lips hover over mine.

"You may be able to hide your thoughts, but you can't hide the way your body responds to me." Confidence oozes from his voice, and I hate how attractive it is.

"How do you know the response is something positive?" I ask, breathless. "Maybe the hate I harbour for you has become visceral."

"Because I bet if I reached into your panties right now, you'd be a sopping mess for me." He smirks, and I almost reach out to touch him.

"You're delusional."

"Am I?" His fingers brush the side of my neck and trail down over my nipple, sending a shock throughout my body. "Is that why I can see your nipples through your shirt, begging for my attention?" He runs his fingers underneath my shirt, and the electric pulse of his skin on mine is unmistakable.

His raw masculine magnetism pulls me in, and I find myself breathing quicker. The walls I've worked so hard to build begin to tumble down brick by brick as he undresses me with his eyes. His fingers drop to my shorts, and I try so hard not to respond. I haven't been touched in years, and it makes me feverish to even imagine Nicholas's hands on me, but it doesn't come close to how hot he makes me feel when he's just inches away.

"I could make you feel things that you didn't know were possible." The corner of his mouth pulls up in a sly smile when he leans in closer, his lips almost on mine, teasing me.

"You have a mighty high opinion of your ability to please a woman."

He chuckles at my response. "I could make you come quicker than you can spell your name."

My stomach flips, and a pulse races straight to my pussy at his words.

"No one is *that* good with their fingers."

A devilish smile spreads across his face. "I never said I'd use my fingers."

"Sorry, Nicholas…" I smile, desperately trying to ignore the arousal coursing through my body. "You're going to have to live the rest of your life with your dick in your hand." I push past him and don't look back because if I do, I know I'll cave, and I will *never* give in.

Not to Nicholas Casella.

Not Never.

Peering into Nicholas's room, I see him sleeping on his stomach, his entire back tattoo on full display, along with his toned ass. I peel my eyes away and focus on why I'm awake at three in the morning. Making my way down the stairs as quietly as possible, I pry open the front door of the villa and pad outside barefoot. The rocks, sand, and dirt dig into my skin, but I'm too focused on the task at hand to care. Reaching the end of the driveaway, I check the letterbox, finding an old burner phone inside. I swallow, looking around, hoping no one saw me, and sprint back to the villa, all the way up into my room.

I shut the door slowly and sit cross-legged in the corner to begin dialling, sweat pooling on my upper lip as I focus on getting my breathing back to normal.

"Did you do what I asked?" The gruff voice fills my ear.

"I can't."

"We had a deal."

"There's no way I can do what you want. There's no room to breathe here."

"Find a way."

"Please, is there anything else I can do?" I plead.

"If you want your freedom, this is the price."

He hangs up, and I'm left wondering what the fuck I've gotten myself into.

I call the only other person who could help me, and I know that even with all the rest of his problems he has to face, he would.

He answers on the first ring, and there's silence on the other end before he speaks, tears stinging my eyes at the sound of his voice. "Darcy?"

"It's me."

"Are you okay?"

I cover my mouth when tears roll down my cheeks. "I can't do what they're asking of me, I just can't."

"Okay. Whatever you do, stay with Nicholas."

"They're coming for him."

"I'm coming for you."

"I can't ask you to do that."

"Darcy, you're family."

I bite my hand to stop the tears, but they continue to flow. "No, if you come here, things won't end well."

"It's about time *something* ended."

He hangs up, and I fall apart, wishing more than anything that I could be at home. Not at the Brayford mansion, no, that wasn't my home. My *actual* home, in my own bed.

I hold myself together, and eventually the tears stop. Pulling myself off the floor, I walk outside to the back of the property with a small shovel I took from the garage and begin digging. I dig until the hole is deep enough to my liking, then place the box that houses the burner phone into the hole and cover it back up.

Stay with Nicholas.

CHAPTER EIGHTEEN
Nicholas

The rain patters against the top of the car whilst Darcy, Asher, and I sit in silence, waiting with Ezra and Jackson in the car alongside us.

Enzo Petrucci's words ring in my ear, and I close my eyes to fight them off. I haven't told Ezra about his threat, and even though I should have, I couldn't admit to just how monumentally fucked everything has become. I have three days to do as he asks before shit gets sour, and I consider how I'm going to pull this off. The letters on the screen in the car begin to mesh together, and I squeeze my eyes shut, shaking my head, trying to rid my body of the effects of the poison still plaguing me. When I open my eyes, I spot black cars parking a few spaces in front of us.

The place is empty—just grass, trees, and mountains that look like shadows under the full moon. Sometimes I think even nature can sense the impending violence—a warning that echoes in the rustle of leaves and a silence that stretches beyond the vast lands under the night sky.

Asher takes a deep breath and releases it. "I'll go."

"No." I reach for the door. "You stay here with Darcy."

"Stop treating me like a child," she chimes.

"Do as you're fucking told," I warn her before stepping out and slamming the door behind me, not giving her another chance to speak.

Three men approach me, and I smile. "Gentlemen." I greet them with my arms out wide. "Such nice weather we're having tonight." The raindrops hammer down on my face, slowly soaking my shirt, and the man in the middle scoffs, throwing a duffel bag down in front of me as it slides on the mud before coming to a stop at my feet.

"Tell Ezra we no longer owe him anything."

"Come now, there's no reason to be bitter. You owed us a debt, and this is you paying it off, like a good sport."

He sneers at me. "Don't forget who we work for."

"Ah yes, the Della Torre family." I pick up the duffel and open it, inspecting the cash inside. "Tell me, does Dante ever want to expand outside of Falcon's Keep?"

"Falcon's Keep has been its own entity since before your grandfather was even born, son. Have some respect in the way you talk about the Della Torre family."

It's been known that the Della Torre family set themselves apart from the rest when they declared sole ownership of imports and exports out of an island close to Italy during the war.

"No need to get prickly, I was merely asking if he's ever going to step out into the real world."

The man slides his gun out of his holster, aiming it straight at me, and I know I've hit a nerve. My heart picks up speed at the sound of the car door slamming shut as Darcy races in front of me.

"What the fuck are you doing? I told you to stay in the car!" I pull her behind me, now shielding her, when Asher steps beside me, pulling out his gun. Panic unfurls in my chest as the air becomes thick with tension. Ordinarily, I would salivate at the chance of a fight, but with Darcy standing behind me, it makes me sick to my stomach.

"Now, now, let's all calm down." I place my hand on Asher's gun and force him to lower it to the ground.

"You Casella boys think because your father pissed on Big Ben that you somehow have more power than God," he scorns.

"God is nothing but a pretty picture people have painted in their heads, bowing to something that doesn't even exist." My eyebrows draw together.

"So when the nights get dark, who do you pray to, boy?"

Another car door slams shut, and I watch as Ezra walks in between us, right up to the man in the black suit.

"Me." He leers at the man.

There's a silence that befalls the cliff face, and no one moves.

The man finally speaks. "Dante Della Torre's debt has been paid."

"Send my regards to Dante and mind the way you speak to my family." I don't have to see Ezra's face to know he's mad, and when my brother is angry, there's a chance someone could lose their eyes…or their soul.

The man quickly nods and waves a hand at his men, and within seconds, they disappear. I turn to Darcy, who is now completely drenched with the rain, her clothes sticking to her every sensual curve.

"I told you to stay in the fucking car!" Gripping her wrist, I pull her towards the car, but she escapes out of my hold.

"I'm not a dog!" she shouts, her hair now stuck to the sides of her face.

"All right, boys, let's leave the couple to sort out their differences." Ezra, Asher, and Jackson all file into one car and drive off, leaving me and Darcy alone.

"Why would you do that?" I ask, noticing the way her breasts rise and fall with each breath she takes. "Why would you put yourself in harm's way? Fuck Darcy, don't you *think!?*" I yell, my heart thumping wildly beneath my ribcage at the thought of her hurt. I have watched many die before me, pleading for their lives, and some of those were my brothers, but for reasons I cannot place, the pain wouldn't come as close to seeing Darcy in pain…because of me.

"I don't know, okay!" she roars in frustration, pushing the wet strands of her hair away from her face. She looks up at me, tears mixing with the raindrops running freely down her cheeks. "Nicholas, I—"

"Fuck it." My mouth covers hers as I taste the words on her tongue, her arms swinging around my neck, her body pressing against mine. My cock strains against my jeans as I press it into her, her tongue moving against mine, battling for power and hungry for more. I lift her, and she instinctively wraps her legs around my waist as the rain pelts down harder, thunder now brewing in the dark clouds above us, the taste of her salty tears on my lips.

She rests her forehead on mine. "This is wrong," she whispers, fighting something behind her eyes.

"My whole life I've felt like I've been doing all the wrong things, *fenice*, I know what wrong feels like, but this is not it." Lowering her onto the bonnet of my Bugatti, I admire the way her shirt clings to her when she slowly peels it off, revealing her breasts almost spilling out of her black lacy bra, and it makes me so desperate for her that I groan at the sight.

"Fuck," I breathe, biting my knuckles when she removes her bra.

"Show me." She bites her bottom lip, and within

seconds, I'm on top of her, taking her nipple in my mouth, sucking and licking the droplets of rain from her skin.

A moan slips from her throat as she paws at my shirt. "Take it off."

I waste no time and remove it, the rain feeling cold against my skin. My mouth hovers over a large scar in the middle of her breasts, and her eyes meet mine, scared that I'm going to pull away, but what she doesn't know is just how beautiful these scars make her and how much of myself I see in her pain.

"You're devastatingly beautiful, *fenice*." Placing my lips on her scars, my hand slips into her shorts and panties. "Never think anything less of yourself, because those are not scars I see, but marks of survival." Sinking two fingers into her already soaking pussy, she arches her back, moaning.

My mouth continues to work on her nipple as my other hand grasps at her breast.

"Nicholas," she breathes, and her voice sounds like an angel whispering the promise of heaven.

The rain continues to hammer down hard on us, and I feel myself growing harder with her loud moans filling the space between us. Pressing my thumb on her clit, I graze my teeth up toward her neck, and she cups my face in her hands, bringing my lips to hers. Her hips buck like crazy, pleading for me to give her what she wants.

"Tell me how much you want it," I growl, and she moans. With the way she fought so valiantly, I want to hear her say it.

"I need it, please."

I hook my fingers, touching the delicate spot inside her, and she comes undone, shuddering as she comes all over my fingers. Pulling them out, I bring them straight to my mouth, dying to know what she tastes like, and her eyes go wide, watching me relish her deliciously sweet arousal all over my tongue.

She reaches for my belt, undoing and removing it, throwing it beside her, but I catch her wrist and she looks up at me. "Once we do this, there's no going back," I warn.

"Are you scared?" she taunts, making me chuckle.

"No, but you should be." I leer when she licks her lips and lowers my pants to pull out my cock. "Because once I fuck you, the only thing you will crave is my touch, my mouth, and my cock. This, I promise you."

A smile creeps onto her face, and it makes me want to wrap my hands around her delicate neck. "Prove it."

CHAPTER NINETEEN
Darcy

Lust fills my every pore as I watch Nicholas stroke himself in front of me.

He's big.

And the piercing on his crown has me doubting my ability to follow through on my threat. He stands tall, the rain cascading down his muscular frame, and slowly, I peel my shorts and panties off, tossing them next to me to part my legs, showing him all of me.

His eyes leisurely wander south, and he groans when they land on my pussy. The mud splashes when he drops to his knees, sliding me down the bonnet as his mouth lands on me, his tongue gliding flat against my pussy, reaching my clit, then sucking hard, causing my body to buck. His warm hand presses my stomach down holding me in place as my hands thread into his dark, wet hair.

"More," I plead, pulling his head into me, and he gives me exactly what I want by closing his entire mouth over my pussy, devouring me like a meal. His tongue pushes into me, then moves up and down over me. His teeth graze over my clit, and his tongue follows, soothing the sting. Sucking me into his mouth again, he flicks my clit with his tongue, teasing me, and I grind my hips over his mouth, inching closer to euphoria.

The past few weeks, all I've wanted was for an escape,

to leave and never think about this goddamn world again, but now, watching Nicholas's tongue work over me, I feel a sharp sting in my chest at all words I've left unsaid, the secrets that lay heavy on my shoulders, and my mind wages war with my fragile heart.

"I can't take much more…" he breathes, standing to lean over me. "I need to be inside you."

I wrap my legs around his waist, feeling the tip of his cock slowly pressing into me, and my heart pounds in my ears as I feel him stretching me slowly.

"Don't treat me like I'm fragile," I whisper, biting his neck, needing him to make me forget about everything I'm hiding.

"Do you know what you're asking of me?" He grips my wrists, forcing them above my head.

"I'm asking you to *take* me." Because that's all I want to feel. The hate. The fiery, red-hot hatred that has seemed to become non-existent between us.

Within a second, his mouth is on mine when he forces himself into me to the hilt, filling me completely, the weight of his body feeling like everything I imagined it would.

A growl rips through his throat as he rams into me again, the droplets of water falling from the tip of his nose onto my cheek. "I love just how wet you are for me." Slowly pulling out, he thrusts back into me, the piercing on his cock hitting the right spot each time. He releases one of my wrists and wraps a hand around my neck, pushing me into the bonnet, causing my pussy to clench, watching him thrust into me and dominate me.

"Is this what you want?"

Thrust.

"Yes," I breathe, and his hand closes tighter on my

neck, the blood in my veins pumping harder when he pulls out of me, and he turns me over like I weigh a feather, my hands smacking onto the bonnet and slipping on the slick hood. I ground myself with one foot on the wet mud as he lifts my other leg, bent up on the car.

"Don't say I didn't warn you." He enters me, his hand twisting in my hair and pulling back with force. "I will give you what you want, *fenice*. I will fuck you like I hate you…" he whispers into my ear, sending a shiver down my spine. "Even if that hate has slowly morphed into something else."

He pounds into me mercilessly, my body jerking against the car as my whimpers fill the grey sky, and I brace myself with my hands when he jerks my head back, the stinging in my skull sending a zing of pleasure straight to my pussy. I feel his hand land hard on my ass, and I moan, my hand slipping between my legs. Before I can get to my destination, he yanks it behind my back. "You come when I tell you to come."

"Nicholas—"

"I'm not even close,"

My pussy feels raw with how hard he's fucking me, but it feels too good to stop.

"And I won't stop until I have you a teary, sopping mess before me."

His words fill me with excitement as he continues to fuck me harder. Both his hands snake around the front of my neck, pulling me back as he thrusts into me, and my stomach flips when the wave begins to build inside me. "I-I need to come," I plead.

The sound of his skin slapping against mine echoes through my ears, and my eyes slowly roll back. No matter how much I fight it, I can't seem to stop wanting more.

More of his hate to make me feel better about the things I have left unsaid.

"Is that what my greedy wife wants?"

"Yes," I breathe. "Please."

"Come all over me, *fenice*." His hand closes tighter around my neck. "Show me how much you hate me."

My nails scrape against the paint of the car as he thrusts harder into me, his hand coming between my legs to rub my clit, and I feel the vibrations of my loud moans when I clench on his cock, squeezing my eyes shut as the world slips out from under me.

"That's it." He chuckles. "So much hatred," he mocks.

My arms falter, and I land on the hood of the car, panting, his arm wrapping around me to turn me over as I stare up at him. Leaning over, he slides into me. "I want you to look at me when I come inside you…I want you to see just how fucking deranged you make me feel."

My heart falters at the way his eyes pierce into my soul, awakening something I forced myself to bury and ignore for the rest of my life. They pull every single emotion I've tried so desperately to ignore, making this moment something more than just sex.

"Stop talking and show me," I challenge, and his eyes turn onyx as he drives into me harder, his hands holding the back of my knees, forcing them apart. He watches himself enter me, and the pleasure in his expression is probably the sultriest thing I have ever experienced.

"Fuck," he hisses as the sound of our flesh pounding against each other surrounds us.

He lowers himself on top of me, his tongue now swirling against the skin of my neck, and I let a moan slip through my lips as I run my nails down his back when our eyes meet again, water droplets falling from his open mouth onto mine.

"*Fenice*," he growls, filling me with his warmth.

The breeze from the storm softly blows through the large doors of my room, fanning the sheer drapes as we lay in bed. We didn't last two minutes after stepping into the house before we were all over each other again. I know I promised myself I wouldn't cross this line, especially with Nicholas, but I don't know what came over me. My stomach was in my throat when that man had his gun on Nicholas. I couldn't just sit in the car and wait for something to happen. What I didn't know was how he would react, and now things are so much more complicated than I wanted them to be.

Nicholas pulls out a cigarette and lights it, sucking in the poison, staring at the ceiling, laying beside me, and I can sense he's tense about something.

"Do you regret it?" I ask in a soft voice, and he turns his head toward me.

"Never." He smiles, taking another drag, soothing my doubts for just a moment.

"Then what's on your mind?"

He sighs. "Enzo Petrucci."

"He wants me to do something that I know will start a war between the families here in Italy, and that's exactly what he wants."

There's a silence between us as he takes another drag.

"What happens if you don't?"

He blows out a puff of smoke and turns his gaze to the ceiling again. "I don't get what I want."

"And what's that?"

"My half brother."

My chest cracks, but I ignore it. "What is he asking you to do?"

"Kill someone I've known for years, whose family swore allegiance to mine since before we were born."

That's the reality with this life, no matter which family you come from or what your intentions are, there will always be that one person who is hungry for more, who wants to be on top. Although Nicholas likes to act like he doesn't care, I know he has an unhinged side to him. I have seen it with my own eyes with how he murdered that innocent man at the club with an axe, but I have a feeling he doesn't like to kill when it isn't justified.

To him.

"Have you told Ezra?"

"No." He pauses, and his expression changes. "My brother has enough on his plate. He told me he's leaving for London tomorrow because the Dixons have ransacked a few of our clubs."

"What about the reason we came here?"

"It's up to me now, I can't fuck this up." He sighs.

"Nicholas—"

"Darcy, I need to know you're with me." He looks at me again, and every bit of hate that was left inside me crumbles.

"What do you mean?"

"I know you've felt the shift too."

I pause, swallowing my nerves. "The shift?" I ask.

"Something happened between us at the hospital. I felt it in the way you looked at me."

I look away, unable to face him with the truth, and he reaches out to grasp my chin. "I was worried about you... that's all."

He pauses, his eyes dropping to my lips. "I'm sorry."

"For what?"

"For the worry that will constantly be there, reminding you that you have a soul that is purer than mine will ever be." He puts out the cigarette in the ashtray beside him to step out of bed and stands to full height. I admire him as I rest my head on my pillow, the hard lines on his back accentuated by the moonlight flowing in from the doors, and the guilt is back. It rushes through me as I think about everything I'm still hiding, so I pull the covers up over my shoulders and close my eyes to push the thoughts away, hoping that, by magic, it'll just be me and Nicholas in this villa until the end of time.

CHAPTER TWENTY
Nicholas

My phone rattles on the bedside table, jolting me from sleep, and I roll over to answer.

"Ezra."

"Meet us at the tarmac in an hour."

"Done."

I check on Darcy, only to find the bed empty and soft jazz music filtering through the villa as I make my way downstairs into the kitchen. A smile spreads onto my face as she comes into view, white powder smeared on her cheek, noticing me.

"I made pancakes." She grins.

"It's six in the morning."

"I couldn't sleep." She averts her eyes from mine and continues mixing the batter as I watch her elbow work, stirring, the heat coming off the pan on the stove.

"Is this how you cope with a sleep debt?" I ask, leaning over the breakfast bar.

She shrugs. "Better than some of *your* coping mechanisms."

Ouch.

I guess I deserved that.

She pours some of the batter on the pan, creating a perfect circle as I come up behind her. "I can show you another coping mechanism that could work in *both* our favours." Lowering my lips to the side of her neck, I graze my teeth up to her ear. She smells fucking divine, her flowery shampoo burning my nose.

Wrapping both hands around her hips, she opens her mouth to speak, but when I slip my hand inside her shorts, she bites her bottom lip, swallowing the words she was about to say.

"We have thirty minutes before we have to be in the car." My fingers slip into her pussy, and she leans back into me, my hard cock now pressing against her ass. My eyes close as I imagine what it would feel like to fuck her tight ass, and a shiver rolls down my spine at the warmth of her body against mine.

"You got lucky yesterday," she breathes, pressing her hips back. "I hadn't been touched in a really long time."

"So you think it'll take me longer to get you off?"

"Probably," she challenges me, making me chuckle.

"How about this…" I massage her clit with my fingers as my other hand slips under her shirt, grasping her breast. "If I can't make you come before you can recite the Founder's Code, I will let you walk right out that door."

"And if I come?"

I feel the corner of my mouth twitch when she whimpers, knowing I have her right where I want her, my fingers now sliding back inside her. "I will fuck that beautiful ass."

She moans, resting her head on my shoulder, moving her hips like her body has been possessed. The pancake sizzles as she lowers her shorts and panties and I almost lose it when she bends forward to push her ass out. "Tell me when to start reciting." She looks back at me with a twinkle in her eyes, challenging me.

I pull out my cock, rubbing it along her, and fight to

stifle a groan, the skin on her round ass rippling when my palm connects with it. "Code one." I push inside her, and she braces herself on the counter with both hands.

"*Silenzio,*" she whispers, gasping as I move in and out of her. "The oath or 'code of silence,' never talk to the authorities." Tangling my fingerings through her hair, I yank it back, burying myself deep inside her. "Fuck!" she cries, her breasts bouncing from the force of my thrusts.

"Two."

My fingers enter her mouth, hooking her jaw down. "*Etnia.*" Her words come out garbled between her panting. "Only men of Italian descent are allowed to become made men…" She pushes her hips back into me, and I grip her hair tighter, making her pussy clench.

"You're forgetting the associates." I grin at her state, bouncing on my cock and taking what she's desperate for, the hate she often spoke of nowhere to be seen or heard.

"Associates, partners, and allies have no ethnic limits."

"Good girl." I grit my teeth when she arches her back, my hand moving over her throat, saliva now covering her chin. "Three."

"*Segreti…di…famiglia…*" she says between thrusts. "Nicholas." I pull her into me, her shoulders pressed against my chest. "I—"

I chuckle, feeling her pussy beginning to tighten. "Already *fenice?*"

"Four," I continue, pushing into her, my hand tightening on her throat as the pancake burns and sticks to the pan beside us.

"I can't."

"Continue or I won't let you come," I warn.

"*Sangue per sangue o occhio per occhio.*" I force her face

down, now flat on the countertop, dangerously close to the fire burning on the stove as I drive into her.

"In English."

Her eyes begin to roll back, and I slide out of her completely.

"Nicholas!" She practically begs to have me back inside her.

"In English!" My hand lands hard on her ass, and she cries out, making me enjoy torturing her with my cock.

"Blood for blood or an eye for an eye!" She tries to lift her head, but I force it back down. "Please…" she beseeches this time, causing my self-control to slip away from me. I want to take her, to make her scream and cry as I wipe her tears with my tongue.

"We're not even halfway, *fenice,*" I torment. "Five." My hand caresses the smooth skin on her back until I meet her ass, her moans ricocheting off the walls when I enter her again, my cock filling up her pussy and my thumb caressing her tight hole.

"I can't breathe." She sighs.

"Such a greedy little slut, aren't you?"

"Mm-hmm," she whimpers, and I gather her arousal with my fingers to spread it over her ass, yanking on her hair again, forcing her chest out.

"Five." My voice is stern.

"Fuck," she hisses, and I thrust into her hard. "I'm coming." She clenches on my cock, her cries piercing the room like a bell ringing in triumph in my favour.

"That's my good girl." My lips curl into a smirk at the sight of her panting, sprawled over the counter before me.

"Nicholas." Anxiety coats her tone when she speaks, and I slip out of her and turn her around to grab her chin, forcing her to face me.

"Don't worry, *fenice*, I'm going to save it for later… when I can savour it most." My tongue darts out, tasting the desire on her lips. "Right now, I need to feel you come undone once more as you scream my name."

My gaze drops to my cock, her cum covering me, and her eyes follow mine, a rosy flush adorning her cheeks in stark contrast to her skin. "Is that—"

"That's how much you hate me, *fenice*." Grabbing her behind her legs, I lift her onto the countertop beside the burning pancakes. "That's proof…" I slide into her, earning me another moan. "That even though your lips utter words of hate, your body will *always* belong to me."

"I will *never* belong to you," she whispers, the familiar fire in her rising to the surface again. Then her mouth is on mine, her arms around my neck as I grip her ass and pound into her. My skin feels like it's on fire at her touch, pleading for relief, my knees almost buckling as she takes me deeper. Her mouth lowers to my neck, and I hiss when she bites me, sending a sting of pleasure and pain straight to my core.

"You said you like pain?" The green in her eyes turns ominous. "How much of it do you want?" she whispers.

"Give it all to me." My fingers dig into the skin of her ass harder. "Let me bear it all."

She reaches for the knife block behind her, grabbing one in her hand and holding it beneath my collarbone.

"Do it." My teeth graze her bottom lip as the tip of the knife pricks the surface of my skin. "Mark me." I thrust into her hard, the knife digging in deeper as it slices down my chest slowly, and I think I fall just a bit harder for her, the wall between us thinning the closer we become.

"Fuck," I hiss, my eyes closing as I chase my release.

Her moans echo through my ears, bringing me closer

to the edge as she glides the knife lower, marking me. "You feel so good," she groans, dropping the knife and giving in to the feeling of losing control. "I think I'm— Nicholas!"

"Fuck!" Her pussy clenches around my cock, and I burst inside her, my head coming to rest on hers.

The euphoria slowly dissipates as we both come back down to reality, the blood trickling down to my stomach as she pulls back, assessing the wound. When I think she couldn't surprise me more, she does something that makes me want to put my grandmother's ring on her finger and declare to the world—*for real this time*—that she is *mine*. Her eyes lift to mine when she slides off the counter and bends down, running her tongue up from my stomach, collecting the red drops of blood into her mouth. Slowly, she stands, smearing my blood across her lips, and I run a hand down my face at the feeling of freefalling.

"I may have lost the bet, but you just lost a piece of yourself to *me*." She grins, like she knows exactly how fucking hard I'm falling for her, and I know she's enjoying every moment of it.

I grab her from the nape of her neck and whisper, "I would lose *all* of me to you if it meant you'd truly be mine."

If it weren't for Ezra, I'd gladly be fucking my wife in the villa the entire day, but the weight of what's about to come weighs heavily on my shoulders now. She stands beside my motorbike, waiting, shifting from one leg to the other as Ezra's bodyguards load our jet with his bags.

"It's up to you now, brother." He squeezes my

shoulder as if it'll give me some sort of comfort or motivation. "As soon as I straighten out the shit that's been happening in London, I'll be back, but I need you to take over here."

I nod and watch Jackson disappear, entering the plane.

"Asher will be with you along with the two other bodyguards, but if you need someone else to turn to, Antonio is your best bet until we send more guards."

"Antonio is a club rat, drunk off his daddy's money, I doubt he'll be much help," I scoff.

He pins me with a glare. "Take this seriously, Nico."

"Yeah, yeah, don't stress, brother." I placate him because I know no matter what happens here, it needs to be straightened out without Ezra, which means I can't let him down.

He glances at Darcy, then back to me. "Did something happen between you two?"

"She's the daughter of our nemesis." I reinforce what I should still believe, but the truth is, what I feel for her is a lot different to when I caught her running away from our wedding.

"She's your wife now," he reminds me like I don't already fucking know. "You need to protect her."

I nod. "Say hi to Aries for me."

He smiles and nods to Darcy. Still speaking to me, he says, "Do you remember the day you told me how lucky I was to have found Aries?"

"What of it?" I ask, wondering where the hell he's going with this.

"You might not see it yet, but the way she watches you, I'd say you've found what you were missing."

I glance back at Darcy, and a small sparkle appears in her eyes, sending the organ in my chest into a fucking frenzy…a feeling so foreign to me. When I look back to Ezra, he's smiling and sliding his sunglasses over his eyes.

"Don't fuck it up!" he calls, walking toward the jet, and I don't know if he's talking about Darcy or about the war I'm about to start.

CHAPTER TWENTY-ONE
Darcy

The sun peeks through the awnings on the balcony of the bar, and it feels nice to be out of the villa, even if it is to be sitting on the sidelines as Nicholas deals with whatever business he has here. My skin crawls at the shudder that rolls down my back with the thought of what the near future is going to look like for me, but I quickly pull myself from the thoughts and strain my ears to hear Nicholas and Antonio's conversation from across the room.

The bar seems different during the day, almost like it'd be the perfect spot to bring a book and relax, sipping on a cocktail, but the atmosphere right now is anything but peaceful.

"I swear to God, Antonio," Nicholas grips the gun on the table. "If you know something and you're not telling me." He pauses, driving his point home.

"Nicholas." His voice shakes. "I promise, we have given you all the information we know."

"Why does he want Sara dead?" he questions, and Antonio sighs.

"There's been a conspiracy amongst the families that Sara's family owes Petruccis money."

"Fucking money." Nicholas slams his fists on the table,

making me jump. "Everything revolves around money," he says with disgust.

Antonio smiles solemnly. "Unfortunately, in our world, money is everything." His eyes meet mine, sending a cold wave of fear rushing down my spine and I look away, rolling the ice in my glass.

I've learnt a lot from the twenty-seven years I've been on this earth, watching my parents, learning from my uncle about how our half lives. Even though it never sat right with me, I never spoke up because I had a plan. It was cemented in my fucking chest that one day I would make it my reality. I wouldn't quit, even if it meant I'd leave a mountain of bodies in my past. It may be selfish, but for once in my life, I deserve to be selfish...to want a better life. One far away from here and from them.

"What are you going to do?" Antonio asks, and Nicholas runs a hand down his face.

"What I do best."

I swallow the guilt into my stomach and stand to walk over to the open doors that lead to the beach with Asher on my tail, no longer able to listen in from the squeeze in my chest. Sliding off my sandals, my toes slip into the soft sand, the breeze pushing my hair behind me. Watching the waves roll off one another, I take a deep breath in and pretend I'm anywhere but here. I don't know how long I've been standing here, but I stiffen when I feel someone's presence next to me.

"He doesn't like this either, you know?" Asher's voice fills the calm air, and I look beside me, his focus on the waves.

"He sure makes that hard to see," I admit.

"He's been doing it a long time." He shrugs, and it makes me curious.

"Why are you here?" I ask, genuinely wanting to know why he and his family follow the Casellas so fucking blindly.

"*Lealtà.*"

Loyalty.

"My family and his go back to the very beginning." He looks down to me, the grey in his eyes swimming with something he wants to tell me but can't. "He's my brother. I've seen him witness things that made me think he wouldn't survive, that he wouldn't be able to pull himself out from…but he did."

"Why are you telling me this?"

"I don't want to see him hurt." There's a warning in his eyes.

"Are you accusing me of something?"

He can't possibly know anything.

Turning to face me, his boots brush sand onto my feet when he moves. "I know you view all of us as an enemy, Darcy, but I don't blame you for it. I don't blame you because we were kids when we were fed these words of hate."

His eyes soften when he glances back up at where Nicholas sits, still talking with Antonio. "But here's the funny thing about the hate we keep in our hearts…when it lingers for too long without reason, it becomes just like smoke that floats through the air and disappears before us."

I chuckle at his words. "You think something like hate is not permanent?"

"Nothing in life ever is. Especially in the one we live." His eyes soften, and the words cut me like a knife.

"He may hate you for what he believes you stand for,

but the truth is, the root of that hate was planted by somebody else."

The problem with being involved with the darkness is that it's hard to get out. No matter how much you claw at it, it's like quicksand, sucking you deeper until it smothers you.

"Thanks for the words of wisdom, I think I know what I feel without you mansplaining it to me." Sarcasm taints my voice, and he grins.

"Darcy, if I wasn't clear before, let me be frank." He leans in, causing a trickle of fear to fall down my spine. "If something happens to Nicholas, *you* are the first person we will be coming for."

I don't miss his tone of accusation, and I know for a fact he means every word he says.

"I am *not* my family," I say through gritted teeth as my breath shakes at his insinuation, the guilt trapped inside my throat, cutting off the air I so desperately need.

"Maybe not, but I have yet to see something in you that tells me you are not a threat to my brother."

"Maybe you need glasses," I harrumph and turn to head back into the bar when his large hand clasps around my elbow, stopping me.

"Snakes like to hide in dark, secluded spaces, but they also aren't afraid to appear in plain sight."

I stare out the window of Nicholas's Bugatti and watch the landscape pass us by as he drives, the leather hot on my skin, the air thick with tension between us. Neither of us wants to acknowledge what has happened.

I feel it, just like he had asked.

The shift.

It's transformed the dynamic between us, and there is no denying it anymore.

"What did you speak about with Asher?" He breaks the silence, pulling me back into the present.

I fiddle with the hem of my sundress. "Not much."

Except for the fact that he pretty much threatened me.

His face twists with something I can't place before he speaks. "I need to be somewhere tonight." He grips the steering wheel, his knuckles going white. "But I can't take you."

"What?" I ask, and his eyes meet mine with apprehension. "I'm not staying with Asher."

"I can't, Darcy." He shakes his head, returning his eyes to the road. "It's too dangerous."

"How many times do I have to tell you I can take care of myself?" I almost yell.

"No." He smacks the steering wheel with his palm, frustrated. "Dammit, Darcy, just fucking listen to me."

I turn my body to face him, and he looks at me, determination churning in his chocolate hue. "I will find a way to follow you if you leave me behind." It's a promise and one that I can deliver.

"For fuck's sake." He swerves the car and comes to an abrupt stop on the side of the mountain, facing me. "Do you have any fucking clue what is about to happen?" he asks, and I think I hear a hint of fear in his voice.

I shrug my shoulders. "I don't care. I'm with you." I feel a squeeze in my chest as soon as I say the words, but I steel my spine, and he looks down at his hand on the steering wheel, making me anxious to know what he's thinking.

"This is not a game anymore, Darcy." He doesn't call me by my nickname, and that's how I know he's serious. "It's war," he whispers.

"I've lived through them before, if you have forgotten." There's more malice in my tone than I intend, and he hears it.

He fists his hand on the wheel and his jaw tics. "Not after the stunt you pulled the other day." He means the day we were intimate. The hot sex we had on the bonnet of his car, and my cheeks flush at the memory as I press my thighs together at the recollection of what his cock felt like inside me.

"I can't have you do that shit again."

"I promise, I won't." It's utter bullshit because I know if it came down to it, I would do the same thing over and over again.

His gaze shifts over my body slowly, and I feel my nipples harden beneath my bra at his unapologetic stare. "If you so much as *think* about putting yourself in danger again." He leans over to me, our lips just inches apart. and gently brushes the hair away from my face. "I will make sure you can't walk straight for a week."

We pull up at the large house nestled between the trees, and an uneasy feeling settles right on my chest. I can feel that we shouldn't be here, almost like if we enter this place without a forward invitation, we might not make it out with our limbs intact. Asher exits his car along with two other men I haven't seen before, then my car door is swung open, and Nicholas waits as I exit, closing the door behind me.

"One of you at the back and the other at the front, let's go," Asher orders, and the two men waste no time in heeding it. He turns to me, eyeing me, and I glower at him before he shakes Nicholas's hand. "Ready when you are, brother."

Nicholas nods, clasping my hand in his, and we move toward the front door. It's now dark since the night settled in an hour ago, and a rustle in the tree has me jumping to see two large eyes watching us. A low chuckle sounds next to me as Nicholas tries to stifle his laugh. "It's just an owl." He smiles, his hand tightening around mine. "I thought you said you can take care of yourself."

I glare at him as we stand on the porch, Nicholas on my right and Asher on my left. The wooden boards creak, and I watch them raise their hands in surrender, mine still clasped around Nicholas's hand. The door opens, and a woman appears, dressed in an all-black dress.

She is stunning.

"*È così carino da parte tua visitarlo di nuovo.*" She smiles, staring only at Nicholas, not even acknowledging me or Asher. The only thing I understood from her sentence was *visit* and *again*.

"*Non sono qui per giocare, Sara.*" There's no emotion in Nicholas's face when he replies.

"We played quite a lot back in the day, Nicholas, have you forgotten?" she says in her Italian accent and her eyes lower to me, a smirk on her lips and a fiery rage in my belly, taking everything in me not to make a scene at her obvious flirting.

"We have important business to discuss…" He lowers his hands. "Are you going to let us in?"

She looks back at him and crosses her arms, her eyes running over his body.

Is this bitch fucking serious?

"Fine. I will give you ten minutes to explain." We step through the door and into a room crowded with paintings that no doubt cost more than my inheritance. "But please." She motions to the lounge, and we sit. "Do not leave out the reason you've brought a *Brayford* into my home."

I feel Nicholas tense beside me, his eyes shooting up to her. "She is a Casella." His defence sends my heart into a fluttering mess, but I rein it back, knowing everything I'm keeping from him.

"*Lei è una traditrice!*" Her voice booms across the space between us, and I grit my teeth.

I definitely understood that.

She is a traitor.

"Her family made decisions she was not a part of." Nicholas composes himself. "She is not why I am here." His voice lowers, getting her attention off me.

"The Petruccis," he whispers and fear flashes through her eyes momentarily. "They're after you, Sara." She rights herself as quickly as that flash of fear disappears.

Waving a hand at one of her guards, he places a tumbler filled with brown liquid in her hand. "What makes you think I do not know?" She tries to regain some of the power she lost.

"Sara—"

"Ah, Nicholas, you have always been one of the good ones…" She offers him the glass in her hand and he takes it. "But I'm afraid it's that type of thinking that will bring you to your end." Panic rises in my chest at her words, and I look to Nicholas, who is eyeing her without saying a word. Her heels click and clack on the wooden floors as she walks over to a table by the large window, picking up an envelope, walking back to us, and tossing it to our feet. Wads of cash flow out of the lip, covering Nicholas's boots.

"*Maledetto Bastardo,*" Nicholas mumbles under his breath.

"This, and four along with it."

"Enzo is a smart player." She looks at me and flicks her hair behind her shoulder. "He will use everything and *everyone* against whatever stands in his way of power."

"How do you know it's from him?" Nicholas asks, and she picks up the envelope. Reaching in, she pulls out a single card, one that has been taken from an Italian deck of playing cards.

"This is his trademark." She hands it to Nicholas, and his brows pull in, deep in thought.

"What does he want?"

"Whatever it is, it will not end well."

CHAPTER TWENTY-TWO
Nicholas

I t starts with one threat—one that can have the ability to come between the most notorious, most powerful of family ties. Then all it takes is an offer someone cannot refuse, and that empire will crumble to its knees quicker than flames can take down a building.

"È potente e saresti dannatamente stupido se pensassi che non ti ucciderà." He is powerful, and you'd be fucking stupid if you think he won't kill you.

Her tone is harsh, and I know it's because she still cares for me in the same way she did all those years ago, but truth be told, my feelings for her were never there. We shared a small part of life together, mostly bonding over our shared trauma, but I never once imagined a future with Sara, and I know it broke her heart to keep things going with me, but she did it anyway.

"Ci conto." I'm counting on it. I smirk, a plan formulating inside my head the more I think about Enzo and what his next move might be.

Sara eyes Darcy sitting next to me and tips her chin up, her words aimed at me, *"Ti fidi di lei?"* Do you trust her?

"È con me da quando abbiamo messo piede in Italia. Non è una minaccia né per me né per te." She's been with me since we stepped foot in Italy. She's no threat to me or to you.

"Questo è il problema delle minacce, di solito sono dirette ma non puoi proteggerti da un coltello alla schiena."

That's the thing about threats, they're usually direct, but you cannot protect yourself from a knife in the back.

Her eyes fall back to mine, and I see the clear warning in them. Her heels click on the floor as she steps toward me and places a palm on my cheek, Darcy stiffening beside me.

She's jealous.

"Tell me, Nicholas…" Her eyes sparkle as I place my hand on Darcy's knee beside me, more to keep her calm than anything else. "Do you miss it?" she whispers, and Darcy springs to her feet, chest heaving, visibly irritated. I stand beside her, and Sara steps back, dismissing her like she was as unimportant as a pesky fly on the wall. The only person in the room who knows the depth of her question is me, and the answer is *fuck no.*

Do I miss getting high every fucking night and passing out in front of the gates of my parents' house only to have Ezra bring me in and hide my sins?

Do I miss almost dying more times than I can count on my fingers?

Do I miss the vomit-covered embarrassment?

Fuck. No.

I can't say I don't crave the feeling of numbness, the want and need still constantly gnawing at me from within, selling me false promises, but I sure as fuck don't miss being that desperate man.

"Sit down, miss," one of her lackeys declares as she takes her place back on the lounge, crossing her arms with defiance written all over her face.

"I think it's best we speak alone, Nicholas." Sara lights a cigarette.

"Fuck no," Darcy chimes in, and I hide my smile at her boldness.

She's so goddamn sexy when she fights.

"It'll be fine, Darcy. Wait outside with Asher," I command, and she stands to face me with Asher beside her.

"Are you fucking kidding?" she says, her tone incredulous.

"Go wait outside," I reiterate, hoping she listens when she turns to Sara, her eyes assessing her, and Sara smiles, waving her out. The tension between the two women is corded, and I feel it from where I stand. Darcy and Asher move toward the door, and she looks back at me with a last look of warning that if I don't explain everything to her when I'm done, she will pull it from me word by word.

Once she's out of earshot, Sara begins explaining the elaborate plan she's been drafting. My eyes find the bags of pills strewn about across the room on a buffet table, and the demon within me lurches inside me, thrashing about, begging to be freed. The sweat trickles down my temple as I focus on my breathing, steadying the nausea in my stomach, the need to use growing strong again.

She continues to speak, her words becoming distorted as her mouth moves, her voice muffled as I try to focus on her lips moving, desperately attempting to ignore the sickness inside me. Since I did the cocaine at Enzo's order, it's become stronger again, the need to use, but I want to try to be better. Better than the pathetic, vomit-covered version of myself.

I'm hoping that by coming to Sara about Enzo, it'll help me ascertain her trust and aid in finding my half brother.

Once Sara and I agree on our plan, I exit and walk

over to where Darcy and Asher stand by the car, and when she sees me, she opens the car door, climbs in, and slams it shut before I get the chance to say a word. I chuckle, making my way around the other side and into the driver's seat. I try to get a better read on what she's feeling, and by the look of her crossed arms, staring out the window...I just know this car ride back to the villa will be entertaining.

On my behalf, at least.

"Want to tell me why you almost cost me an ally?" Starting the ignition, the engine roars to life beneath us as I'm met with silence.

She wants to play, huh?

I pull onto the exit, taking us down the mountain when a smile threatens to break through my poker face at the memory of her staring down Sara. It was attractive watching her get all jealous and possessive.

"Were you...*jealous?*" I keep my tone even, and she bites.

"If I were to be jealous of every woman you've ever fucked, I think I would develop heart disease and die prematurely," she huffs, spitting her words like daggers, and I laugh, reaching a hand over to place it on her thigh, but she swats it away immediately.

"*Fenice,*" I drawl. "It was a long time ago."

"Does *she* realise that?" she questions, and she still hasn't looked at me.

I floor the gas, thrusting us back into our seats at the force, gaining her attention as she gasps, clutching the handle and dash.

"Nicholas," she warns. "Slow down!" Her eyes dart to mine with fear blazing through them, and my cock springs to life beneath my jeans, watching her chest heave, her breaths becoming short and sharp.

"Not until you admit you were jealous."

"What!?" she yells in disbelief.

The road begins to get smaller as we approach a bend in the mountain and the adrenaline peaks. "You have about eight seconds before I take us over that fucking cliff."

"You wouldn't," she dares, and I smile wryly, watching the needle on the speedometer hit one-sixty, my ribcage vibrating with the pulsing of my heart as we approach the bend, and in a couple of seconds, she yields.

"Fine! I was jealous, okay? I was fucking furious when she touched you, and I hate myself for it!"

Bingo.

I pull the steering wheel, stepping on the brake, and the car spins, coming to an abrupt stop right at the edge of the cliff. She stares out her window, down the cliff side, and returns her eyes to me, red-hot fury emanating from her every pore.

"You are *unbelievable.*"

"I get that quite a lot." I grin, and she slaps me, the sting on my cheek sending my dick to attention.

Grabbing her wrist, I squeeze. "I dare you to do it again," I growl and she doesn't back down, her other hand slicing through the space between us before I catch it in my other hand.

She's becoming predictable.

"You could have killed us!" she exclaims, and every cell in my body screams at me to leap over the console between us and take her like a man depraved.

"If this is what it takes to get you to admit even a sliver of those feelings you try so desperately to hide from me, I will bring us to the brink of death every fucking day," I breathe, making my intentions crystal clear.

She pulls her wrists out of my hold, and I let her go,

watching her shift in her seat. "You don't have to comfort me," she whispers, and the look on her face almost shatters me to pieces because of the way my heart is beginning to beat…for *her*.

"She means nothing to me," I reiterate, and her eyes find mine. "Want me to show you?" Guiding her hand in mine, I place it over my rock-hard cock beneath my pants and roll my hips into her hand.

"Fuck," I whisper, closing my eyes at her touch when she grips me tighter, moving her hand over me, and I jerk my hips into her hand.

She leans over, pressing her lips to my ear, her tongue darting out to lick my lobe. "Your turn."

The metal on my belt clanks when she unbuckles it and slides my zipper down, freeing my cock. My eyes open, and I stare into her emerald ones as her thumb glides over my crown, smearing my precum over my cock. "Now you admit something to me." She fists her hand around me, and I place my head on the headrest behind me, revelling in her control.

"That night I came home, and I saw what you did to my bike…" I begin to speak when she lowers her head, her wet tongue licking along the side of my shaft. "Fuck…I wanted to punish you for it." Her mouth closes over the tip of my cock, and I hiss when she twirls it along the sensitive spot beneath it. "But when I saw you in that fucking dress, all I could think about was tearing it off your body and worshipping you on my knees." My confession earns me a smile when she lifts her eyes to mine and continues to stroke me.

A moment passes, and I feel a rattle in my chest at how hard my pathetic heart is working to stay in the present, but all I want to do is get lost in her. In what we could become…together. A part of me wants to abandon all my responsibilities and take her with me to the edge of the world to hide together in our sins. The logical side of me dismisses the thought as soon as it appears, bringing me back to the moment as she climbs over the console and straddles me. I make her more comfortable, bringing the seat back and giving her more room.

"This is dangerous," She cautions, running her fingers through my hair, pressing her breasts against my chest, making my cock jerk beneath her as she rolls her hips.

"I was never one to back down from danger," I smirk, sliding my hands up her dress and cupping her ass. Something crosses her mind as her face changes in a split second and if I wasn't watching her as intently as I am, I would have missed it. I raise my hand to grip the hair at the base of her neck and pull her forehead to mine, "Let go." I whisper and she closes her eyes clearly fighting with herself.

"Nicholas, I don't want this." Her voice shakes, her eyes brimming with tears and panic seizes my lungs, "I don't want this life."

I swallow, "I know."

"I never did." She admits, a tear rolling down her face, and I damn near hear the crack in my chest when I wipe it away with my thumb.

"Can you do something for me, *fenice?*" I ask, and she hesitates before nodding. "Can you trust me?"

Her brows furrow, and I feel her uncertainty when she presses her lips together as if going over every single thing our families have done to each other. There's been nothing but violence and animosity in our history, and I can just imagine that she believes history will repeat itself.

She grants me this small victory, nodding, and I grind

my hips when she lowers her hands beneath her dress. I'm beginning to allow my heart to beat for her, and it fucking terrifies me. There is not one woman on this earth that could make me act this absurd, but she does it so fucking effortlessly, and all I crave right now is to break down the high walls of her gilded cage, even just for a small glimpse into her heart.

I've never met a woman more determined than her, and when she looks at me now...I know she sees more than an enemy.

I watch with bated breath as she reaches to grip my cock in her hand and guides the tip to her wet pussy. The heat cloaks me when she lowers herself onto my cock, and I caress the pads of my fingers down her supple breast, pulling the material of her dress down, causing them to spill over the edge. Pulling her nipple into my mouth, I suck hard as a low moan vibrates through her body, my fingers pressing into her hips as she grinds herself on me, taking her pleasure. The sight of her above me, free like the phoenix I've claimed her to be, sets alight to a part of me that was beginning to burn for her. Except now, that part of me is entirely up in flames, uncontrollable like a bushfire, spreading for kilometres until it incinerates everything in its path.

She leans down, her lips so close to my ear, I can feel her need pulsing through her when she whispers, "I don't want this to end."

Her words surround me, solidifying my thoughts.

I will never let her go, not ever. She has to know this by now. She has to know that she is with me, and I will see to it that it remains this way.

I pull her into me, my hips jerking up to meet hers and

she moans as I pound into her. I'm not ready to let her go, not yet. Not until I can make her see that she's mine.

"Nicholas…" she breathes through my thrusts as I hold her tighter in my arms, afraid that if I let go, I will lose her. "I lo—" Her hips grind over me, shuddering all over my cock.

CHAPTER TWENTY-THREE
Darcy

My heart is in my throat as I frantically search for the phone I buried in the garden. The wet soil splatters as I dig with my hands, throwing the shovel to the side, the dark soil cementing itself beneath my nails.

No, no, no, this cannot be happening.

The rain lashes down when I almost give up until my nails scrape onto something hard, and I heave a heavy sigh, pressing my weight back onto my heels. Opening the box, I give my wet hand a wipe on my shirt and yank the phone out, frantically dialling.

My heart stops when he answers, and I don't know how to tell him.

"Darcy?" His tone is low, almost like he's hiding as well.

"I can't."

"I told you to stay with Nicholas. What's changed?"

"So fucking much." A tear rolls down my cheek as I feel the weight of the decisions I have made. Heavy enough to bury me six feet deep in the ground, and I wish I was because death would be easier than admitting to what I've done.

"Don't." His voice hardens. "Don't tell me what I think you're about to do."

A sob leaves my throat as I stare up at the night sky like a prayer. A prayer for Nicholas to forgive me.

"He's just as broken as me." I sniffle. "He's human. This whole time I was blinded by someone else's hate, and I won't be…not anymore." I rephrase the words Asher spoke to me.

"Goddamn it!" I hear something crash on the other end of the call before he speaks again. "You cannot trust them, Darcy. Whatever he's told you—"

"He's as much the victim as me."

"No, you don't get to call them *victims*, they are *anything* but victims." He tries to veil the maliciousness in his tone, but I hear it. I know it all too well because I once spoke of Nicholas the same way, and the reality of my emotions pins me like an anchor sitting on my chest.

He pauses before he speaks again, leaving a silence to linger. "Listen to me. I don't care whatever he's told you to sink his knife that deep into you that you are sitting there *crying*…for *him*…but you *cannot* trust him."

I close my eyes, feeling the rain begin to slow. "I fear it's too late."

"Don't fucking do anything stupid, Darcy. You hear me?" I know his words were intended to incite fear, but I know better than to let fear cripple me again. "I'm on my way."

"I can't let you come here. Not with shadows watching your every move."

"I said *stay with Nicholas*," he reiterates. "And Darcy?"

"Yes?"

"Don't you dare forget your promise to me. A promise we both made when you were sixteen."

"How can I?" A lump forms in my throat, and I swallow. "It's all I've thought about."

The call ends, and I'm forced once again to fight my demons alone. Placing the phone back into the box, I bury it again and head back to the house to peel off my wet clothing, and shove them into the bin out front to hide any evidence that I was up to something. Peering up into the void, I sigh in relief when I don't hear movement. Nicholas has shown me how much he's trusting me by removing the guard that was watching my every move, and after what I have just done, the dormant guilt resurfaces.

There's not much I could give him...not now. If he were to catch me, I would be forced to come clean, and I don't think he could ever forgive me for everything transpiring behind his back...because of me.

I consider making my way up to Nicholas's bed to crawl back into his arms, but my mind races with one too many thoughts. So instead, I walk quietly to the back and dip my toe into the pool, the image of a future filled with violence and vengeance becoming clear as day. I need to be ready...ready to fight the one person who shares the same broken pieces as me, the one I would have never imagined could get under my skin...the one who I once believed was my enemy.

The water rests at my ankles as I step onto the first landing, ignoring the chill that rushes down my spine at the temperature submerging my naked body.

Cold. Like your fucking heart, Darcy.

It isn't until I'm neck deep into the water that I notice the sound of the door opening.

"What are you doing up?" he asks in his sleepy voice, pulling on my fucking heartstrings yet again, standing there under the moonlight in his black boxer briefs.

"I couldn't sleep." I give him a half smile.

"And you decided swimming would help?" He steps

into the water without flinching, and I admire the way the reflection of the water dances on his inked chest.

"Be thankful I didn't raid your cellar again," I say in jest, but the crack in my heart at my deception reminds me I cannot give in to whatever has evolved between us, not fully.

He enters further into the water, wrapping his arms around me and pulling me into him. His eyes find mine and I want to look away, ashamed of myself.

"What is it, *fenice?*"

His heart beats in tandem with mine, and I want to give him something, anything that could potentially paint me in a better light, but I know the truth. No matter what I say, in the end, it'll be me he detests.

"The secrets my family kept…I fear that even I did not know the full extent of them."

He rests his forehead on mine. "You've told me what you know, and if there's more, we'll deal with it. Together." His words are meant for reassurance, carving through me as he lifts my chin, forcing my eyes to his and claiming my mouth…taking the last pieces of myself I had been holding onto.

The rain patters lightly atop the water as I run my fingers through his damp hair, pressing myself further into him, needing to be close, afraid of him letting me go. I lift my legs to straddle him as he walks us to the edge of the pool and places me down on it, removing his briefs and tossing them out of the pool. I swallow at the sight of him standing there, his muscular frame towering over me, his dark ink illuminated by the light of the moon and water. He lifts a hand, raking it through his hair, and my heart almost implodes at the action, the water droplets trickling off the ends of his hair.

"What are you doing to me?" I whisper, and he grins, lowering himself above me, invading my space so beautifully.

"Same thing you're doing to me." His soft lips caress mine. "And I'm loving every fucking second of it," he murmurs, splaying a hand on the centre of my chest and pushing me back onto the cool travertine. His tongue flattens on my pussy as he forces my legs apart with his hands behind my knees, and I moan at the pleasure he awakens within me. He starts slowly, giving me just enough to warm me up but not enough to tip me over the edge, sucking my clit into his mouth and plunging his tongue into my already wet pussy.

Grabbing his hair, I pull him into me even further, grinding my hips over his face and feeling the tip of his nose brushing my clit with every buck. My breathing becomes jagged when he sinks two fingers into me, pumping them in and out, his tongue flicking my clit. It's when he looks up at me, the smile so clear in his eyes, that I realise I'm so much deeper into this than I had anticipated to be. From the time he cornered me in the woods as I ran from him until now, so much has changed between us that I'm finding it hard to process and fully understand how we ended up here. From what I know about the emotion fluttering inside my chest is that it's never up to our minds to decide, the heart chooses for itself when and how to feel.

I must have been too entranced in my thoughts to notice he has pulled himself up out of the pool, and his body now hovers over mine. His tongue swirling around my nipple jars me as he sucks and bites.

"How do you feel, *fenice?*" he whispers, and I buck my hips, feeling the crown of his cock slide along my pussy, making me crave his friction.

"Like I'm falling into a black hole and the only person who can pull me out is falling with me," I answer honestly. He doesn't say anything, but he doesn't have to. I see it in his eyes. The clear passion and affection he feels for me.

He takes me with one swift thrust of his hips, burying himself inside me as he groans. I feel sore from the amount of sex we've been having, but we can't seem to stop. It's like my skin beckons his touch and his caress no matter where we are, and it's staggering just how much I've come to love it.

Tears sting behind my eyes, and I squeeze them shut, pulling Nicholas into me, feeling him move in and out, savouring his passion. Our tongues fight for dominance in a different way as I taste myself on his tongue and feel every strong beat of my heart in my throat.

I can't pull away, not this time.

I wondered all my life if my parents ever knew the moment they truly fell for one another, and tonight, I have my answer, because in this moment, I've fallen, and there is no force strong enough to pull me out.

"The way your body moves with mine is like finding the missing piece of my soul," he rasps, moving effortlessly above me. "And when it comes to you, there isn't anything I wouldn't do to ensure your safety." He caresses my hair and lowers his lips to my forehead, placing a gentle kiss on my skin. "Know that you're safe with me, *fenice*."

My lip wobbles when I almost tell him I love him, but I bite my lip to hold back my tears as they continue to form. "I lov——" A sob leaves me, and I see him smile.

"I know." He kisses the tear that escapes, licking them off my face as they continue. "But what I don't know is why you're upset about it." His brows pull in with concern now that he is watching me.

"I just—" I stop mid-sentence and pull him into me, my mouth crashing over his with the need to be consumed by him.

I will not lose you.

I roll him over and straddle him, the sight of him beneath me, giving me control, makes me feel more alive than I ever have before. Grinding my hips over him, I feel his cock hitting the right spot over and over, his rough hands running up my torso to grasp my breasts and squeeze them tight.

"You are so fucking beautiful." He moves his hips, mimicking my rhythm as I tip my head back, the stars sparkling down on us in the dark sky. I quicken my pace, and the euphoria starts to build within me as he sits up to wrap his arms around me and we move as one, my fingers threading through his wet hair.

A weak moan leaves my body as he runs his tongue from the middle of my chest to the side of my neck, his hot breath making my skin itch and ache for a release.

"You're the anchor I've been searching for this whole time," he groans, nipping at my ear. "It's like you were made just for me."

Shivers run through me at his words, and I move my hips faster, chasing the release I can feel within my reach, forgetting the guilt and shoving it into the void.

"Fuck," he moans, scraping his teeth over my shoulder.

I rake my nails over his back, pushing my breasts into his face, his cock hardening inside me, and his hand coming up to circle around my throat when my eyes meet his.

"Fucking mine."

My body quivers as I come undone, his lips crashing

into mine, stealing the air from my lungs as he rocks my hips with his hands, erupting inside me.

The sun beams down onto Nicholas's ridiculously toned back, and I wonder who he's talking to. We stayed up until morning, exploring every line on each other's bodies, and I just know I will be paying for it today because when I move, the ache between my legs spurs the memory of last night's passion, reminding me that it did happen and I didn't dream it. After we tired ourselves out, we ended up laying on the plush rug on the floor, curled up in each other's arms. I don't remember how I got on the lounge, so I assume Nicholas put me here.

My attention turns to the ticking clock on the wall.

Twelve *p.m.*

Nicholas is usually out by this time and sends Asher to watch me, but not today.

I don't miss the way his brows pull in at whatever exchange he is having on the phone outside, and my curiosity peaks. Padding slowly toward the door, I slide it open just enough for his voice to filter through.

"What is it going to take?" His tone is all business as he pulls out a cigarette from the packet of smokes in his pocket.

"You know my word is worth everything, so don't fuck with me on this." He sounds pissed, and no matter how much I strain my ears to hear who the person on the other line is, I'm too far away.

"I know," he says as he turns, and before he spots me, I shield myself behind the wall.

It's no secret that we both have things we are afraid to share with each other, and that will always remain the reason for an empty void between us, stopping us from truly being together, truly seeing each other. The heart wants what it wants, but when secrets as big as the ones we both carry loom over us, it becomes impossible to see a future together—at least not one with promise.

CHAPTER TWENTY-FOUR
Nicholas

A sher grins at me as I watch Darcy kick a stone by the water, her white dress flowing freely in the wind, the sun slowly taking its rest behind the trees, almost disappearing into the horizon, and I revel at the sight of her illuminated by it.

"Fuuuck." Asher chortles, following my line of sight to Darcy. "You're done for." He laughs, lifting his beer glass in my peripheral to his lips. "Never thought I would see the day."

"Neither did I," I admit, not bothering to hide from Asher. He's been through a lot with me, so I let him savour this rare moment.

"As long as you know what you're doing, Nico."

"I have no fucking clue," I confess, bringing my eyes back to his. "The only thing I know about women is how to please them with my mouth or my dick."

He chuckles. "That's for sure."

"I never bothered to explore anything further...until her." I sit back against my chair, and a comfortable silence falls between us. There was never a time where I thought I would be sitting across from Asher and professing my love for a woman, let alone my enemy.

He dips his chin, staring into his lap, before he looks at me. "Are you ready for this, brother?"

I know what he's asking, and I can't help but take in a breath. The plans we've made together over the last week are slowly coming to fruition, and I can't help but feel a little anxious about how they will play out. I have not one but two people counting on me now.

"The Dixons were spotted in Sicily yesterday, and we have confirmation on where they are staying." He watches for my reaction, and when I don't give him one, he continues. "You know why they're here, don't you?" he asks, accusation in his voice.

"Their reason for being here doesn't matter. What matters is they keep their distance," I declare.

"You know I'm not one for questioning your strategy, Nicholas, but if this backfires, there's a chance everything will turn to shit." He leans forward, and I see the warning in his eyes.

"You've lost faith in me, Asher." I smirk, my eyes fleeing to Darcy who is now seated on the sandbank.

"My faith in you doesn't change the probability of the outcome, Nico."

I'm getting bored and restless with this conversation.

"Tell me, did you bring me what I asked for?" I question, changing the subject, and he reaches into his pocket, handing me the item.

The rumble of the motorbike courses through me with Darcy's arms wrapped tightly around my middle. She presses her front to my back as I speed through the roads, intent on making this night one she will never forget. One that she will look back on and remember me for the man she made me.

We come to a stop, the sea thrashing against the rocks by the same cliffside I threatened to throw her off. It's dark, but the full moon provides us enough light to illuminate the glow of her porcelain skin as she steps off my bike and joins me to stand, watching the ocean.

"Why did we come here?" she asks, placing the helmet back on the bike.

I search for the words I want to say, but there are too many in my head that I can't seem to formulate a proper sentence. Something foreign batters beneath my heart, and no matter how much I try to calm myself, it continues to reverberate through me.

"*Fenice…*" I begin as she watches me intently. "There is a lot I want to say, but I fear I don't have the right words."

Her hands intertwine with mine as she steps closer, her goddamn scent enveloping me, and I become powerless to its compulsion.

I take a deep breath, steading my thoughts and composing myself.

"Lately, whatever has changed between us has made me realise that hate I felt toward you wasn't fair. It belonged to a broken part of me, one that I thought I would have to wrestle with every day for the rest of my life. Still to this day, I crave it, and I can't lie to you or to myself," I declare as she squeezes my hands, her way of silent support.

"I had a stash hidden away in the villa in case I needed it, and *fuck*, I wanted to. I wanted to so fucking bad…but I didn't." Sliding my hand out of hers, I grip her by the nape of her neck and bring her forehead to mine. "I couldn't because I didn't want to disappoint you. I no longer wanted you to see a broken man before you, but one who would battle his demons not just for you but for himself."

She sighs, and I release her, wanting to read whatever expression is on her face.

"I know it's hard."

"You have no fucking idea," I counter as a tear rolls down her face.

"I'm so sorry you had to live through that trauma." She leans in and plants a small kiss on my lips.

"That trauma is what made me who I am. I'm not sorry it happened, but I do feel the guilt eat at me every night for those who have worried for me," I admit. "The reason I wanted to bring you here tonight was to apologise for how I treated you that day." I step back and pull out the platinum necklace, holding it flat in my hand.

Her eyes drop to the necklace and lift back to mine. "A phoenix," she whispers.

"*Fenice.*"

She lifts the necklace in her hands and admires it before clutching it to her chest.

Clasping her face in my hands, I lift her eyes to mine. "I never want you to forget who you are."

Her arms wrap around me, crushing me into her, and I breathe in her scent, etching this moment into my mind before she slowly steps back. I take the necklace from her as she turns around, lifting her hair, and I clasp it around her neck.

"It's beautiful," she whispers, turning around to reach up and place her palm on my cheek. "Thank you."

My mouth hovers over hers, our souls finally giving in, her white cotton dress blowing in the passing breeze, her fire-red hair framing her perfect face. A face that graces my dreams, chasing away my nightmares. I lift her as she wraps her legs around me and place her on my bike, her back resting between the handlebars as I straddle the bike and she straddles me.

"Let's rewrite the past," I whisper on her lips between the dance of our tongues, and she moans in response, bucking her hips, her hands moving down to my belt, unbuckling it, then pulling my zipper down and freeing my cock. I groan as she squeezes me in her hand, mine now running along her thighs and tugging off her panties.

"Fuck me," she demands, and I glide her dress up her chest, exposing her breasts, yanking down her bra and slipping my hand between us. I slide two fingers into her as she rests her head on my bike, closing her eyes.

"Nicholas…" she moans my name, and my cock twitches with the need to be inside her.

"You're making a mess," I tease, my fingers sliding out and coating her pussy in her arousal.

If it were any other night, I would have taken my time with her. I would have had her shuddering on my face and fingers before I took my pleasure, but not tonight. I need to be inside her, and I need it now.

Her eyes meet mine, and I see her plea just as I give her what she wants, rubbing my cock on her pussy, spreading her legs wider and pushing into her, both our moans slicing through the dead of night. Her hands skim down my chest, her breasts bouncing from the force of my thrusts, and the sight is fucking wonderful, one I will be storing inside my head for the rest of my life. Picking her up, I flip her over, face down, with her legs on either side of my bike.

"Should I collect on what I am owed?" I ask, wanting

to know if she would scream my name just as hard if I were in her ass.

Her eyes clash with mine over her shoulder, hesitation written all over her face.

"N-now? But I've never done that before."

"You're more than ready, *fenice*. You're dripping all over my bike." I comfort her, spreading her arousal to her ass with my cock. She bites her lip, and I pause, waiting for confirmation from her.

"I've never—"

"I'll go slow," I promise, and she closes her eyes, nodding, her anxiety evident in the way she grips my bike.

Spitting on my hand, I fist my cock, wetting it and priming her as I push the tip of my finger into her ass. Running my hand slowly up and down her back, I notice her responding to my touch. Sliding another finger into her, I grasp my cock with my other hand, watching her take both fingers, making me throb to be inside her. Slipping both fingers out, I spit on my hand again, covering myself with more of my saliva as I slowly push the tip of my cock into her ass.

"Lucifer, have mercy," I whisper, squeezing my eyes shut at the pleasure of her tight ass around my crown. Continuing to rub her back, I lean over her and brush her hair behind her ear. "You okay, *fenice?*"

She nods, her grip remaining strong in the middle of the handlebars.

"Focus on my voice and the way it makes you feel," I whisper into her ear, caressing her hair as I push into her further, eliciting a moan from her. "You're the fiercest woman I've ever met," I admit, pushing a little further, feeling her stretching around me "Your body was made just for me. For me to play," I whisper, pushing in further.

"For me to taste," I groan as I fill her completely. "For me to fuck."

She whimpers as she begins to move her hips, rubbing her clit on the seat of my bike, and that's when I know she's ready. I remind myself to take it slow even though I want to fuck her into oblivion.

Moving my hips in a slow rhythm, I grip her hip with one hand and stabilise myself with the other on the handlebar as she builds more confidence and moves with me, the muscles in her legs tensing when she uses the balls of her feet to push against the frame on either side of my bike. It's everything I imagined it would be, with someone who I never thought I'd have this connection with. If I believed in all that bullshit about soul mates, I would probably say she is mine, but I don't because soul mates are traditionally known to be your perfect fit and we are anything but perfect.

She is a mirror—a mirror that shows me everything I am worth. She shows me the parts of myself I try so desperately to hide in shame and forces me to deal with the parts I despise. She fights, and it's her fight I love.

"Nicholas," she breathes, rolling her hips faster. "It feels amazing," she moans as my cock thrusts in and out of her.

"Fuck, I'm going to come just by watching you mount my bike," I grunt, pushing into her harder and threading my fingers through her hair, my belt clanking against the metal on my bike as my hips work. My legs strain on either side of the bike as I pull her hair. Watching her body take me so effortlessly has my cock pulsing, and I feel myself getting close. Slipping my fingers into her pussy, I work them faster, tightening the grip on her hair, ramming my cock into her, and meeting her hips with each thrust.

"I'm so close," she whispers, and with a few more

thrusts, I feel her body shudder as I spill every last drop inside her, and when I pull out, I admire my cum dripping out of her ass and onto my bike. I watch as she lays there with her back heaving. Massaging her plump ass with both hands, I search her face when she turns to me. "Talk to me." I press light kisses up her back until I'm hovering just next to her ear. "Did you enjoy that?"

I feel instant relief when a small smile covers her features, and her emerald eyes look back at me. "That was...phenomenal."

I chuckle, lifting her and repositioning us so she is now straddling me.

"We should clean up." She eyes the bike.

"No."

"What?" She looks at me, confused.

"I want you to feel me dripping out of you." I slide two fingers between her ass, taking the remnants of my pleasure and sliding it back into her.

CHAPTER TWENTY-FIVE
Darcy

Asher moves his pawn forward two spaces as the warmth of the sun settles into my skin. It's been a few days, and every single one has been filled with Nicholas meeting Sara or Antonio. All they do is sit and plan. I'm never allowed in on the strategies, which is not surprising, but I don't even know if I want to be.

"Your move." Asher motions to the board, and I stare at it, willing my pieces to move on their own because the last thing I want to focus on now is beating a Guerra at a chess game. My mind is far across the world to where my decisions will take me if what I have wanted my entire life is still what I want now.

"Who taught you how to play?" I ask, hoping he will extend a friendly conversation back.

He smirks. "My father, actually. Who taught you?"

I swallow at the razor blades pressing against my throat, thinking of my mother and I sitting at the large kitchen table with my father's glass chess pieces. "My mother," I answer, reliving the memory in my head.

I place the castle in front of his black pawn, and he eyes me. "Your strategy could use some work, though." He chuckles as his bishop takes my castle.

"Nicholas must trust you." I move another pawn.

"I trust him with my life, and he trusts me with his, so you understand why I had to say what I did."

I nod.

I understand him, and a piece of me wishes I had someone like Asher in my life, someone who would lie for me, steal for me...die for me.

The closer I feel to Nicholas, the more I want to pull away. How can something so unexpected develop so quickly and with such passion? I'm beginning to think the line between hate and love doesn't really exist and is just an illusion.

As I grab the queen to move her to the square behind my pawn, an echo of engines rumbles through the trees, and within minutes, gunfire erupts through the bar.

"Get down! Get down!"

Bile surges up my throat, threatening to explode as Asher pulls me to the floor and flips the wooden table, pulling me behind it, our chess pieces clattering to the ground. My eyes dart to Nicholas, who has his guns in his hands, and relief rushes over me at the sight of him unharmed. I squeeze my eyes shut and cover my ears as an explosion vibrates the floor.

"Fuck," Asher mutters, reloading his gun and aiming to shoot.

"Give me a gun." I look at him with an open palm.

He looks to me, then to my hand, visibly fighting with himself on if he wants to arm the one person he knows he shouldn't.

"I said give me a fucking gun!" I yell over the gunfire, and he swears, slapping his other gun into my palm. I haven't held one in a long time, but the weight in my hand is all too familiar as I cock the gun and scan the threat. Spotting a man between the bushes, I take aim and pull the trigger, the first shot missing him by an inch. My aim is rusty, but the second shot lands straight in the middle of his forehead, and he drops to the ground. Adrenaline spikes throughout my body when Asher looks at me in my peripheral, probably with a shocked expression, but I don't stop. I continue emptying the magazine until I've shot four people. Taking cover, I throw him the empty gun and he reloads it, then passes it back to me. The gunfire slows and then stops altogether when I hear Nicholas.

"Who the fuck sent you!?" he shouts at the man kneeling before him.

I hastily run to stand beside him, and the man smirks up at me. "Someone who wants you dead."

"Enzo?" Nicholas asks, and the man gives him nothing.

Nicholas's knee slams into his chin as he roars in pain, blood trickling down his chin, his spit now filled with blood.

An eerie laugh springs from the man when he looks up to Nicholas. "You have no idea what you've started, do you?" He shakes his head, and my palms clench at my sides. "You should've killed her. Now, it's you who will die."

I watch something flash across Nicholas's eyes, but it's gone as quickly as it came.

"Don't say I didn't give you a chance." Nicholas cocks his gun and aims it at his forehead.

"You're just as arrogant as your brother."

"Ezra and I share many similarities, but unlike him, I don't like to play with my prey." Gunfire echoes, and the man thuds to the floor, his eyes wide.

Nicholas eyes me, checking me over, and I shrug out of his hold. "I'm fine," I say as he places his gun in his waistband.

"I don't think this will be the last we see of them."

Antonio assesses the damage to his bar, holes in the walls, and scattered furniture.

"How did they know we were here?" Asher questions, and Nicholas purses his lips. The Petrucci family has influence all over the city, so I wouldn't be surprised if there were a few people tailing our every move.

"Antonio, find out," Nicholas demands, and Asher pulls out his phone.

"Ezra mentioned he was sending a few guys for backup; they should be here tomorrow night," Asher confirms, and Nicholas nods.

"You better watch your back, Nico, she doesn't just know how to use a gun, she's a dead shot."

Asher gives me a wry smile, and I can't help but feel a small sense of pride swell within my chest, and I don't miss the way Nicholas's lips almost curve into a smile at that remark.

"Get some guys here to help Antonio restore this place," he tells Asher, grabbing me by the wrist and dragging me into the building, now filled with bullets.

"I'm sending you back to London." He sighs, waiting for my reaction.

"What?" My heart pounds so loudly through my ears that I don't hear the next words that come out of his mouth. "I'm not going anywhere." Sidestepping, I attempt to step away from him, but his hand flies out, clasping around my throat and pushing me back into the wall.

"Do. Not. Argue." He speaks through a clenched jaw, and rage rushes through me.

Grabbing his wrist with both hands, I look him dead in the eyes unflinching. "I will not, and you can't make me."

A loud bang echoes through my ears when he slams his fist beside my face and roars, "I'm trying to keep you safe!"

"I don't need your protection!" I shout, watching as he pulls away, sliding a hand down his face, clearly frustrated. It's too late to hide behind Nicholas or anyone else for that matter. I know what they truly want, and it's not him. Whether or not he knows this, I can't be certain, but I will not leave him to suffer the consequences of my family's actions. It's time things changed, and I will be the first to admit I am no saint, but I will not bow to a bunch of thugs playing dress up in suits. "After what just happened, I would think that's pretty fucking clear!"

"What? After you shot four men?" He snickers, and it makes me livid.

"I saved your fucking ass, and you criticise me for it?"

"No, *fenice*, this is me telling you it's not safe in Italy anymore." He crowds me again, his eyes pleading for me to reason with him. "I can't protect you if I'm constantly worried about you."

"And you think sending me away to London will ease that worry?"

"You'll be safer there, away from all of this." He pushes, brushing my hair behind my shoulder, and silence befalls us as we stare at each other, the energy crackling around us each time we fight for what we want, what we truly believe is the right thing to do.

"No." My voice is firm, and he closes his eyes, no doubt trying to decide if fighting me is going to be worth his while.

"I have other ways to get you to say yes to me." A devilish smirk appears on his lips, and I look around to notice Asher on his phone in front of the building and Antonio picking up the furniture by the beach.

"You wouldn't," I challenge, reading his mind, and sure enough, he accepts by forcefully pinning me to the wall by my throat, my eyes darting to the two men outside. "Nicholas," I warn, but he's too far gone to hear me. In a flash, his belt clatters to the ground, and I watch as he undoes his bloodied pants. "Nicholas!" I breathe, trying to get him to listen.

"You want to fight?" he questions as he slips my panties to the side underneath my dress, hooking one of my legs around his waist. "You do it with my cock buried deep inside you." He pushes into me with force as I squeeze my eyes shut at the intrusion and press my lips together to stifle my moans.

His piercing caresses the spot I've come to know all too well in the past weeks, and as he thrusts into me, it becomes harder and harder to argue, my thoughts slipping away when he tightens his hold around my throat and brings his lips to mine.

It's fear mixed with lust when he takes me against the wall with an animalistic need.

I release one hand from his wrist that is still gripping me, and push him away just enough to land a hit right in the middle of his face. He groans at the impact, my hand now thumping in pain, but he doesn't budge an inch when blood leaks out from his nose and flows down to his mouth and chin.

A sinister smile appears slowly on his lips, the blood now flooding into his mouth and staining his white teeth. The sight should have me terrified, but it leaves me wanting more of his wrath.

"Came to play, *fenice*?" He sinks himself into me further, closing his hand around my throat even tighter than before. "I can play," he whispers into my ear, and I rock my hips into him, ignoring my instinct to fight…to fall apart in his hold and give in to his lust. He grabs my wrist with his other hand and slams it into the wall, holding me in place as he has his way with me.

"This is how I want to spend the rest of my days with you. Fighting, with my cock so deep inside you that you can't form the words to deny me." Grunting, he thrusts into me harder, taking his pleasure. "I want the remnants of me dripping from your pussy even days after I've had you." He lowers his mouth onto mine, forcing it open, and slides his tongue inside, his thick blood now smearing over my face, the metallic taste lingering inside my mouth when he pulls away. "I want you to taste just how much I crave your fight."

He loosens his grip on my throat and slides his hand into my dress, pulling out my breast to cover it with his bloodied mouth. When he releases it, he looks up at me, and it's in this moment that I know that no matter what Nicholas says or what he does to me, I will never live another day in my life wondering if I'd ever feel the love I knew I deserved.

In his own ruined way, I feel it.

He loosens his hold on my wrist as if sensing my thoughts, and I wrap my arms and legs around him as he crushes me into the wall harder, burying his face in my neck. He pounds into me relentlessly, my loud moans echoing through the building, uncaring as to who might hear as we both chase our release.

"I will fight you until my last breath," I manage to say through his thrusts, and with one last drive, we both explode together, groaning as we give in to our bodies and ride the wave of pleasure coursing through our blood. When the wave resides, he slips out of me, his release sliding down my inner thigh.

Placing himself back into his pants and buttoning

them, he pulls his belt back on as I smooth my dishevelled hair and fix my breasts back into my bra. Heat rushes to my cheeks when I notice Asher walk in from the front with a grin on his face.

"Finally. Feel better now?" he says in jest to Nicholas, handing him his phone. "It's happening tomorrow."

"What's happening tomorrow?" I ask.

Asher and Nicholas look at each other, and a silent question forms between them before Nicholas turns to me with a devilish grin. "Damnation for those on the path of war."

CHAPTER TWENTY-SIX
Nicholas

I fill the magazine to the brim, forcing it back into my pants with a huff as Darcy stands behind me, watching my every move to make sure I haven't missed loading any of the guns splayed out on the table.

"Are you going to help?" I ask, eyeing her.

"No, I think you're doing a good enough job." She nods to Asher. "But I think he might need some help."

I turn to Asher, struggling to fit some of the bullet packets into a duffel, and he gives Darcy a look of frustration. "Well, if you want to do it, be my guest."

The bag slams to the ground as he storms out of the room, the tension in the air almost tangible as we all prepare for the war to come. Call it intuition, but I just know somewhere along the line that something is just not going to go the way I want it to because it never does, and Darcy, being the stubborn woman that I love her to be, won't listen to me. So, I'm forced to take her with us.

"I need you to reconsider, Darcy," I implore her, pulling her to me, and she looks up into my eyes, her emeralds not backing down, not that I expected her to.

"No," she says calmly, placing her hands on either side of my face. "I'm not leaving you."

"If you get hurt, I swear to God…"

"You don't believe in God," she retorts, pressing her body into mine, making me lose my breath yet again.

"No, because he's a selfish bastard." I give her a half smile, and she presses her soft lips gently onto mine. "This is the last time I'll ask, even if I know your answer."

"You need all the manpower you can get."

"We will have more than enough," I reassure her, but she shakes her head. "Darcy." I pause, watching her intently. "The Dixons are in Italy."

Her body tenses in my arms, her eyes darting away from me when she steps back. "I think this is a bad idea." Her voice shakes as she fidgets with her hair, suddenly wary.

"Why?" Confused, I watch her for an answer, even if she doesn't give it to me verbally, she almost always shows me how she truly feels with her body.

"It's a trap." Grabbing my hands, she squeezes. "Nicholas, please listen to me. Don't. It's a trap."

"What do you know that I don't?"

"Think about it! Why would the Dixons come here after they just lured Ezra back to London?" she questions, and I pause.

"This is what I've been trying to warn you about," Asher chimes in, strolling back into the room. "And how do you know so much about the Dixons, Darcy?"

There's no mistaking the accusatory tone in Asher's voice, and I know he doesn't trust her, but he doesn't know her like I do, and I know things had to have changed after the nights we've spent in each other's beds.

"Stop it, Asher," I warn.

"Have you not once asked yourself who she spoke to on the phone in that club all those nights ago?" He steps toward me, and I clench my hand in a fist. I don't want to fight my best friend, but I will annihilate anyone and anything standing between me and Darcy.

"We handled that."

"Are you sure? Did you look into it?" he probes.

"Fuck you, Guerra!" Darcy exclaims.

"Everyone, just fucking relax!" I slam my fist on the table, the guns vibrating at the impact. "Nothing about this plan is changing!"

"She's coming with us?" Sara glances at Darcy in the passenger seat beside me and chuckles, shaking her head and getting into the car behind us.

"I knew my family made a lot of enemies, but I didn't realise just how many." Darcy speaks softly beside me, and I place my hand on hers.

"Don't forget, *fenice*, there is a fine line between love and hate." I smirk. "I think we are a perfect example of that, wouldn't you agree?"

She smiles softly in response as we make our way to our last stop, Antonio's bar. Adrenaline starts to churn in my gut as we approach the dark building, and I consider just turning away and taking Darcy to the nearest safe house. I'm desperate for her to be as far away from all this, but I know she would do everything within her power to find me, and at this point, she is safer with me than without. I can't have her wandering the fucking streets in search of me.

Pulling up to the bar, I shut the car off and grip Darcy firmly by the back of her neck, pulling her to me. "Listen to me this time, please."

A coy smile spreads across her lips. "Did you just say please?"

"Darcy, I mean it." My lips crash into hers, her need matching mine as she unbuckles her belt to straddle me, our tongues moving fervently together, not wanting to waste another second of being apart. Just as her hand slides into my shirt, a loud knock beats on my window.

Sliding Darcy off, I exit the car to find the place empty.

What the fuck?

"Where is Antonio?" I ask Asher, and he checks his phone for a missed call or message.

"He said he would be here." Raising his phone to his ear, he paces the entrance as I walk through the front doors and search the place.

A sick feeling rises from the bottom of my stomach, and every fibre of my being tells me to get back in the car and turn around, far away from here. I waste no time to heed the visceral warning and exit the building, but as I do, my heart free-falls when I see Darcy struggle in the arms of a man—the same arms I was hoping to sever tonight. I take a deep breath and draw both my guns from my waist, Sara's cars lining up behind me, and her men filing out to stand beside me. Antonio smiles from across the space between us making my hand twitch with the need to pull his fucking lungs out.

"Just couldn't help yourself, could you?" I'm the first to speak. "Had to run your father's hard work into the fucking ground."

"I don't know what you're talking about." Antonio looks to Enzo, who has a firm grip on Darcy, his gun pointed at her temple. She struggles in his hold, but he's twice her size, rendering her efforts useless. "In my eyes, I'm extending my family's reach."

"By supporting someone who's as selfish as Enzo?" Sara questions, stepping beside me and aiming her gun at Enzo. "You didn't truly think I'd fall for your bribe?"

"Non sei mai stato il bersaglio."

You were never the target.

His words send a shiver down my spine as I see James Dixon emerge slowly from behind them. Swallowing, I finally realise what their plan had been all along.

Darcy.

No, no, no.

"Let her go." I focus on keeping my voice calm, but the thrashing whirlpool inside me wants to swallow up everyone in my path to her.

"Why would we do that?" Enzo chuckles, cocking his gun, when I take a step forward. "Uh-uh, I wouldn't do that if I were you," he warns, pressing the barrel into her temple.

"Eat shit, asshole." Darcy grunts as she continues to fight.

"She's got a dirty little mouth on her, doesn't she?" He licks his lips, sending fire into my lungs, and I grip my pistols harder in both hands.

"Now the question is, what should I do with you?" Enzo cocks his head to the side, eyeing me.

"Take me instead."

"What the fuck are you doing, Nico?" Asher questions, his voice low enough that only I can hear him beside me.

"Let her go and take me. I know everything she does."

A sickening laugh echoes through the darkening sky as Enzo lowers his gun from Darcy's temple to her neck. He leans into her, inhaling her scent, and needles prick my skin at his proximity to her. "Have you not been honest with your husband, *Mia caro?*"

Her eyes meet mine, the tears pooling in them, and the thump in my chest quickens when her expression changes into something that resembles remorse.

The gravel crunches on the ground as another car rolls to the front of the bar, and I watch multiple men file out one by one, pulling out another from the back with a mask over his face. He's a lot bigger than the rest of them, so it takes three men to push him to his knees beside Darcy.

"Your dear wife has not been entirely honest with you, Nicholas," he taunts as the kneeling man struggles in the hold of the others.

"What the fuck?" Asher whispers as the man's mask is removed, and Darcy roars in Enzo's hold.

"No!" she screams as his eyes meet hers, and it takes everything in me not to react. "I told you not to come!" she cries, the man looking over to me and back at her.

"I couldn't leave you here." He tugs on his restraints, the muscles in his arms coiling at the tension.

"Someone get their phone out." Enzo gives me a wicked smile. "I'm going to want to watch this back."

My mind races with the endless possibilities of what is unfolding in front of me, and I look to Asher, who looks just as confused as I feel.

"Say hello to the man you've been searching high and low for." His voice echoes through my mind as I struggle to make sense of the situation.

"You're a fucking monster!" Darcy spits, biting his arm, and Enzo roars, kicking her behind her knee, causing her to fall beside the man I've been searching for this entire time.

The grip on my pistols tighten as I cement my feet firmly to the ground.

"Oh, *I'm* the monster?" Enzo squeezes her cheeks,

causing her mouth to pout, tears now travelling down to her jaw. "I'm not the one who lied to Nicholas."

"You told me you buried him," I seethe.

"Oh, I did." He chuckles as his fist meets the man's jaw, whipping his face to the side. "Care to share how you escaped, Rafael?"

My half brother spits a mouthful of blood. "Suck my dick." He bares his teeth.

My heart cracks beneath my chest at her deceit, and blood rushes to my ears.

"I'm sorry, Darcy, I couldn't protect you," Rafael admits, and it makes me sick to my stomach watching her wrap her arms around him.

"All right, all right, you two will have plenty of time to catch up. First, I need to decide what to do with dear old Nicholas Casella." Enzo steps forward, closing the distance between us. The only thought I have in my head is lighting everyone on fire to burn together…to make them feel my pain.

CHAPTER TWENTY-SEVEN
Darcy

Hot tears fall from my eyes, my worst nightmare taking place right in front of me, and I can't do anything to stop it. The one thing I had asked from Rafael was to stay away, but he came anyway, and now there's a chance we will all die. I wish I had more time — more time to right my wrongs, to admit to my mistakes and make things right between our families— but I failed so fucking miserably. I knew the secrets my family kept would lead me to a moment very similar to this, and I was right. I was too much of a coward to come clean to Nicholas, still ensnared in my fucking fear.

My eyes meet Nicholas's as he shakes his head, unable to look at me.

Please don't hate me.

I beg him with my eyes as Enzo paces in the space between us.

"I think I may have an excellent idea." He stops pacing and turns to me, gripping me by my hair. My legs drag behind me as he pulls me in front of Nicholas, forcing me onto my feet. "There's something quite poetic about this moment."

"You're a sick fuck." I sob when Enzo grips me by the chin, forcing me to look at Nicholas, and my heart shatters into a million pieces at the visible hurt in his eyes.

"I want you to look at him one last time," Enzo spits, jerking my head. "Watch his love for you fade with each minute that passes."

"Let her go." Nicholas speaks through gritted teeth, his eyes glued to mine. Enzo releases his hold on me, and it takes every bit of control I have left not to throw myself into Nicholas's arms.

"Nicholas." I sob, tears blurring my vision at the overwhelming guilt surrounding me. "I'm sorry."

His jaw tics as he takes in a deep breath, bringing his arm up to lower Asher's gun.

"Get it over with," he utters, his words aimed at Enzo.

"Nicholas! What are you doing?" Sara exclaims, looking to Asher for backup, but he gives her none.

Bile rises up my throat when I feel Enzo slip a pistol into my hand and raise it to aim at Nicholas.

"No!" I protest.

"Do it, or I will kill Rafael right in front of you. Make your choice." Enzo's words ring in my ears as I stare at the man I've come to love. Taking a couple of steps back, Enzo raises his gun to Rafael as a warning, leaving me with an impossible decision.

The horror builds, and I hear Nicholas's guns clatter to the ground, taking a step forward to me.

"Stop!" I yell, "I won't shoot him."

"You will."

My head whips around to Nicholas. "What?"

"I want you to know one thing before you do." He reaches out, brushing a strand of hair behind my ear. "If you want to kill me, *fenice*, you better make sure I die tonight." His fingers curl around the gun by the barrel, placing it directly on his chest. "Because if I don't, I won't stop until I find you."

I choke back tears when my hand begins to shake. Gripping the gun with both hands now, I sob even harder, wishing the ground would swallow me whole.

"If this is the end for me, make it hurt, because I'd rather feel the pain of the bullet than the lifelong suffering of your deceit and betrayal."

His words slice through me, creating scars deeper than I ever thought possible, and I know in this moment, there is no coming back for us. There is not a chance in this world that he would want to hear my reasoning. The twisted part is that I did this for him just as much as I did it for me. I was trying to keep him safe because knowledge is power, and when you have it, everyone wants a piece of it. The secrets I keep, I keep for the sake of guarding the peace because the biggest one of all could tear down the entire world the founders have built, and if I wanted my freedom, it was best kept unsaid.

Nicholas grips the barrel tighter. "Do it!" he yells, making me flinch, and my cries fill the empty air.

"I can't!" I sob harder. "Please, I can't," I beg, but no one listens.

"You're running out of time, Darcy." I hear Enzo speak as he cocks his gun, pushing it into Rafael's temple.

The phoenix pendant burns a hole through my chest, a symbol I wish he never associated me with because right now, a phoenix would be heroic and light themselves on fire rather than make a choice between the man she loves and the man who had been there for her since she was a child.

"I love you," is all I can manage to say through my sobs. Squeezing my eyes shut, my finger resting on the trigger, I hope that by some miracle this is just a dream and, in a moment, I'll be woken up by Nicholas in bed beside me.

CHAPTER TWENTY-EIGHT
Nicholas

I made peace with death years ago, but when she came into my life, she changed everything, even if she didn't mean to. She changed the one thing I thought I'd be stuck with forever, and now I'm forced to face the familiar demon of death, except this time it's in the hands of someone I love. It's not at all how I pictured it, the way our lives have entangled, but I am grateful I got the chance to experience it with her.

"Do it, *fenice*." I whisper, and she closes her eyes. "Man's immortality is not to live forever; for that wish is born of fear…"

"Each moment free from fear makes a man immortal," she utters, her voice only audible to me with her proximity.

Finally, gunfire rings through my ears, my chest vibrating when everything around me slows, but all I feel is her. The smooth touch of her porcelain skin, her lips on mine, and the brush of her hair on my cheek. I know my body thuds to the floor because I stare up into the sky, replaying our time together in my head.

Shrieks, screams, and cries echo in the distance around me as I watch the stars dance in the sky above when hands are on me, the distant gunfire and the screech of tyres surrounding me as my body tries to respond, to move, to breathe, to swallow the blood pooling in my throat.

Fenice.

Black clouds fog my vision, and I give in, surrendering to her heavenly smile pulling me under the unknown, yielding to the familiar rush of peace.

Part Two

CHAPTER TWENTY-NINE
Darcy

SIX MONTHS LATER

The muscles in my arms ache as I haul the bags of groceries into the kitchen and place them on the counter, sweat sliding down my back at the unbearable heat, and out of all the places Rafael has chosen, this one has an equal part hate and love to it. The house is small, but just enough for what we need to stay hidden. I glance at the calendar hanging on the dingy fridge, covered with smudge marks.

Six months.

Six months from the worst day of my fucking life.

Rafael walks in with supplies in hand and runs his fingers through his thick, dark-brown hair.

"It's fucking hot," he says, lifting his shirt to wipe the sweat off his forehead.

"You couldn't have chosen somewhere with a milder climate?" I joke as he gives me a *"good one"* look.

"So, the days you've spent laying in the sun on the beach aren't good enough for you?" he toys, and I give him a small smile back. There's a pause when he steps toward the kitchen to lean over the counter. "It's okay to move on."

"You don't get it, Raf—"

"I get it." He slides a bottle of water toward me. "You fell in love, but now it's time to turn the page. It's been six months."

"Six months of running," I reinforce.

"Would you rather go back to those fuckers and have them torture you some more?" His temper surfaces, and I look away because he's right. "Look, you knew from the moment you spoke to me what was going to happen when you didn't share everything with him."

"You're saying it's my fault?" I ask, astonished.

"Maybe we should talk properly about this some other time."

"You've barely said two words to me about Nicholas," I admit. "In the entire time we've been running, you've barely even mentioned his name."

"Because I knew you were hurting!" he yells.

I swallow, trying to calm my breathing as I muster up the courage to ask what I really want to. "Is he alive?"

His ocean-blue eyes meet mine, and it's hard to look away from the fear of his answer.

"Darcy—"

"Tell me the truth." My voice is stern.

"I don't know," he admits, blowing out a breath and running a hand over his face. "God, this is so fucked."

"I had everything under control. Why did you come?" Tears begin to sting my eyes, and I storm out the back door straight onto the sand with Rafael on my tail.

"I came because you were in trouble, because you needed me."

I whip around to face him. "I needed you to keep yourself safe!"

His jaw tics as he stands there, staring at me.

"I told you to keep yourself far away from these

fucking people, and you didn't listen to me. Now, we must spend the rest of our lives running from them because of the secrets we still fucking keep!" I exclaim. "Because of fucking fear!" I blow out a breath, the tears now falling freely. "I just needed more time." Dropping to my knees, I cover my face with my hands as sobs rack my body. "I think about him every goddamn day, Raf."

He kneels beside me, cradling my shaking body into his. "I know."

"I loved him," I admit more to myself than to him, and he stays silent, wrapping me in his arms as we kneel on the sand.

"You can still have a life." He tries to console me, rubbing my back.

"What kind of a life?" My breathing slowly returns to normal against his chest. "One filled with fear and the constant worry that one day they will find us?"

"It's still a life, and I have a plan." He pulls away to face me. "But I need you to be on board."

"What did you get mixed up in?" I ask, and he remains quiet. I knew it was only a matter of time before the boy I knew would be sucked into some sort of crime-filled life, but I wanted more for him than that. Our exchanges always consisted of him bragging to me how he was on top of his classes, but eventually he dropped out of school and started making a lot of money doing some very questionable things.

"Let me worry about that."

I pull the luggage out of the back seat of the old utility vehicle, moving yet again, and stare up at the beautiful wooden house sitting atop the hill. This is easily one of the most beautiful places we've stayed. Rafael takes my bag and hauls it up the many steps, reaching the front door. After a day or two we spent travelling, from a plane ride to hours inside a car, I can say it was quite worth it when the door opens and I am greeted by the smell of pine needles. Stepping into the living room, I glance around to find a small TV tucked in the corner of the space with a lounge pointed directly to it with an old-school flute fireplace on the wall.

"Is this better than the last place?" Rafael asks with a coy smile.

"Shut up." I smirk, rummaging through the magazines on the coffee table.

He rolls the luggage to the side of the entry door and approaches me. "We can stay here as long as we like."

I stare up at him, his tall frame towering over me. "What do you mean?"

"I have a *friend* who can guarantee us safety here." He grabs my shoulders. "You can have a life here if that's what you want."

I swallow at his words, a part of my heart jumping for joy knowing that I can finally have the freedom I have worked so desperately hard for, but another part of my heart aches for Nicholas to be beside me.

"Maybe this is what I need."

"But—"

"Don't tell me what I think you're about to," I warn, holding my finger up in his face.

"You'll be safe here without me, Darcy." He tries to reassure me, but it just makes me furious.

"You're not leaving me, Raf."

"Not yet." He pulls out a deck of playing cards. "Not until I give you a whooping in rummy."

Grabbing the cards, I take a seat on the sofa as he settles on the opposite side of the coffee table. It's big enough to play at, so I toss him a pillow for him to sit on.

"You know, before we saw each other again after all those years, I imagined you to be taller," Rafael says as I shuffle the deck.

"Yeah?"

"By the way you spoke over the years of getting to know you, I just thought you'd have that height-to-mouth ratio," he jokes, and I roll my eyes.

We play a quick round, and as I guessed I would, I win.

"Damn, when did you get so good?"

"When you became sloppy," I jape, drawing a card. "Raf?"

He looks up at me expectantly as I consider if he really wants to know what I'm about to ask. "What will you do?"

He stares down at his cards again, rearranging them, then placing them all face up. A full hand. "Show them who I am."

"I don't want you to worry about me." He takes the pile of cards I placed in the middle, joining them with the others, and begins shuffling. "I want you to build a life here, one that you want."

"What if I don't know what I want anymore?" I whisper, pulling the sleeves of my shirt over my hands when he places the cards in the middle, waiting for me to cut the deck.

"Then figure it out."

CHAPTER THIRTY
Darcy

The breeze sends a chill through my bones as I wipe down the last table for the day. It's been a week since Rafael left, so I forced myself to become a part of society by getting a job at the nearest local café. The owner pays me enough cash to support myself, and I've been lucky enough to land something with the minimal skill set and next-to-nothing resume I have. I'm about to close when a man on the street begins waving his glove-covered hand, walking over to me.

"Oh god, you're not closing, are you?" He blows into his hands and rubs them together. "I would be grateful for a cup of coffee." His smile reaches his green eyes as he pleads.

I check the time on my watch and think about turning him away but decide against it. Smiling, I wave him in. "I can keep it open for another ten minutes."

"You are my angel." He slips past me, taking a seat on the bench as I shift behind it, grabbing a pot of coffee. "Where are you from? I don't think I've seen you in this town before." His question, although normal, has me clamming up.

"Somewhere across the ocean." I smile back at him as he takes a sip of his coffee.

"Judging by the accent, I'm going to guess the UK?"

I don't give him a definitive answer, and he nods, acknowledging my silent wish to keep it to myself.

"When did you move here?"

"Two weeks ago."

"Well, you have some timing. There's a blizzard on its way soon." He looks outside at the snow falling from the sky, then back to me.

"Luckily I'm used to cold climates."

He smiles at my response and takes another sip of his coffee. "Thank you, I really appreciate this."

My eyes run over him, noticing his carved jaw and large build underneath his black coat. "It's no problem, really."

I return his smile as he continues to sip his coffee, and I begin to reorder and pack things away, getting ready to close before the cold hits. I don't mind working here, it's close to where I call home nowadays, and it leaves me with a sense of accomplishment, like I've truly left my old life behind. Like I have a chance at remaking myself into a part of society and living a *normal* life.

I feel a twinge in my chest as my memories of that night resurface, and almost on instinct, my fingers clasp over the pendant I still wear around my neck.

"That hold some significance?" the man asks, taking the last sip of his coffee.

I press my lips together because how can I tell this perfect stranger that it holds the best of memories and the worst at the same time?

"Something like that," I admit, looking away, trying my damn hardest to force the memories out of my mind. It's been a constant battle to remember the techniques I've been practicing with my therapist. Of course, I couldn't give her my actual name, so I've been using the one on my fake passport.

"What's your name, sunshine?" The endearment sounds foreign coming from his lips.

"Brigid," I respond with a smile as he places the bills on the table beside his coffee.

"Oliver." He nods. "Thank you for your hospitality, Brigid. I look forward to seeing you around town." Grabbing his gloves, he gives me a wink and steps out the door into the cold, leaving me thinking about the one person I shouldn't.

Placing the cup in the washer, I give the bench one last wipe down and grab the keys as I pull on my coat. White clouds of smoke form in the air when I exit and lock the café. Sighing, I walk up to the old utility vehicle Raf left for me and slide into the driver's seat. It's not the life I was used to, and it definitely isn't the life I dreamed of, but it's better than living in a nightmare surrounded by gilded cages.

It seems to always get colder and lonelier when the nights come, and try as I might, I struggle to keep the wandering thoughts at bay. The what-if's—they're the biggest time wasters and joy suckers—and yet, I dwell on almost every single one that crosses my mind in the dark of night.

Dahlia purrs as her tail curls around my leg, welcoming me home, and I pick her up to give her loving scratches on her head. She appeared one night on my walk to my car after a long shift, and I spent all of my weekend searching for her owners, but she wasn't chipped nor did she have a collar, so I ended up taking her home with me. It's only been a few days since she's been here, but it's been a little less lonely with her by my side.

Throwing a large piece of wood into the fireplace, I light a match and begin burning the paper in the fireplace to warm up the space. Turning on the dusty record player in the corner of the room, I begin prepping dinner. There are days when I struggle to get out of bed, and there are days like this where it isn't as hard and I'm thankful for these days when I feel closer to human and closer to *normal*. It's become *mundane*, and a part of me is thankful I get to experience this part of life—one that doesn't include countless murders and blood-soaked hands.

"Here you go, baby," I whisper as Dahlia pads toward her food bowl I set on the floor.

Grabbing a glass, I pour some wine I spoiled myself with this week and take a sip. There will come a time when I'm okay with my past, when I can sit and enjoy a moment of peace without my heart tearing in two every time I think of him, and until that moment comes, I will hold myself accountable in every guilty thought and in every tear I shed. I thought I knew what I was doing by dragging the Dixons into this whole mess, but I clearly underestimated their power and reach. The families of London are no doubt powerful, but the notorious ones remain in Italy, hardened by their past. It shouldn't have come as a surprise that James consorted with Enzo, but that night, it was.

The skin around my arms burns as I stare at Nicholas's lifeless body, the tears running freely down my cheeks to my neck. Nails dig into my skin as I'm forced to my feet, but my eyes remain on him...on what I had done. Red crimson streams from his body with Asher hovering over him, pressing his hands on his chest, and a loud roar rips through me as I struggle in the hold of two men.

"Nicholas!" I cry, hoping I didn't kill the only man who could ever love me. "NICHOLAS!" Sobs shatter through me as I'm thrown into a car, the sight of him slowly getting smaller and smaller as I thrash my body about, desperately trying to escape their hold.

"Someone shut her the fuck up," Enzo barks from the passenger seat when I feel a sting in my neck, the liquid slowly oozing down into my chest, creating a warmth comfortable enough to slip into. My eyelids become heavy as my voice weakens, my screams morphing into silent pleas as I feel my body slowly falling into sleep. I fight it for as long as I can until I can't anymore.

I live through the memory seared into my brain from that night, wondering how long it's going to take for it to fade just enough to give me a small sense of peace. There isn't a day or night I haven't thought of this memory or lived through the trauma seared into my bones. I'm working hard with my therapist to become better at controlling my anxiety and paranoia, but trauma takes time to heal, especially when guilt intertwines so closely with the events that unfolded.

Opening the fridge, I consider making a nutritious meal but decide against it. I just don't feel hungry, and lately, it has been a recurring event. I had never seen a psychologist before, and I always wondered if it was beneficial. So far, all I've done is talk about my past in a way that doesn't incriminate me because I still have no trust in people, and I don't think that will change.

Reaching for my phone, I pick it up, the text from Raf blaring from the screen.

Hope you're doing okay.

I capture a photo of myself and Dahlia by the fire and hit send, then type a message.

Better than you are right now.

I don't doubt Raf has likely gone back to Italy, and it makes me anxious just thinking about what might be happening, but it's out of my control, and right now, I want to focus on what I *can* control because, my entire life, this is all I've wanted and all I have worked for.

Reaching into my bag next to me, I pull out a book I picked up from the local bookstore and open it up to the first chapter, getting comfortable to read when I notice a flash in my peripheral. My heart begins to hammer in my chest, and almost sensing the change in my body, Dahlia jumps onto the ground when I look out the floor-to-ceiling windows, but it's too dark to see anything. Feeling spooked, I draw the curtains and race over to the front door to make sure it's locked. Padding over to my bedroom, I kneel and pull out the box under my bed, which houses a pistol that Raf left for me. I haven't needed it and hoped I wouldn't, but I'm not stupid enough not to think that there's still a chance someone could find me here.

Checking the bullets, I cock the pistol and hold it out in front of me with both hands as I head to the door to unlock it, the icy wind hitting me in the face when I slide out and close the door behind me to begin my search. My toes almost freeze over as the ice crunches beneath my weight, slowly making my way around to the other side of the house where the windows are, but I see nothing, just trees swaying in the wind and an owl sitting on a branch, judging me.

"You'd be paranoid too if you were me, okay?" I whisper to the owl, placing the safety back on my pistol and putting it in my waistband, then head back toward the front door.

It's nights like these where I feel Nicholas's absence the most because somehow in my chest, I can still feel him with me, and when the trees sway in a storm as snow builds on the driveway, I feel his warmth surround me when I sleep. Some nights I wake in sweat after reliving that day and the days following, but other nights I see him in my dreams, reminiscing about the times we spent together, waking up with tears mixed with my sorrow.

CHAPTER THIRTY-ONE
Darcy

Another week of storms and snow, trapping me in this house and forcing me to live through my memories, and I thank the weather for easing up just enough for me to be at work today. If I were to spend another minute in that house alone, I think I would have lost my mind. My struggles with falling asleep have not wavered in the slightest, and I wonder if they ever will. I've considered asking my therapist for something that will help, but anytime I do, Nicholas appears right in front of me, strewn across the chair, his skin pale.

"Oh, sweetie, are you okay?" Clara, my colleague, begins to wipe the water I've spilled on the counter, and I rush to help her. "It's no biggie, honey. Let me clean up."

I step back and place the jug of water on the counter.

"What is it?" She places her hand on mine like a supportive mother would, and I bite my lip.

"It just gets a little lonely in a small town." I chuckle as she smiles, the bell atop the door chiming when someone enters.

"I have been inviting you over, but you always decline."

I look down, not knowing how to tell her that I don't trust anyone.

"It's like when you're working, you're so focused on

your task, dear, that you're in another place." Her brows pull in, a worried look on her face.

"It must be the cold. I hate going anywhere when it's this cold," I admit and hope she won't ask me any more questions. Grabbing the tray, I begin clearing some of the tables when I spot a familiar man sitting in the booth far across the room. He smiles at me, but I struggle to remember his name.

Pulling out my notepad and pencil, I walk over to him. "What can I get for you?"

"Do you remember me from the other day?" he asks, placing a hand on his chest. "Oliver."

Right. The guy who kept me open past closing.

"Oliver. Yes, sorry, I'm not good with names." I give him a half smile, and he nods, fiddling with the menu in front of him. "I don't usually do this, but would you like to go see a movie sometime?"

His question takes me by surprise, and I stutter. "S-sorry?"

"Oh man, I shouldn't have asked." He runs a hand through his dark hair nervously and looks back up at me. "Let's just pretend I didn't—"

"No, no." I chuckle. "It's fine, I wasn't expecting it, that's all."

"I'm sorry if it's forward, but…I think you might enjoy this town if you gave it a chance." He smiles, his green eyes sparkling like a golden retriever would after you've given them a treat and they're waiting for more. "Not obligatory, of course, but I can't help but notice you don't have a ring on your finger, so is it safe to assume you're single?"

"Look…" I sigh, shifting my weight from one foot to the other, uncomfortable with this conversation. "I don't think you really want what you're asking."

"Why wouldn't I?"

Everything within me screams to say no, struggling to find the words.

"Okay, you know what? I'll convince you."

"You better have impeccable influential skills because my mind is quite made up."

"You won't know what hit you." He winks, and I can't help the smile that spreads onto my face at his playfulness. "I'm a local around here, so you'll be seeing a lot of me."

"Oliver," Clara drawls, walking over to us. "I see you've already met dear Brigid."

"We met a week ago, actually. She was kind enough to keep the shop open to pour me a coffee."

"Ah, that's just like her." Clara gives my hand a squeeze and disappears behind the counter.

It hasn't been long since I've been working here, but I can feel that she trusts me.

"So, can I get you anything?" I ask Oliver.

"Just a coffee, please." He smiles, handing me the menu.

Weeks have passed, and Oliver has spent almost every single morning inside the coffee shop trying to convince me to see a movie with him. I will admit to myself that although I still don't give my trust away freely, I do feel an attraction toward him. He works at a hospital in town as a nurse, and I think it is the most endearing choice of career for someone to have. What better way to leave your mark on the world than by saving a complete stranger's life when they owe you absolutely nothing and leave them with that memory in their hearts their entire lives?

"Today's the day, Clara. I feel it," I hear Oliver say as I slip through the door for my afternoon shift.

"What day might that be?" I ask with a smirk on my lips.

His green eyes find mine, his lips creeping up into a full smile. After shedding my coat, I take a step behind the counter and tie my apron around my waist.

"The day you succumb to my charms." He winks, and I roll my eyes with a wide grin. "Would it help if I said you could pick the movie?"

"You asked me this last week." I chuckle.

"Well, maybe you didn't hear me."

He's persistent, I'll give him that. "Oliver."

"How about if I take you skating?" he offers.

"Skating?"

"What better way to charm you than on ice?"

"You skate?" I ask, bewildered by the things I've come to learn about him.

"Grew up learning ice hockey, then played in school as a team sport, and now skating is just what I do in my spare time." He shrugs.

"Spare time?" I chuckle. "If you're not at the hospital, you're here."

"Doesn't that prove how much I want to take you out on a date?" He smiles, and for the first time in months, I feel a spark within my chest I thought was snuffed out, never to be lit again.

"Non-obligatory?" I ask, raising my brows.

His face instantly lights up at my words, and he nods. "Of course."

"How's tomorrow?" I smile, watching him stand and

raise his arms up in the air like he won a huge prize. Clara looks at me with a laugh and shakes her head.

"Tomorrow is perfect. Pick you up at six?"

I nod. "Works for me."

"Great." He raises his cup to his lips, sipping the last of his coffee, then placing his gloves on. "See, Clara, I told you today was the day."

CHAPTER THIRTY-TWO
Darcy

My legs wobble on the ice as I struggle to stay upright. The last time I was on ice was when I was in high school at some rink in London with my girlfriends. None of us knew how to skate, but we all just went down to the rink every now and again to have fun.

Oliver glides effortlessly by me, and things would be a lot easier if this were an ice rink because then at least I'd have the dasher boards to cling to, but no, we're out in the open air on a fucking lake. A lake bigger than any I've seen back home. Oliver skates to a stop beside me and takes hold of my hands, steadying me.

"Have you lived in Alberta your whole life?" I'm not sure why I ask because I don't plan for this to go any further, it just feels nice to be in someone else's company.

"My family moved here from the States when I was only little, so I guess you can say I have." He gives me a warm smile. "Should I ask about you, or will you just give me the silent treatment like you have been?"

Guilt stabs me in the chest at his words, and I wish I could tell him, but I can't, so again, I stay quiet, and he nods like I've answered his question with my silence.

"You can tell me whenever you feel ready to, but right now, let's skate." He gently tugs me along with him as he skates backward, the wind picking up as we gain speed, gliding on the ice. I can see why he enjoys this. The wind in your face, the strength in your legs carrying you as your skates cut through the ice.

The freedom.

"That's it, you're getting it!" Oliver says excitedly, slowly releasing my hands until I'm skating on my own. Laughter bubbles up inside me as my legs work to glide over the ice, picking up speed, taking in my surroundings, and it's the first time I've truly seen the beauty of this place. The bubbles in the lake formed like clouds beneath the thick ice, the mountains are covered in white powder, looking like something off a postcard. In my wildest dreams I'd never even considered it would be possible to live in a place like this, and even in the circumstances I am in now, it is still something to be grateful for.

"Brigid, check this out," Oliver says as I watch him show off on his skates.

I chuckle at his attempt to woo me. "I bet that got you all the schoolgirls you wanted back in your day."

He places a hand on his chest, acting hurt. "You think I was a playboy?"

"Look at you." I motion to him up and down.

"Oh, thank God, here I was wondering if you were attracted to me at all." Ice sprays up off his skates as he stops next to me.

"I never said that."

Here we go.

The guilt begins to creep into my chest, and again, all I want to do is crawl back into my shell and run home. I shouldn't be out here having fun with this gorgeous man. I should be at home living out my life by myself because that's what I deserve for all the things I have done, the lies

I've told, and the people I've hurt. Especially the one person who put his trust in me when he had every right not to.

"Maybe I should go." I begin to retreat off the ice toward the bank with Oliver on my tail.

"Wait, what happened?" He grabs my wrist and spins me around, my body bumping into his. "I thought we were having a great time."

"I just…I'm not ready." I try to be as honest as I can with him because no one else deserves to be lied to, and that's one reason I keep myself locked up inside my house because I refuse to lie any more than I have to.

"Look, Brigid, I want you to know that whatever secrets you hold in your past, I don't need to know." He clasps my hands in his. "We can start fresh."

I feel the sincerity in his voice, and as much as I want to start fresh, I don't know if that will ever be possible for me, not with the demons I carry.

Not when Nicholas haunts me in my dreams.

"Starting fresh isn't something I think I can do, Oliver."

His face falls, and it hurts me to hurt him after all the effort he's put into convincing me to go on a date with him, but he nods anyway, helping me to the bank and motioning for me to sit on a large fallen tree trunk, then begins undoing the laces on the skates he brought for me.

"I won't force you into anything because I can see you're still holding on to something. Even after weeks of being here, you're still not fully here."

"I'm sorry." I speak softly, feeling the all-too-familiar sting in my eyes. His eyes catch mine, and he stops, immediately comforting me with a hug.

"Hey, hey, it's okay." He pulls me back gently and gives

me his warmest golden retriever smile. "I'm not going anywhere."

"So, how was your date, you two?" Clara asks, nudging me on the shoulder as she places the coffee in front of Oliver.

"Well, she's not a skater." Oliver chuckles. "But she sure knows how to leave skate marks all over one's heart."

Clara looks at me and cocks her head to the side. "Oh, honey, what did you do?"

"No, no, Clara, she has me wrapped around her finger. I won't be going anywhere." He sips his coffee and glances at his watch. "Shit." Picking up his gloves and his to-go cup, he grabs his coat. "I'm late for work, but I'll see you when I get off?"

I nod. "I'll be up."

Oliver's been doing long shifts at the hospital and finishing late, so I offered to cook him dinner tonight as an apology for last week's tears. We agreed to stay friends in the meantime, until I'm ready to take things further, but when I look deep inside myself, I don't know if I could ever love someone else. Not like I loved Nicholas. That love was unlike anything I had experienced, it was fuelled by both our fires, our desires, hates, and lusts, and with that kind of love, I'd bet on my life that it would only appear once in a lifetime.

Dinner is finally done just as a knock raps on my door and Dahlia skitters into my bedroom at the sound.

"Coming." I walk over to the door and open it to find

Oliver dressed in his black coat, white snow dusting his shoulders.

"I went home to shower." He admits, "I didn't want to come here straight from the hospital."

"It's fine, dinners ready now actually, you have perfect timing."

We sit at the table and Oliver pours me a glass of wine.

"How was work?" I ask and I can't believe the life I'm living, sitting across from a man asking how his day was.

It's so…normal.

"Ah, it was a hard day today." He frowns, pouring himself a glass. "A woman passed away under my care."

"Oh, I'm so sorry."

He shrugs. "It's part of the job. I've seen many deaths in my career."

I can't help but think about Nicholas, yet again comparing the two men when there should be no competition. Oliver helps people, and Nicholas killed them.

Stop it, Darcy.

I take a bite of my chicken, and an uneasy feeling washes over me, like someone was watching me. My eyes dart to the windows, but it's pitch-black outside, the only light coming from the crescent moon.

"Is something wrong?" Oliver asks, turning to follow my gaze.

Returning my attention to my food, I shake my head. "No, nothing, just a little paranoid, that's all."

There's an uncomfortable silence between us, and I can tell he's waiting to ask me a question he's been desperate to ask since we met.

"Brigid, are you running from something?"

CHAPTER
THIRTY-THREE
Darcy

How do you tell a stranger that you were born in the Mafia and watched four founding families fight for power your whole life?

You don't, which is why I dodged Oliver's question last night by diverting the conversation back to him.

"How are you feeling lately, Brigid?" Emma asks, sitting across from me in her obnoxiously large yellow armchair.

Tired.

Paranoid.

Lonely.

"Just tired, I guess." I fiddle with my pendant as she scribbles on her iPad.

"And why is that? Working long shifts?" She nudges her glasses higher on her nose.

Because I'm staying up all hours of the night thinking about the one person I love and wishing they were still alive…because I see him everywhere I go, no matter what I do.

"Yes," is all I can manage to say.

"How are you managing your time? Are you getting enough physical exercise?"

By physical exercise, do you mean walking around the perimeter of my house, waiting for the ghosts of my past to appear?

"I'm trying to." I lie.

"Hmmm." She scribbles on her iPad again.

Lately, these meetings with her seem pointless as I can't share anything else about my past without uncovering my identity, and I can't risk the Petrucci family or others finding me. Raf still hasn't been in touch, and I'm completely in the dark as to what's happening over there.

"Brigid, for me to be of help to you, I need you to be transparent with me, and from what you have told me, I can't help but feel there are parts of your story that have significant blank spots." Placing the pen down, she taps her fingers together.

"I'm not comfortable sharing more just yet." I cross my arms and watch as she removes her glasses. Although Rafael continues to wire me money into an account he created for me, he made me promise him I'd talk to someone, even if I couldn't share all of my past with them.

"Have the nightmares stopped?"

No.

"Yes."

"Great, well, I'm happy we're seeing some improvement." Placing her glasses back on, she scribbles on her iPad again. "If they start again, please let me know."

Driving out of the parking lot, I begin heading to work for an afternoon shift. Clara opened today and needs me to cover part of her shift so she can see her grandchildren this afternoon. I usually don't like to work weekends, but I rarely ever say no. How can I after she trusted me?

Pulling onto the main road, I turn up the music on the radio and tune the rest of the world out for a few minutes. It isn't until I reach the café that I notice a car I haven't seen before parked across the road. It's a small town, so I've made a note of who comes and goes so I'm not blindsided by any unwanted guests. Parking in front of the café, I head inside to begin my shift.

"Thank you dear for doing this." Clara gently places her hand on my arm.

"It's no problem, honestly." I smile. "Clara, do you know who owns that car?" I ask when she slips her coat on, hoping my reasoning behind the question isn't too obvious.

She glances out at the black Range Rover and chuckles. "They are not from around here, that's certain. Don't forget the lock on the bottom of the door is a little fiddly." She smiles at me and steps out onto the street, leaving me to wonder about the owner of the fancy Range Rover.

It's a little past nine when I get home, and the days seem to be getting colder. I'm no stranger to the cold, but *this* is a whole new level of cold. Shivering, I light up the fireplace again and pour myself a glass of wine. I'm lucky on the days I have an afternoon shift because our chef never allows me to go home on an empty stomach. Taking a seat on my couch, I grab my book and continue where I left off, taking small sips of my wine. My body begins to relax as tiredness sets in and it becomes harder to keep my eyes open.

"Fenice." Nicholas's voice echoes through the air as I work to breathe, my lungs seizing from the lack of oxygen. Terror is the only thing I feel as my legs work to carry me through the trees. Pausing, I work to

gather my breath, looking up at the full moon in the sky, hoping he won't catch up to me.

"You can run, but I will always find you."

My legs work to keep me going, pushing me further into the dark forest as I check every direction for any sign of him when thunder rumbles and lighting cracks, illuminating a man's silhouette, and my scream rips through the air as I see it move toward me.

"I will have my revenge, fenice, even if it means the spilling of your blood." His voice rings through my ears as I struggle to run and trip over a boulder, my hands breaking my fall.

Large hands close around my neck, the sweat dampening my clothing.

My chest heaves as my panicked cries reverberate off the windows and walls. I'm covered in sweat as I force myself up from the couch and my eyes dart around the room.

Just a dream.

Clutching my chest with one hand, I will for my heart to slow, and I reach for my glass of wine, downing it in one gulp. A loud noise grabs my attention, and I whip my head around to face the window where it came from. The residing fear from my nightmare remains, and tears sting my eyes as frustration sets in.

For once, I just want to feel like I'm free…like I don't ever have to worry about them finding me.

Grabbing my Glock, I stomp outside and around to the side of the house.

"If you're here, what are you waiting for!?" I yell into the blackness of the night. "Just fucking get it over with!"

The silence is deafening as I stand here and wait for nothing, the echo of my voice lingering in my mind. A tear glides down my cheek, the cold almost freezing it. "I'm not fucking scared of you!" My chest hammers as I yell, "You hear me!?"

I notice a familiar set of large eyes peeking out from the tree, and instantly feel like a lunatic for coming out here. Pulling out my phone, I begin to write a text to Raf.

> You didn't tell me this place creaks.

Almost instantly, he responds.

RAF

Are the nightmares back?

> They never stopped.

CHAPTER
THIRTY-FOUR
Darcy

The rain drums steadily onto the roof as I get ready for work. Placing my hair into a sleek ponytail and grabbing my bag, I check myself over in the full-length mirror once more. Today, I've chosen a satin button-up long-sleeve shirt and paired it with black jeans and thermals underneath. Combat boots are my new best friend because they tend to hold their grip the most on the snow.

Throwing on my coat, I give Dahlia a goodbye kiss and head to the car. It doesn't take much time to get to work, and once I do, I'm thankful Clara is with me today. Carrying out a shift on a Friday by yourself is hectic, and I'd rather have help. We're not usually open nights, but the people of the town hire out the café to hold their meetings and events in, and because Clara is practically an angel, she opens for them without a fee, as long as they eat.

"Don't forget the rat problem we've been having at the school," a man says whilst the woman beside him takes notes.

"The rat problem wouldn't exist if we stopped allowing children to keep rotten fruit in their bags. Tell the parents to clean out their backpacks every once in a while," another woman chimes in.

I place the coffee and tea in the middle of the table,

and everyone reaches for their drinks. The local school committee is gathered here tonight, and although I know nothing about the school, I can see just how much they care for it. The conversation is fuelled by passion, for their school and the kids.

Clara sets down a few of their orders as I head to the kitchen to retrieve the rest.

"How's things going with our boy Oliver?" Johnny, the chef, asks.

"What?" I chuckle, placing the dishes onto the tray. "We're just friends."

"Mm-hmm." He nods sarcastically. "That's how I look at my friends too."

"He's lovely, it's just…" I pause, waiting for the right words to drop into my lap.

"Ah, don't worry about it, dear. If it were right, you'd know it." He flips the burger meat on the flat stovetop.

Would I?

What if I already had the right one?

What if I never feel a love like his again?

The night goes by achingly slow, and finally, after everyone has left, I see Oliver look through the window with a smile on his face. Letting him in, he gives me a hug.

"Where have you been, stranger?" I ask, looking him over.

"I've had to do a few night shifts. It's been hard on the hospital lately with the staff shortage. How did the meeting go?"

"To be honest, I didn't pay much attention, they were talking about rats," I admit, and he chuckles.

"Ah, they're still working through that issue? Wow." He smiles and shakes his head. "I just came by to ask if you were free tomorrow morning."

"I have a shift until ten, but I'm free after that," I say.

"Great, I can pick you up from here if that's easier."

"Sure, but are you going to tell me what we are doing?" I ask, and he smirks.

"It's a surprise."

Once the cafe was clean and in order, Oliver offered to take me home, but I declined because I had driven to work.

Shutting off the car, I look up at the house, now riddled with the shadows of the night and wonder if I should be trying harder. Harder to move on or trying another way to deal with my past. Slipping out of the car, the snow crunches as I make my way toward the front door when an eerie feeling suddenly suffocates me.

Cold leather clamps over my mouth as I'm pulled backward into a hard body, and every cell within me reacts in fight. Dropping my bag, I cement my feet onto the ground and bring my hands up to curl my fingers over the hand grasping my face. Even if I were to scream, no one would hear me. The more I struggle, the tighter their hold gets, and as much as I try to manoeuvre myself to get a look at my attacker, it's no use, they're too strong. I feel a sting in my neck, and horror fires through me as I'm transported back to that goddamn night.

No, no, no.

My body gives into whatever they forced into my blood, and as much as I fight to stay awake, my muscles refuse, lulling me into the darkness once again.

CHAPTER THIRTY-FIVE
Darcy

The room spins as I battle to open my eyes, willing them to stay open, and when I try to move my wrists, I notice the pain and shackles around them, chained to both walls of the room. I pull, hoping there's some slack in the chain, but remain disappointed when there's no give.

You got too comfortable.

The voice in my head wastes no time attacking me when I'm already on my knees when the door opens, the light shining into the room, causing my eyes to squint from the brightness. The man's face is riddled with shadows so I can't make out who he is, but as he gets closer, my heart drops into my stomach, fresh tears threatening to escape.

This must be a dream.

"Y-you're—"

"Alive?" His familiar, husky voice surrounds me like a hug I never knew I needed. "No thanks to you, *fenice*." Pure malice oozes from his tone, and rightfully so. I let the tears fall, my sobs echoing through the empty room as he stares down at me, relieved that I didn't kill the man I love, that I have a chance to make it right.

"I'm sorry…" My loud cries vibrate through my chest. "I'm so fucking sorry, Nicholas. I had no choice."

He stays quiet and crouches down to my level, assessing me.

"You have to know, and I will tell you everything, please," I beg.

The pad of his thumb brushes my wet cheek, and he brings it to his mouth, tasting my tears, and silence befalls us as he stares at me without a word.

"Are you going to speak to me?" I ask, now desperate for his words.

Standing, he slides his hands into his pockets, still assessing me, his jaw ticking away as if he's weighing up his options on what to do with me next, and in another breath, he retreats, slamming the door behind him, leaving me alone with the crushing weight of my resurfaced guilt.

He left me alone the entire night in this cold room, with no idea as to where I am. For all I know, he could've taken me back to London. My joints ache from the temperature, and I thank what lucky stars I have left that I wore thermals beneath my clothing. My tongue darts out to lick my dry, cracked lips, and I don't think I've ever felt as thirsty as I do now.

Is he going to kill me?

Is he going to starve me and torture me?

The thoughts haven't stopped for the hours he's left me here, eating away at what's left of my soul, and in all the time I spent running, I never once allowed myself to truly believe he was still alive.

The door creaks open as Nicholas walks in, looking a lot more dishevelled than before, his black jeans splattered with dark blood, his shirt buttons ripped open, his tattoos also covered in thick, red blood. He runs a hand over his face, the sound of the chair in his hand scraping against the concrete floor echoing around us. He faces me, straddling the chair, and I can't bear to look at him.

"Tell me," he demands, his voice soft at first. "Tell me how you betrayed me." Hurt flashes in his eyes when I look up to them, and I swallow back the lump in my throat, denying myself the tears.

"I promise, I—"

"Don't feed me anymore of your fucking lies!" he explodes, standing and kicking the chair to the side to grip my face in his hand. "Tell me how you stabbed me in the back without remorse and moved on with your life..." He squeezes harder, forcing my lips to pout and my cheeks to sting. "Tell me how the one person I fell for deceived me and pulled the trigger that almost ended my fucking life!"

A tear falls down my cheek and over his fingers as I begin to sob.

"You'll need an ocean of your tears to convince me of your regret, *fenice*." He speaks softly, releasing my cheeks.

"I had to! They would have killed Rafael," I answer him.

"There are so many questions that have plagued me for months, and you have no idea how much I want to torture you as I pull the answers from you one by one, to watch you hurt just like you hurt me." He takes a sharp breath in. "I want to watch you *burn* for the things you did to me."

"Do whatever you want to me, Nicholas, it won't change how I feel about you." I pull on the chains, rattling them. "It won't change how *you* feel about *me*."

He scoffs, taking a step toward me and crouching so we are at eye level. "If you think I feel *anything* for you after what you put me through, I can only hope for your sake the next few days go by quick."

I swallow at his words, afraid of what's in store for me.

"W-what do you mean?" I stutter, my mouth feeling drier now.

Without warning, he yanks on the chains shackled around my wrists, pulling me forward, my face just an inch away from his, and I stare into the shadowy irises I've longed to see. "I will keep you here until you share every piece of your soul you kept hidden from me when I was baring mine to you."

CHAPTER THIRTY-SIX
Nicholas

FIVE MONTHS EARLIER

Everywhere hurts.

Every single part of my body is in pain, from the bullet in my chest to the screaming in my head. If there was a hell, this would be it.

Betrayed, shot, and still alive.

Opening my eyes, I glance around the room to notice Ezra with his head in his hands, the light from his mobile flickering as a call comes in. I search the room for the one person I've grown accustomed to seeing every day, and when I don't find her, I lose it.

Anger, frustration, and the feeling of betrayal lay heavy on my chest as I open my mouth to scream, but nothing comes out. I must have moved because Ezra is now by my side, his face contorted with worry, but all I feel is anguish.

"Nico, stop." He places his hand on my arm.

Hot tears streak down the sides of my face as I let it all back in, the flashbacks from the moment piling onto me like bricks, forcing the betrayal even further down my throat.

"Darcy...." I croak, clenching my weak hands into fists.

"Just take it easy. You're lucky the bullet went right through."

Lucky.

I want to laugh in his fucking face. Nothing about this is fucking lucky. Asher enters the room and rushes to my side.

"Oh fuck, Nico." He runs a hand through his hair. "You scared the shit out of me, man." He stares up at Ezra as I focus to breathe through the searing pain.

"Do you need something? I can get the nurse," Asher offers, and I shake my head.

"No." I look to my brother. "I want to feel every second of pain she inflicted on me, so I know how much more to give her."

I look to Asher as he glances from Ezra to me. "We haven't been able to find her."

"How long have I been in this fucking bed?" I ask, both of them now looking at each other, afraid to tell me. "Tell me how fucking long!?"

"You've been in critical care for a month." Ezra releases me and reaches for his phone.

A month?

"The doctor said you're lucky to be alive," Asher comments.

"*Lucky?*" I force a chuckle, the pain in my chest radiating to my stomach. "Death would have been a gift compared to living through this."

"I'm sorry, Nico." Asher hangs his head and closes his eyes. "I should've—"

"No." I cut him off because if there's anyone to blame here, it's me. "There's nothing you could have done, but I need you to do something for me now, Asher." I look up at him, and he nods. "Find her."

Rage. That's all I've felt in the weeks I lay in this goddamn bed with no fucking outlet. Rehab has been a fucking cunt, to put it nicely, and it's like learning to walk all over again, learning to stand like a fucking toddler. Weeks of people telling me to be patient like I don't already know that I should be. Weeks of seeing my failure every time I look at Ezra and weeks of planning exactly what I'm going to do when I find her. It's dizzying how much I want to make her suffer and make her hurt. I thought we shared something in the months we knew each other, but it was obviously one-sided. The trust wasn't there, and this lesson was mine to learn.

I swallow down my orange juice and watch some show playing on the TV above my bed. They've moved me from critical care down into a private room, but I still hate it here. I hate that every six to twelve hours someone needs to check on me, like I'm a flight risk or at risk of causing myself harm. Picking up my phone, I call her number again, but all I get is a dial tone.

I don't know why I expected anything different. It's been weeks of me calling her phone in the hopes she will pick up, that I'll hear her voice, but again and again I'm left feeling disappointed and betrayed. She's likely changed her number, so I don't know why I do it. Maybe a part of me hopes she's hurting, that the guilt is eating her alive.

Anytime I ask Asher for an update, all I get is the hang of his head and silence. No one can track them, and it's pissing me off.

Lifting the remote, I shut the TV off and do the only

thing that's been silencing my mind these last few days. I begin slowly, doing one push-up and then another. I refuse to be the weak man she saw when we were first married, I refuse to let her into my heart again, and now that I'm clean, I can use my body for what it was meant for.

Revenge.

An eye for an eye until the whole world is fucking blind.

CHAPTER THIRTY-SEVEN
Nicholas

FOUR MONTHS EARLIER

Pain radiates through my jaw and into my mouth as thick blood runs down my chin. Loud roars fill the space as I circle my opponent in the ring. I've found a new way to deal with the resounding agony I live through every single day, and the answer is *more pain*.

My opponent lifts his chin as if to say, "Come on," and I give him what he wants. This is our third round, and neither of us wants it to end because the look in his eyes mimics the same in mine.

Pure thirst for rage and blood.

"Get him down Nicholas!" someone from the crowd screams when my opponent throws a punch, missing me.

My knee flies through the air, landing into his ribs, and even through the roar of the crowd, I think I hear a crack as he topples over, clutching his ribcage.

The bell sounds and the crowd loses their minds as my arm is lifted, crowning me the winner, but I couldn't care less about the title. All I want is more pain. Night after night and day after day, that's all I crave, to feel closer to her. Someone smacks their hand on my shoulder as I enter the makeshift dressing room, and I look up at a set of dark eyes just like mine.

"Enjoy the show, brother?" I ask, smiling through the blood that's no doubt stained my teeth.

His eyebrows crease when he talks. "You've been out of the hospital for a month, and you're already looking for a way to kill yourself?"

"Nah." I walk over to the sink and begin unwrapping my hands. "Just looking for some entertainment."

"I know what you're doing, and it's not fucking healthy."

I chuckle at his words. "I don't think you should be dishing out advice, Ezra."

"Look—" he begins when I cut him off.

"Don't fucking stand there giving me advice when *you're* the one who forced me to marry her…when *you* said I had no fucking choice!" I yell at the top of my lungs. "I did it for our family, Ezra, and look where it's gotten me!" I bring my arms out wide, gesturing to the underground fighting club.

His jaw tics as he holds back whatever he was about to say and takes a deep breath. "We will find her, Nico, I promise you."

"I want her alive," I say, returning to unwrapping my hands. "And *I* want to be the first one to see her."

He nods through the mirror and places his hands in his pockets.

"Asher has traced a tail to Rafael," he mentions casually, as if the news isn't something we've been waiting for.

I turn to him and wipe the blood from my chin. "And?"

"She's not with him, but we know where he's heading." Ezra slips out his phone and holds it to his ear and, after a moment, he places it back into his pocket, taking a step toward me. "I need you to be ready for what's about to happen, because when it does, life as we know it will change."

"If this change welcomes revenge, count me in, brother, because I want to see them squirm."

"You're fucking crazy," Asher says from beside me as I lay in the chair. "Are you seriously going through with this?"

"I am."

The tattoo gun buzzes, and I make myself comfortable, closing my eyes, welcoming the numbing calmness of the needle. Asher's decided on a forearm piece he's been wanting for a while, and he finally made the decision to go ahead with it.

"Is that ten needles?" Asher asks in shock, and Gideon chuckles.

"Try one hundred and twelve," he says, and Asher winces at the number.

I knew getting a blackout tattoo would be a lot more painful than any regular tattoo, but this is what I want. It's time to erase the past and fill the present with something new.

"All right, man, you ready?" Gideon asks, and I nod. "You're one hundred percent sure you want this?"

"Yes," I confirm, waiting for him to start already.

"Okay, it's going to need at least a month to heal before I can tattoo over it with white ink."

"Just fucking start, Gideon." I feel my patience wearing out, and then the needles are in the skin of my back as I melt into the sting.

CHAPTER THIRTY-EIGHT
Darcy

PRESENT DAY

My eyes are heavy, resisting the urge to fall asleep. Exhaustion settles into my bones, pulling me down into the dark, and just as I'm about to close my eyes, the door opens and the chains rattle when I wobble to stand.

"Please." My voice comes out croaky as Nicholas holds a glass of water to my lips, and I drink like I've been living in the desert without it. He only lets me have half the glass and pours the rest over me, drenching my top.

"Nicholas." I choke on my own spit as he places the glass onto the lone table by the door. "The chains."

"You don't deserve to utter my name, *fenice*." He removes his jacket, displaying his muscular arms beneath his shirt. He's a lot bigger in size now, and it has me wondering if he has been looking after himself. I want to smile at the thought. "The chains remain in place until I have answers to my questions."

He takes a step closer to me, his scent overpowering my every sense, leaving me yearning for his touch.

"I'll tell you whatever you want to know."

"There's only one way I know you'll tell me the truth."

The back of his fingers brush down my wet chin, toward

my chest, and linger on the buttons of my blouse. My eyes meet his when he yanks my blouse open to reveal my black lace bra. I plant my feet firmly on the ground, readying myself for a fight I know is coming, and he sees it too. Smirking, he slides his hand up my chest and around the nape of my neck, clearly aware of how he still affects me, even after all this time.

"You've still got that fire," he whispers, his lips brushing mine gently. "I wonder what it'll take to smother it."

I stay silent, hoping it'll earn me some points, but all it does is make him angrier.

"Let's start with your new boyfriend." He pulls out his pocketknife and opens it, the blade shining as he holds it out to me, pressing the tip to my cheek. "Do you love him?"

"He's not my boyfriend," I answer honestly.

"Right, and I'm a fucking saint," he retorts, tracing the tip of the blade down to my neck, resting it above my jugular. "Did he touch you?" His tone is veiled with possessiveness as his dark eyes roam over my breasts.

"No. I told you; he is *not* my boyfriend." I pull on the chains, the echo of the rattles surrounding us.

His jaw tics as he lowers the knife, placing pressure in the middle of my chest where my bra meets. "Why did you hide?"

"It was the safest thing to do," I admit, and he presses the knife down further, the sharp blade cutting through my bra, causing it to fall open and my breasts to spill out. He doesn't take his eyes off mine as he glides the blade over my nipple, the sharpness of the blade nicking me, bringing my body back to life with a single shock.

He speaks through a clenched jaw, holding back his anger. "Did you think of me, *fenice?*"

Every fucking day.

I nod, not having the courage to say the words out loud.

"Did you think about how you betrayed me and went on to live out a life you so desperately dreamed of as I rotted away on a hospital bed, waiting for you to come back to me?" His tone is littered with malice and hurt, his words digging through my scars, opening old wounds that I've tried desperately to heal.

I look away, unable to meet his gaze, and he forces my head back, squeezing my cheeks.

"Oh no, no, you don't get to run away, not this time." He steps into me, our bodies almost touching as he glides the blade down my torso. "I want to watch the suffering in your eyes as your soul breaks in two. I want to watch the woman who broke me live through just as much hurt as she put me through, because only then will you understand how much I fucking loved you."

I swallow back the lump forming in my throat as he undoes the button on my jeans, pulling my zipper down and forcing them off along with my thermals. He stands back, admiring his work, and when his eyes find mine again, I know there's no escaping his wrath. No matter what I say, he wants to watch me burn, and if that's what he wants, I will give it to him because I know I will rise from the ashes, reborn once more to show him the breadth of my wings I've learnt to embrace.

"I've seen the way he looks at you," he whispers, his eyes darkening. "Does he *know* you?" he asks, as he steps forward, tracing the pad of his fingers over my nipple. "Does he know you like *I* know you?" His breath fans over my skin as he leans into me, lowering his lips to my neck, barely touching me, sending shock waves all through my body, aching for more of his touch.

My skin tingles as he trails the back of his fingers down my torso to my navel, raising the hairs on my arms as my body remembers his touch, and I suck in a deep breath when his fingers slip into my panties, the chains rattling as I pull them taught, rising to my toes.

"If you think I'll be giving you what you want, I'm sorry to disappoint you, *fenice*, but I will be taking everything you have left until you're a weeping mess, begging me to stop," he murmurs as his fingers slide into me, a moan slipping from my lips as I tilt my head back. His hand fastens over my throat, his fingers sliding deeper inside me, and I close my eyes, revelling in the pleasure, rocking my hips onto his hand.

"Fuck, I missed the way your body responds to me," he utters, tightening his hold on my throat. I groan at the loss of his fingers when he slips them out of me, and I watch as he brings them to his mouth, his eyes rolling back, a low, pleasured moan vibrating through him and straight into me.

I can sense he's not the same man I left in Italy, but I'm not the same woman I was either. Something about him has me on edge, waiting to see if there is any part of him that feels even the smallest bit of love toward me still, and when his dark irises clash with mine, the only thing I see is rage trapped beneath them, waiting to detonate.

"I've waited for this moment for months," he admits, releasing my throat and sliding his hand into my hair. "Months I spent obsessing over what I was going to do to you when I found you..." Tugging on my hair, he cranes my neck. "And now that I have you where I want, why is it that the only thing I can think of is sinking my cock so deep inside you just to hear you scream my name the way you used to?"

My mouth salivates as his lips hover over mine, giving me just enough proximity to drive me closer to insanity. "Nicholas," I breathe, my nipples hardening. "I'm sorry…" Wetness now coats my cheeks. "I loved you…and I still love you."

His face contorts in disgust as he steps away from me, walking toward a black duffel bag on the table by the door. Reaching inside, he walks over to me with something small in his hand, and my eyes go wide when I realise what it is.

"It'll feel good at first, and then I'll make it hurt, just like what you did to me."

He rips my panties off and tosses them to the floor. Bending my knee, he holds my leg up as he slides the vibrator between my legs, gliding it into me gently. The small tip of the vibrator rests on my clit, the other end firmly inside me, pressing gently on the very spot I've denied myself for months. Reaching into his pocket, he takes out his phone and releases my leg. The legs of the chair scrape on the concrete as he takes a seat in front of me and turns the vibrator on low. I twist my hand on the chains, pulling them taught as a low moan escapes me, the low vibrations of the machine pulsing through my body, warming up the fire I refused to fuel. My toes curl as he increases the vibrations, causing my hips to buck as he watches me.

He wants to see me come undone, to fall apart in front of him over and over again at his control. A twisted smile forms on his lips when he increases the setting, eliciting a loud moan from me that echoes through the empty room, and I squeeze my eyes shut, trying to focus on controlling my body, but it doesn't get me far because within a minute, my hips shake as the pressure builds, exploding through me like wildfire. The toy falls to the floor when my orgasm rips through me, and the cold doesn't bother me anymore because I now feel like my body has been submerged in molten lava.

"Please," I beg, unsure if I want him to stop or keep going.

"Your pleas mean nothing to me anymore."

"I will tell you the truth, just ask me whatever you want to know, and I will tell you." I sniff, holding myself back from breaking down again.

"Oh, I will." He stands to pick up the vibrator and slips it back inside me, turning it up. "But only when I can be sure you're too spent to lie to me anymore."

A tear rolls down my face when the agony behind his eyes reveals itself through the hate he's so desperate to inflict on me. My salty tears now run over my chin and down my neck as I grip the chains, readying myself for another wave of pleasure, and he gives it to me, my body pulsing with euphoria as I come undone all over again.

CHAPTER THIRTY-NINE
Nicholas

Her body quivers, and my cock begins to run out of space in my pants at the sight of her like this before me. Her breathy moans fill the room as I tear another orgasm from her. She's given me six in total, and even though I'm not even close to being done, the questions I've asked myself in the dark nights chip away at my brain. Shutting off the device, I walk over to her, her skin now covered in sweat, her heaving chest flushed with a rosy hue. She looks as exhausted as I felt when I woke up that day in the hospital, and I smile at the thought of breaking her like she broke me.

"Why didn't you tell me you knew Rafael was my brother?" I ask, gently brushing the hair stuck to her temple.

She regains her breath and wobbles to stay upright. "The secret would have either killed you or given you the power you needed to continue the Casella reign over London," she admits between breaths. "I grew up writing to Rafael and came to love him like a brother."

The irony isn't lost on me. "So you kept him for yourself."

"It wasn't like that," she protests.

"Does he know this secret that you're clinging onto?" I

ask, and her emerald eyes meet mine, filled with unshed tears. "I'll take that as a no."

Placing my phone into my pocket, I wipe the tears on her cheek and trace my fingers down to the necklace she still wears. "Brigid," I utter, and she squeezes her eyes shut as she sobs. "Do you know what Brigid means?"

She remains silent when she opens her eyes, pleading with me to stop.

"It isn't a coincidence that you renamed yourself the goddess of fire, *fenice*."

"I didn't want to hurt anyone," she claims. "I just wanted to be free."

"The Dixons promised me my freedom if I handed you over to them—"

Disgust swirls in the pit of my stomach. "And you did so without even a second thought."

"No!" she exclaims, pulling on her chains with all her might. "I didn't! I warned you not to go that night because I had a sickening feeling that something was going to happen, not because I knew! I ceased all contact with them the moment I knew…"

"Knew what? That you loved me?" I chuckle. "Go on, say it again, wear it out because it holds no fucking meaning for me!"

"You can deny it all you want, Nicholas, but we felt it. Which is why I called Rafael."

There's a silence in the air as I absorb her betrayal once again.

"Were you ever going to tell me about him?" I ask, almost not wanting to hear her answer.

"There were so many moments where I almost did."

"Almost." I take a deep breath. "A word that sums us up so clearly. Something that *almost* happened."

"Nicholas." She pleads for me to hear her when all I want to do is hurt her. "Rafael was coming to help us when we got ambushed."

"Not we…" I stare into her eyes, making sure my next words cut her as deep as she cut me. "When *I* got ambushed and you left me to die."

"You think I didn't suffer too!?" she shouts, leaning forward, her face an inch away from mine. "Because I suffered every goddamn day thinking I just killed the only man who could *ever* love me. I lived with the ghost of you haunting me every single fucking day, from the moment I woke up, down to my nightmares. You never left me, not even in the moments I managed to find peace because all I could think about was if you had found yours."

"Why didn't you tell me?"

"Because I feared that the only man who loved me would cast me aside when he found out I had betrayed him from the moment I stepped foot into his home!" She sobs. "Because the second I knew how I felt about you, I wanted to erase *everything* I had done. Please, you have to believe me, I had no idea Enzo and James would work together against you. When I said I couldn't go through with the original plan, James told me to find a way, and that night you saw me in the pool, that night I knew I couldn't." She looks away, the tears rolling down her cheeks. "So I called Raf for help, and he told me to stay with you because he knew you'd protect me, but we both did not anticipate what happened next."

"How did you call him?" I ask, confused as to how fucking blind I was that I missed the signs.

She bites her lip. "Antonio. He placed a burner phone in the mailbox, and I buried it in a box in the ground."

I chuckle in disbelief, the deception opening an old

wound. "So, you conspired with Antonio behind my fucking back."

"You could not stand me at the time, you wanted me gone just as much." She fights the chains, pulling them taught. "You had no right to deny me my freedom."

"And how does it taste now, without me?" I smirk, knowing I've gotten under her skin.

She clenches her jaw shut and speaks through gritted teeth. "I'm big enough to admit my feelings for you, but I will not stand here and have you cut me up with your words purely for your entertainment."

"You have no choice…because I'm not done yet," I say as I walk over to the duffel bag, pulling out the bar and cuffs. Walking back over to her, I place the cuffs on her ankles with the bar resting between her legs, immobilising them in place.

When I stand, her eyes meet mine with a challenge. "You can hurt me as much as you want, but I want you to know that after you're done, even if the anger fades, what you feel for me won't and if my pain is what you need to move past this, then fine, I'll give it to you."

"You're still under the delusion that I feel anything but rage caused by your betrayal." I hook my finger around her necklace, resting the pendant inside my palm. "Forget everything you think you know about me, because the man before you is no longer a broken shell but a rage-fuelled fire, seeking vengeance."

Her loud screams rip through the room when I yank the necklace from her neck, tossing it aside, and her chest shakes as her soft sobs fill the room.

Unlocking the chains on her wrist, I notice the purple bruises they have left in their wake when they fall to her sides, and her legs wobble as I place her on the floor. I replace the chains with leather cuffs on her wrists, tying them to the bar between her ankles. It seems like she's given up her fight as her head hangs, letting me do whatever I want to her.

"Look at me," I say, and she doesn't move. Lifting her chin with my fingers, her head cranes up, and her bloodshot eyes stare into mine. "When I'm done with you, only *I* will be the one able to put your broken pieces back together."

"It's *always* been this way." Her voice croaks as her words send a rush of guilt through my chest. There's always a chance she's telling the truth. There's always a chance I could be wrong, but after what she put me through, a part of me wants to see her burn, and the other wants to cradle her into my chest and hold her so fucking tight that no one would be able to pry her from me.

"There's still a secret you're keeping from me." I lay her flat on her back, the bar spreading her wide open for me to see. "And before the night is done, I want you to tell me."

"Raf should know first," she whispers, her voice barely audible.

"You will tell *me* first," I demand, running my fingers along her thighs as I lower my mouth to her pussy. It's been too fucking long since I've had a real taste of her, and I'm dying to remember what her cum feels like on my tongue.

"Give in to me." I speak softly over her pussy, my mouth closing over her, her hips bucking up into my me, a guttural moan filling my ears. Sliding my tongue along her, I suck on her clit, pulling it into my mouth and releasing it. It's pure heaven being between her legs, having her surrender to me. Sliding two fingers into her pussy, I hook them as I massage the spot I know she loves.

"Nicholas," she breathes my name, and I'd be damned if I said I didn't enjoy the way it slips from her lips.

"Tell me, *fenice*," I utter, flicking her clit with my tongue, my fingers moving in and out of her. She squeezes her eyes shut, grinding her hips as she moans.

"I can't."

"Yes, you can." My other hand snakes around to twist her nipple, and she cries out loud, the pleasure in her body mixed with the pain in her voice making my dick twitch inside my jeans. Sliding my wet fingers out of her, I glide them over her ass and she moans, lifting her hips for me, and it takes everything in me not to take her on the cold floor like an animal.

Pushing the bar further down, her legs spread wider, and I lick her from top to bottom, devouring her with the need that has built up inside me for the months I've thought about this moment. I had a world of hurt ready for her, but the fragile thing inside my chest wants what it wants. There's no denying the gravitational pull she has over me, and I'd be stupid to give in to it again.

I devour her with my mouth, sliding my tongue into her pussy as she cries out my name, wearing herself out, building up to her release. Hooking my fingers into her mouth, her jaw opens, and I slide my fingers in, her tongue wrapping around them, sucking without instruction. She's just as needy as me, and it makes me wonder if she denied herself pleasure during the nights that she spent without me.

"What's the secret, *fenice?*" I ask, continuing to consume her.

"I..." she breathes, a moan slipping from her lips as she rocks her hips over my mouth. "He's...the...son of..."

she moans, pulling her wrists, causing the links in the chain to rattle. "Gabriele Guerra."

With one last lick of my tongue, she comes undone, exploding all over my tongue, and I suck every last bit of pleasure that drips from her pussy, my mind working to catch up to the secret she's just revealed.

CHAPTER FORTY
Darcy

A dull ache forms around my wrists as I look around the back seat of a car, and guessing by the dark ink on the forearms in front of me, I know Nicholas is driving. My body feels drained, like I've been through an intense training session, only the training was with an instructor who cared not for my cries. It feels like I haven't slept in days, and I sigh, feeling grateful I'm no longer chained in a dark room, but my eyelids remain heavy, beginning to become harder and harder to keep open. So I surrender to them, closing them and drifting off as the car jostles over the bumps in the road.

When I open them next, relief floods over me, seeing Dahlia curled up next to me on my bed. She purrs when I give her a loving pat, but my heart sinks when I realise I'm alone. Sitting up in my bed, I check the time, and it's well past three in the morning. I lost all sense of time when Nicholas kept me in the dark room, so I don't even know how many days I was in there.

I had just told him the secret that could ruin the Casellas or make them even stronger, but the part that scares me now is how Rafael is going to react when he finds out who his father is. I kept the secret for as long as I did because I was worried it would create more harm than good with the knowledge, but with the secret now out, I'm riddled with anxiety thinking about what might happen.

My legs shake when I stand, forcing me to stabilise myself against the dresser as I hear clattering coming from my kitchen. Confused, I gather my strength and step out of my room to find Nicholas placing a frying pan into the dishwasher. I'm tongue-tied when he turns around, eyeing me from my head to my toes, then I notice I'm wearing an oversized shirt with nothing underneath.

"How did I get here?" My voice comes out rough, and I clear my throat.

He crosses his arms and leans onto the counter. "You fell asleep after your...*exhaustion*...so I took you home."

I vaguely remember opening my eyes in the back of a car, seeing a blurry moon through the window, but other than that, I don't remember much.

"Why are you still here if you already got what you wanted?" I ask.

"I'm not done with you," is all he says, motioning to the food on the table. "Eat."

"No." I cross my arms even though my stomach rumbles with the delicious smell wafting over to me.

"Don't be stubborn," he warns.

"Tell me why you're still here."

"I made you a promise." He steps towards me, his arms falling to his sides as he eats up the distance between us with just a few steps. "Until you share every piece of your soul you kept hidden from me when I was baring mine to you, I'm not going anywhere." His jaw tics, and his eyes burn through me. "I meant it when I said your freedom would only be a reality when I'm buried six feet deep."

I swallow at his veiled hostility but remain thankful I am no longer in chains.

"Now eat," he demands, and I give in, the smell of home-cooked bolognese filling the house, causing my mouth to salivate.

When I'm done, he instructs me to shower, and as I go to close the door, he holds it open, leaning on the doorframe, watching me. I don't argue, partly because I don't have the strength and because I *want* his eyes on me. I spent months wishing I could have another moment with him, and although he may hate me, I still want him to want me.

Slowly, I raise the shirt over my head and pull it off, letting it drop to the floor beside me as I stare into his eyes, standing here bare for him to see, my skin tingling with the need for his touch.

"I'm not hiding. Not anymore," I whisper, stepping closer to him. He looks away, causing me to stop in my tracks, and my heart to break a little more. "Nicholas," I utter, pressing my body into his, wishing he would wrap his arms around me and hold me close, but he doesn't.

His hand flies up, closing around my throat. "Don't," he warns, the hurt still visible in his eyes when he looks at me. "Don't say my name like I mean something to you still."

"But." I struggle in his hold, my hands clasping his wrist. "You do."

His lip curls into a snarl, pressing me back into the basin. "Is that another lie?"

Anger and adrenaline surge through me as I grip the edge of the basin as my hands come up to meet his wrists, and he hoists me on top of the bench. I take this opportunity, wrapping my legs around him and pulling him into me. "Why don't you come closer and find out?"

I feel the energy between us crackle when he pauses to

run his gaze down my naked body and back up to me. Rolling my hips over him, his hard cock tenses beneath his jeans, and his hand tightens around my throat.

Leaning forward, he presses his lips beneath my ear and whispers when I hear his zipper. "Don't mistake this for anything other than *hate, fenice.*"

The tip of his cock begins to stretch me, and without giving me a moment to adjust, he rams into me, causing a scream to rip through my throat. I know he meant to hurt me, but as the pain fades, as I adjust to him, my body takes over, his scent overwhelming me as I close my eyes, sinking my nails into the skin on his wrist. My head bangs against the mirror as he pounds into me relentlessly, his breathing matching his thrusts as I hang onto him, clinging to every bit of himself he's willing to give.

"Fuck," he moans, the piercing on his cock hitting all the right places inside me, filling up the void I'd created within the months I denied myself. His fist clashes with the mirror just above my head, startling me as he lifts his head to look at me, and I see the crack in the fury behind his eyes, revealing what little emotion he has for me, hidden beneath all the disgust and hatred. His grip on my neck loosens as his anger falters, slipping into a lust we both can't deny. His lips crash into mine as he picks me up and walks us over to the bed to place me down. He pulls his shirt over his head, and I marvel at his physique, sculpted even more than before in all the right places and bulkier in others. He removes the rest of his clothes, and without wasting another second, he's on me, forcing me onto my stomach and gripping my hair, exposing my throat.

"I told myself I wouldn't fuck you because of how you betrayed me…" he says as he bends my knee to my side up to my chest. "But seeing you come over and over for me…

is making me need to feel the way your pussy tightens on my cock again." He pushes into me, and I moan as he fills me, holding my leg in place. "I need to hear you breathe my name when I come deep inside you." He pushes deeper into me, yanking my hair back and my nipples harden as he thrusts into me harder, and I know this isn't for me.

This is for him.

Taking back some semblance of control he feels he lost due to my betrayal, and I let him have it. If this is what he needs, I won't resist, because I want it too. I want his wrath to soothe the guilt I feel.

"Nicholas," I breathe as he hits the right spot over and over again, the tingles in my fingers rising to my arms. I grip the sheets, his tongue on my neck, and with another thrust of his cock, I give in, my pussy clenching around him just as he wanted.

He growls as if displeased with my response and flips me over to my back. "I want it to hurt," he says as he reaches for his belt, wrapping it around my wrists and securing it to the bedpost above my head. My heart races as I lay before him, and he pulls out a bar from the same duffel he had in the dark room, which now lies by the bed and he wastes no time, securing my ankles to each end of it, then smothering his cock in lube. My heart rate soars as I pull against my secured wrists, realising what he's about to do.

"Nicholas, what——"

"Save your strength, *fenice*," he sneers as I feel him insert something into my pussy, and from what I can tell, it's shaped exactly like a penis. I moan when he fucks me with it, his fingers dancing around my ass, rubbing the lube mixed with my arousal all over me. He lifts the bar, causing my knees to bend into my chest. My ass is now perfectly accessible to him, and I squeeze my eyes shut when I feel the tip of his cock enter me.

"I want you to remember what it felt like on my bike," he says, pushing into me a little further, stretching my ass to accommodate himself. "Only this time, I'm not going to be so nice about it." And he does exactly what he says, slipping into me, stretching me further and further as I breathe through his size. Opening my eyes, I see the revenge in his, taking out his anger on me, forcing himself deeper as he pushes the bar further, causing my knees to dig into my ribs. The muscles in my arms ache from how much I'm tensing, pulling on the restraints as I rock my hips, wanting to feel the pleasure and friction.

"I need more."

He gives me what I want by thrusting into me, and I moan from the pleasure that surges straight to my pussy, my breasts bouncing as he powers into me hard, the muscles in his arms flexing as he holds the bar, pressing it into me.

"Fuck," he groans, his face contorting into a mix of pleasure and lust as he chases his release. "The sight of you like this, submitting to me, makes me want to tear you apart until you're begging me to put you back together."

I'm dying to touch myself when I look up at him, his eyes dancing with a dominance I hadn't seen before. He takes exactly what he wants, thrusting into me until he spills every last drop of hatred he's held in his heart inside me. He releases the bar as he slowly pulls out of me and takes the toy out of my pussy. Blood rushes back to my toes when he uncuffs the bar from my ankles and removes his belt from my wrists. Cradling me into his arms, he carries me into the shower and places me down to stand. The water hits the tiled floor, and my breath is taken away when he turns to place two towels on the hangers behind the door. His back is completely covered in dark ink, the phoenix tattooed on with white ink, one of its wings broken where the bullet exited through his back.

I gasp, covering my mouth, and he turns to me. "What?" he asks, looking me over to see if I'm hurt.

"Y-your back."

His eyes soften as he steps into the shower with me, our bodies almost touching, his large frame taking up most of the space.

"Why?" I ask, realising how much he really did care for me and how much I had caused him to hurt when I betrayed him. "Why would you do that after what I did to you?" Tears begin to flow down my already wet face, and he pulls me into him, my face now against his hard chest.

The softness of his cheek rests on the top of my head when he speaks. "Because I never wanted to feel like I lost you." I swallow down the lump in my throat as more tears threaten to break through. "Because without you, I felt directionless, like I had somehow misplaced the one thing in my life that made sense."

Sobs rack through me as I fall apart in his arms, thinking of what he went through and how he must have felt, the guilt thick like blood in my chest.

"Shhh." He tightens his hold on me, holding all my broken pieces together. I pull away slightly, and my eyes find the mark on his chest, the scar tissue thick under my fingers.

"I spent every single day in that fucking hospital thinking about how much I wanted to make you pay..." My lip wobbles as he speaks. "But even when I thought about killing you, all I wanted to know was that you were safe. Because in the end, I knew I couldn't kill you," he admits, shattering my heart all over again. "I can't kill you, because that would mean eradicating the one thing in this world that came to mean more to me than I ever thought possible." I look up, the hatred in his eyes now squashed and replaced with need. "I thought I could do this—to hurt you and leave you with your broken pieces—but I can't because they fit too perfectly with mine."

"I should have told you everything that night in the pool," I confess when he presses me into the wall behind us. "But I was so scared you'd never trust me again because you already hated me."

He chuckles, lowering his lips to mine. "I don't know that I ever truly hated you, *fenice*," he admits, causing my heart to flutter.

"Not even when I ruined your bike?"

A smirk dances on his lips as he shakes his head. "It turned me on how much you wanted to fight me. I was constantly hard when you wanted to argue, and I know you liked it too."

Grabbing my soap, he runs his hand over my breasts, lathering them. "That night you caught me using, you were the first person who didn't look at me with sympathy. Why?" he asks.

Taking a breath, I try to focus on his question and not his wandering hands. "Because I knew deep down you were hurting." His hand travels down to my pussy as the soap clatters onto the floor of the shower. "As someone who has been through a similar hurt, I never judged you for seeking comfort in what you did."

I groan when his fingers enter me, causing me to rise on my toes. "Things happened between us not because we were desperate to feel the love of someone else, but because we hadn't let ourselves have the love we deserved.

We thought we didn't deserve it because of what we had been through, but we deserved more, and that's what we were for each other," he breathes as he crowds me, his fingers sinking deeper into me as I wrap my arms around his neck. Feeling the need for his lips on mine intensify, I pull him into me, crashing my lips to his as my hips buck, riding his fingers. My body is sore, and yet I can't stop wanting more from him, and he meets me at every turn. Slipping his fingers out of me, I pull away from him to slowly drop to my knees.

"I want you to use me," I say, licking my lips at the sight of his large, pierced cock. "Let go of the remaining hurt, release it into me." Placing my hands on my knees, I open my mouth as he slowly guides his cock onto my tongue.

He fists his shaft twice, rubbing the tip over my lips as he grips my hair, and grins when he enters my mouth, his girth stretching my lips as I try to take him deeper. "I won't be gentle," he warns, forcing himself deeper into my throat. "I think I like seeing you on your knees, *fenice.*" I almost gag when he pushes into my throat. "Ah, fuck," he groans, thrusting the piercing on his cock down deeper.

My fingers slip between my legs, and I rub my clit, focusing on breathing through my nose.

"That's it, *fenice*, just like that," he whispers, thrusting into me. "Open wider," he demands, and I do my best to, but he's too big.

I moan around him, and his cock twitches. "Fuck, that's going to make me come." He fucks my mouth more aggressively as he grips my throat, forcing himself to go deeper with each thrust. "Look at you, taking every fucking inch into your throat, like a good girl," he moans, and I can feel his cock hardening with each thrust.

"Do you want to be my good girl, Darcy?"

He pulls himself out and pumps his cock as I stick out my tongue, waiting for the warmth of him. His pleasured moans fill the shower as hot streams of his cum spurt onto my tongue and run down my chin to my neck.

"Wait," he commands, pulling me to stand. I never thought it would be possible to be more turned on with Nicholas, but what he does next both surprises me and turns me on to the point where I'm so hard up, I could come just by his voice alone.

Leaning forward, his tongue darts out, licking from my breasts up to my neck, gathering his cum on his tongue and forcing it back into my mouth. "Swallow." His voice hardens, and I do as I'm told before his tongue dances with mine again.

CHAPTER FORTY-ONE
Nicholas

I curse the day I met her and pray that if there is a God, he never takes her from me again because I'd rather live with the pain of her betrayal with her by my side than live without her. It's a sick, twisted, double-edged sword, but I'm already cutting myself up for her, and the reality behind it is that I don't care.

Yes, she nearly fucking killed me, shot me, and left me to die like some deer in the woods, and I wanted to make her pay. Right now, all I want to do is soak up her scent before I must leave for London, before she finds out we have Rafael. I don't exactly know Ezra's plans, but I know they don't involve a welcome home party.

I glide the pads of my fingers over her porcelain skin, the sheets barely covering her naked body, and she stirs in her sleep when I hear a faint knock on her front door. She turns, and I see her bright green eyes open.

"Expecting someone?" I ask, and she shoots up out of bed, wrapping the sheet around her to head for the front door with me on her tail.

She opens the door to a wide-eyed Oliver, staring at her, then at me.

"I—" he begins, and I cut him off before he can embarrass himself further.

"Thanks, Oliver, we have enough towels." I smirk, and Darcy's elbow flies back into my stomach.

"Oliver…" she begins.

"So, this is why you could never commit, huh?" he asks, gesturing to me.

"You couldn't give it to her the way she wants anyway, Oli." I chuckle, stepping to the side to expose myself to him.

"Oh, good God!" His eyes drop to my dick, and he places a hand in front of him, blocking it from his vision.

"Judging by the look of you, I assume you're the reason she is running from her past."

His words fuel the burning rage in me, and I push Darcy aside to grip him by the throat and slam him into the wall.

"I'd be careful of talking about something you have zero knowledge on." I speak through gritted teeth as he struggles to breathe beneath my clasp.

"Nicholas!" Darcy yells, clawing at me with one arm. "Let him go," she says more calmly.

"Maybe I should show him exactly who we are, since you fooled him so fucking easily into thinking you're someone you're not," I seethe, jerking him back and ramming him into the wall again.

His eyes dart to Darcy, then back to me. "You're fucking crazy, man!" he sputters, and I let go.

"Get out of my sight before I prove you right."

Within a second, he's out the door and sprinting to his parked car.

"You're such a dick!" Darcy huffs as I close the door behind us. "He's my friend," she says, turning to face me, the sheets scrunched up in her fist at her chest.

"Friend?" I ask, stepping into her. "He wanted to fuck

you, and he still does. I should have slit his fucking throat for even *thinking* of you indecently," I snarl.

"You're such a fucking caveman." She rolls her eyes, and before she can turn away, I grab her wrist and rip the sheet off her body.

"If wanting you to myself makes me a caveman, I'll gut him, put him on a spit, and have him for dinner, because *no one* touches what's mine, and I certainly don't fucking share my treasure." I'm surprised at my confession as she stares at me.

"Treasure!? You literally had me chained up for days!" she yells, clearly frustrated I ruined whatever she had going on with that fucker. "Look at my fucking wrists!" She holds up her arms, showing me the bruises around them.

Grabbing them, I pull her into me forcefully. "And do you remember what *you* did?" I speak resolutely, focusing on remaining calm, then her eyes fall to the middle of my chest, where my scar lies in plain sight. She struggles in my hold, but I don't let her go, feeling every inch of her beautiful body against mine.

"Let me go," she warns, and I challenge her with a raised brow. If she thinks, after it took me months to find her, that I'm going to do anything she asks, she can keep dreaming.

Stopping, she raises her eyes to look up at me as unshed tears linger on her lashes, and I feel the bullet in my chest again, burning through my flesh. "We're not good for each other." She sobs, breaking as tears flow down her cheeks.

How can she still believe that after how much we have been through?

How can she even bear the thought of us being apart when it's so fucking clear that we belong with each other?

When *she* was the one telling me how much she loves me?

My lips crash over hers, her hunger matching mine as I lift her to straddle me. Pressing her against the cool window, she nips at my lip, and I taste the metallic blood on my tongue. "How can you draw that conclusion when your body fits so perfectly with mine, *fenice?*"

She says nothing as she grips onto me, wrapping her arms around me tight. "You only think this way because of what you think you felt at the hospital. Not because you love me." She sobs, and I pull her away, her words sending a spear through my heart and fury down my spine.

Gripping her hair, I pull her head back. "Don't tell me what I feel," I seethe. "Because all I've done for the past months without you was *feel.*"

She swallows, a tear running down her chin.

"I haven't touched another drug ever since I woke up in that hospital bed—not for you, not for me, but for us— because I knew when I came back to you, I had to be a better man. I had to be the version of me who could give you all of me," I confess, my words spilling out of me easier than I thought they would. "Tell me, what's stopping us from becoming what we were supposed to be all those months ago?"

She bites her lip in hesitation before she speaks. "I have a life here, Nicholas. I don't want to go back…"

Just like that, reality comes bursting through the peaceful nights we've had, burning any remnants of happiness, and if I were a true asshole, I would force her to come with me. Drug her, kidnap her, and *steal* her for myself, but she would never *truly* be mine.

We're at a crossroads, one I selfishly thought wouldn't be in our reality, and every fibre of my being wants to stay with her, but the reminder of blood and loyalty screams so loudly that it's deafening, and it will continue to be without a moment of peace if I choose her.

Placing her down, I release her and step away to give her some space, letting her words linger in the air so she can absorb them.

If this is what she wants, will I be able to give it to her?

Even after everything we've suffered through?

I know she's built a life she'd always dreamed of, but I believed deep down that she would want me more than anything else.

"Is this what you truly want, *fenice?*"

More tears run like a river down her angelic face as she nods before stepping into me and lifting my hands to her lips. "Stay with me," she begs, laying a soft kiss on my knuckles. "We can have a life here, far away from the bloodshed in London. We would never have to worry about the founding families ever again."

I laugh at her thoughts because she could not be more delusional if she tried. "You know I can't. I have a responsibility, a duty."

"Fuck the duty. Don't you want to be happy?" She stares at me expectantly, waiting for an answer, but I know I won't be able to give her the one she wants.

Taking a deep breath, I lower my lips to hers. "Happiness was never written in my fate."

We lay together as Darcy reads one of her favourite poems aloud by Walt Whitman, silencing all our thoughts for just a moment, allowing us to be present together in each other's company without the burdens of our past or future weighing on our shoulders.

"I celebrate myself, and sing myself, and what I assume you shall assume, for every atom belonging to me as good belongs to you."

Placing the book down beside her, she sniffles and turns her head up to look at me. "Tonight is our last night, isn't it?" she whispers, and I hold her tighter, not wanting this night to end.

"I can't stay with you, *fenice*, because I need to finish what I started," I say, tracing my fingers over her elbow.

Her face falls as she comes to terms with our impending departure. "Promise me you won't hurt Rafael."

"You know that's not something I have a say in. It's up to Ezra." I speak the truth because Ezra is the king, and he gets the final say on who lives or who dies, and depending on what Rafael has to say, I'm hoping there will be no more need for bloodshed. We've had enough to last another generation.

"We've found him and we're working things out, that's why I can't stay."

I feel her leg slide over mine, and she rests her cheek on my chest. "In another life…"

"Don't finish that sentence," I warn because I'm not ready to lose her completely yet.

Pushing herself up, she slowly climbs on top of me, straddling me, her fiery red hair cascading down her naked skin, covering her plump breasts as I marvel at her beauty.

In another life, we could've been happy.

I swallow at the thought, razor blades cutting me up from within as I prepare to say goodbye to the only woman

I've come to feel something for, and yet again, she's going to be taken from me because of family…because of *loyalty*.

Her fingers trace the crest on my chest as she sighs. "Loyalty."

"We'd be nothing without it." I don't know why I say it, but maybe it's because it's what I've been taught from such a young age. I can't help but question all my beliefs right now with her on top of me. "Mine is the original. The heart represents courage, the guns symbolise safety, and the dagger represents the hostility we are capable of if we are ever threatened."

She grits her teeth, her fingers still tracing the lines. "And the wings?" Her eyes find mine, and my heart breaks as I speak.

"Freedom."

She nods slowly, raising herself to lean forward and press her lips onto mine. Words have become obsolete as our mouths devour one another, my hands beginning to roam her skin. Pulling her closer, she rolls her hips onto me, my dick now rising. Surprisingly, it still functions even after the endless times we've fucked over the last few days, but in this moment, it feels like something has changed. Something has shifted into the unknown as her hand curls into my hair, grasping it and tugging my head back as our tongues fight each other.

Gripping her ass, I groan when she rolls her pussy over me again, her slickness sliding over my cock, her chest heaving as our tempo increases until I can't take much more of her teasing. Raising her hips, I lift her until her pussy is hovering over my mouth, her knees on either side of my face. Lowering herself onto my mouth, she moans my name, and it sends an animalistic need shooting straight through to my cock.

"Sit," I say through my licks as she hovers over me still, needing her entire pussy on my mouth so I can taste every inch of her. "Let me taste *all* of you."

She hesitantly lowers herself to my mouth again, and I lose my patience, my hands pressing her down by her thighs, and I groan when all her weight is on top of me, her entire pussy on my tongue. If there is a heaven, this would be it, tasting her, devouring every inch until she can only utter my name.

I suck her clit into my mouth as she squeals, grinding her hips over my mouth, taking the pleasure she so desperately wants. The sight of her over me makes my cock harden, and I roll my hips, lowering my hand to stroke myself for some relief.

"That's it, *fenice*." I plunge my tongue into her as she continues to grind. "Come all over my mouth."

Gripping her breast, her head tips back. "Nicholas," she moans as I grip her hips, supporting her rhythm as she moves faster over my mouth.

Reaching up, I twist her nipple, and her moans grow louder, grinding herself over my tongue harder as I lick and suck her arousal into my mouth like a man starved when she comes undone with a shudder, moaning my name. She falls onto her back next to me, struggling to catch her breath, but I waste no time sliding between her legs, bending her knees back to her chest and spreading her open. I savour every second that I watch my cock glide into her, inch by inch, with the taste of her still lingering on my tongue. Her hooded eyes open as she practically melts into the mattress. and I lower my gaze to my cock again, sliding another inch in.

"I need all of you, Nicholas," she pleads as she bites her lip, and I give it to her, pushing into her until I'm buried so fucking deep that I need to shut my eyes at the way her pussy clenches over my cock. My eyes shoot open when I feel her hand on mine, and she looks at me in a way I've never experienced before, and within a breath, all the promises I made to myself when I was healing in the hospital fade like an imprint in sand during a sandstorm. Only she is the storm, and I am the sand, blowing in the breeze, desperate to cling onto her strength as she blazes past, leaving the shattered remnants of my fucking heart in her wake.

"Don't wait for me," I whisper as I lower myself over her and stare into her treasure like emerald spheres. "Because I can't promise I'll come back to you."

I refuse to watch the tears build in her eyes, so I kiss her instead, thrusting into her, feeling myself become as desperate as she was. For me, the desperation stems from needing to cling onto her, the need to hold her, to be with her, to become so fucking intertwined with her that when we part, the only thing others will be able to see is the missing piece of me.

Her.

She latches onto me, pulling me closer into her as I fuck her, never once taking my hands off her skin, our collective moans bouncing off the walls of her bedroom. I'd give anything to stay like this, but as hard as it was to find her, leaving her will be infinitely harder than anything I've done. Harder than becoming sober because now I have to pry her out of my system, where she's creeped into every crevice and opened my eyes to something I never knew was possible for me. A love I thought was invented by some guy with a moustache in the eighteenth century.

Only now do I see that it's real...and it's her.

Pressing my phone against my ear, I take a drag of my cigarette as the moon shines down on the vast amount of trees that surround her property. She's been asleep for an hour, and as much as I wanted to fall asleep with her, I needed to make sure she has everything she needs to survive and thrive without me.

ASHER

I'll be there in two minutes.

Asher's text lights up my phone, and I place it back in my pocket. Taking another drag, I consider staying with her because, fuck, I want to, but I'm too far gone. Where she has no ties left to this world, I have two. Two that are related to me by blood.

I watch as Asher's sleek black mustang rolls into the driveway, and I step down the stairs to meet him. He greets me with a nod, handing me a thick yellow envelope.

"It's all there, Nico," he says, watching me for a reaction, and when I don't respond, he sighs. "If this isn't what you truly want, just shred it up and forget about it."

"You know I can't fucking do that." I sigh, dropping the cigarette to the ground and crushing the tip beneath my boot.

"If it was me"—he places his hand on my shoulder—"I'd say fuck the rest and be with the woman I love. You deserve it after everything you've been through."

I think about the secret Darcy had been holding onto for years, and my chest aches for my best friend. He is completely clueless that he and I share a brother and that one of our parents shares a history deeper than the bond of our family alliance.

I open the envelope to check the contents. "My mind is made up, Asher. This is how it should be."

CHAPTER FORTY-TWO
Nicholas

The strain in my neck pulses through to my shoulders as I stare down at Rafael, who is sitting and glaring up at Ezra beside him. It's been a few days since I've been back, and I can't seem to get her out of my head. Even when I had been back in the underground, fighting my demons with my aggression against others, she wouldn't leave. I'm stuck being pulled from either side, my mind bending and breaking as I'm trying to be who I believe I'm supposed to.

"Are you going to tell us, or are you going to force my hand into *making* you tell us?" Ezra stands with his arms crossed, and I think it's the first time I've seen him this calm. Usually in situations like this, I would have expected him to have Rafael tied up, stripped, and skinned alive.

Rafael remains still, his poker face unwavering. "What's in it for me?"

"What do you mean? You know we share the same blood, don't you?" Ezra asks, and he nods. "So, fucking tell us how you're connected with the Della Torre and the Petrucci families, and why the fuck were the Dixons involved?"

Rafael sighs, running a hand over his face, and considers whether he should. He still doesn't know who his biological father is, so until we know what we need to, Ezra suggested we keep it this way.

"It's a long story."

Ezra pulls up a chair and takes a seat in front of him. "Why don't we start with how you escaped being buried alive?"

Rafael chuckles. "Fuck, that was the worst day of my life." Looking up at me, he pulls out a lighter from his pocket and flicks it open. "Dante and I have history. One that goes back to when I was banished as an infant to Italy for being a bastard child," he says with malice in his tone. "There was one night I was involved in a gang fight, and they'd beaten me down to my bones and left me to rot by the shores of Falcon's Keep. Dante's father found me and took me in," he admits.

"Did he know who you were?" I ask.

"No, I hid that from him for years. He thought I was just another fatherless kid wandering the streets, searching for trouble." He flicks the lighter again, and the flame alights. "Which I was." His eyes fall to the flame. "He taught me everything I know…"

"How does this relate to you being buried?" Ezra deadpans.

"Dante Senior was many things, but unintelligent wasn't one of them. He knew the Petrucci family would come for them one day, and that's what Dante and I worked towards for years," he admits. "Only, our plans didn't come to fruition because Dante's father passed suddenly from an illness that we both didn't know he had, and when Dante took power, I offered to carry out our mission alone. Only, I didn't anticipate the cavalry due to their newly formed alliances and our betrayals."

Ezra looks at me, his eyes asking if I believe his story, and although every part of me wants to beat him black and blue for hiding Darcy from me, I do believe him. He has no reason not to tell us the truth.

"Why didn't you come to London if you knew who you were?" Ezra asks the question that's been burning a hole through my mind for months.

"I wanted no part in what you both had here. Not when I had everything I wanted and more with Dante," he confesses. "Before Enzo buried me, I made him think he had the upper hand, but what he didn't know was that I was involved with Dante. He thought I was working for him—"

"When you were a double agent," I say with a chuckle.

"Exactly." Rafael smiles, and in a way, he looks similar to Ezra, the only difference being that Ezra looks a lot sharper, more put-together, whereas Rafael has an untroubled nature about him.

"What about the Dixons?" Ezra questions, and Rafael's face falls serious when he looks at me.

"I didn't know they would come. I only found out through Darcy."

I look away, not ready to acknowledge my losses and betrayals as the room falls silent, but the silence may as well be as loud as a fucking horn echoing through my skull and rattling my brain.

"Where do you stand, Rafael?" Ezra finally breaks the silence, and I close my eyes, hoping that I won't have to break Darcy's heart yet again.

My eyes find his as he looks from me to Ezra, flicking the lighter closed. "I think the proper question is, are you willing to admit that you need my help for a war *you* started all because you didn't want to stick to tradition?" A smirk plays on his lips as he snakes his way under Ezra's skin.

My hand immediately flies out to grab Ezra before he can reach Rafael, and I push him into the wall when I speak. "He's our brother," I remind him.

"*Half*," he snarls, his eyes never leaving Rafael.

"All right." I turn to Rafael as Ezra tugs at his suit. "We need your help."

A shit-eating grin spreads onto his face as he stands to extend his hand to me, and I take it. "Dante will be pleased."

The thing with quitting a habit is that when you finally do, all you think about is going back to it. Every single day, that thought is like an itch you shouldn't scratch, a craving you'll never taste, and a memory you'll never forget. Every day seems like one hundred days in a place you wish you could escape, but the only escape out of the prison you've created for yourself is consistency, because the longer you stay consistent, the easier it becomes to tolerate. You never fully forget what it was like or how it made you feel, but you slowly remember why you've stopped and how important it is to feel, because without the bad, there would be no good. Without the hurt, there would be no pleasure. Without hate, there would be no love.

If I could turn back time and take back every substance I abused my body with, I wouldn't, because no matter how much I hate that about myself, it's still a part of me. It's a part of me I've come to appreciate because, without it, I wouldn't know how strong I can be. We all need words of encouragement, affirmation, and love, but for me, all I need is her. She's the one who taught me that in order to heal, we need to feel, and without her, nothing in this fucked-up world makes sense anymore.

The cool night air feels foreign without her here, and all I want to do is go back to her, take her into my arms, and take her to the furthest corner of the world to keep her all to myself. Music blasts through the speakers in my helmet as I speed down the highway in the dead of night. There are hardly any cars out at this time, and I take full advantage by revving my bike as the light beads of rain patter against my helmet. The next phase of our plan is going to be the toughest one of them all because it means we will all have to come to terms with the risks. It's a great deal to have the Della Torres on board with us, given our rocky history, but even still, it makes me anxious that we will be going against everything we have been taught.

The darkest sides of me have been making themselves known a lot more the past few days, and I'm holding out because I know if I give in, it'll be over for me. The months I spent in rehab, the months it took for my brain chemistry to return to normal, even though it'll never be the same again…I just can't chance it. Not even once.

My mind wanders to her, and I hate it as I rev my bike faster, speeding down the highway. There's no fucking way I can go back to my apartment, not without her. I haven't been back there since I've been back in London, and tonight is no different.

After a while of riding aimlessly, I hold my helmet in one hand as I make it up the steps of the home I practically grew up in. The door opens as I raise my hand to knock, and Asher steps aside, letting me through without a word, and I set my helmet on his mahogany dining table.

I know I can always count on Asher because he has seen it all, and aside from Ezra, he's the one who knows me best.

"Another late night on the town?" he jests with a smirk as he pours some tea into a mug and places it in front of me. "I'd offer you some of the heavier stuff, but I like the Nicholas you're becoming."

I don't answer him as I take a seat and place my forehead in my hands.

Sighing, he takes a seat beside me. "I get it." I feel his compassion as he places his hand on my shoulder. "She's the one, isn't she?"

"There will never be anyone else," I confess with a heavy heart.

"Then why did you ask me for the papers?" he questions, leaning back and crossing his arms in front of him.

"Because—"

"And don't give me any of this fucking bullshit that you can't have her," he says in a harsh tone.

One reason I kept Asher close to me all these years was because he never once skirted around the truth, and I think that's one of the reasons why I came tonight. To hear it straight. Maybe that's what I need to move on.

"She deserves better, Asher. She deserves a life outside of this. It's what she wants."

"But is it what *you* want?" His question stabs me in the chest, because no, it isn't what I fucking want. It was *never* what I wanted.

"What I want doesn't matter, I'm part of this fucking family, aren't I?"

Sighing, he wipes a hand over his face and shakes his head. "*Lealta,*" he whispers as he stares at my helmet.

"That's not why I came here tonight," I admit as his

eyes meet mine and my heart thumps beneath my chest in anticipation of his reaction to what I am about to tell him. Asher is relatively calm, unless provoked, and I truly don't know how he's going to respond to this.

"Rafael…" I begin, unsure of how to tell someone they have a brother who they knew nothing about until this day. "He's not only my half brother, but yours also."

A moment passes before he speaks, and I almost think I lost him until he lets out a small chuckle. "What?"

"Your father—"

"No, no, my father would never cheat on my mother." He stands, taking a step back, running a hand through his hair, and I feel sick to my stomach for having to tell him this way.

"It's true. We did some digging, and my mother confirmed it."

More silence as he processes this, giving me a chance to gather my words.

"What does this mean?" he asks, and I take in a breath.

"For our families or for the war we're about to incite?" I ask.

He shakes his head, almost like he's refusing to accept it. "Fuck."

"We still don't really know what this means, partly because it all depends on Rafael, but no matter what, it won't change our loyalties." I try to comfort him.

"Have you forgotten the code?" he asks, visibly anxious.

"Ezra would never make such an order." I know my brother, and as crazy as he may be, the Guerra family has been by our side since we were able to breathe. There's no chance he would eradicate them.

"This is so fucked." He chuckles with an exasperated

breath. "Where the fuck do these secrets keep coming from?"

"Your guess is as good as mine," I say as I stand to walk over to him, gripping him by the shoulders as his eyes meet mine. "We are brothers, Asher, and now we are tied through blood. Forever."

CHAPTER FORTY-THREE
Darcy

My eyes are sore and puffy as I stare down at the envelope on my coffee table. It's been days since Nicholas left, and in those days, I have done nothing but stay holed up in my house feeling sorry for myself.

Why did I think he would choose me?

Sighing, I take out the papers and go through them again. Sifting through the endless stack, I stop at the second-to-last page, one box with Nicholas's signature as bold as he is and the other, empty, waiting on mine.

This is what you wanted, right? To be free?

I trace his signature with my fingers, feeling every groove the pen had made on the surface of the paper. Months ago, I wouldn't have dreamed I would be holding divorce papers in my hands and contemplating whether or not I should sign them. Months ago, I would have signed them in blood if I had to, and now all I can think about is burning them in a fire.

I clutch the keys Nicholas left behind as I sit here in my sweats and wonder if I'd been destined to be miserable for the rest of my life by being born into it. Nothing can match the yearning I feel stabbing through my stomach, pulling me to physically be beside Nicholas, and I have never in my life felt something like this—the pure agony that comes from being miles away from him. I thought I had a home here, I thought I could build one and start anew, but like a fucking comet, Nicholas came crashing back into my life, destroying any hope of that ever happening.

Dahlia wanders her way over to me, probably sensing my state as she jumps up to curl in my lap. It's late, and too many times I've considered heading back to London, but the need today is stronger than I have ever felt it. Not knowing what else to do, I grab my phone and call the number I know I can depend on, but even Rafael doesn't answer.

Worry ebbs its way into my mind, and I can't keep it from wandering.

What if he's hurt?

What if Nicholas or Ezra has hurt him?

Rafael has been in my life longer than anyone else, and it was by pure accident that we crossed paths, or so I thought at the time. My parents had travelled to Italy one summer for reasons I had no idea at the time, and I saw him sitting by the beach by himself as two men stood behind him. My first instinct was to approach the lonely boy who was playing with shells when my mother warned me not to talk to strangers, but the way he was all by himself with no friends broke my little heart, so I did what any other child would.

"Hi." I smile as his eyes meet mine, looking around me to my parents chatting with a man. Taking a seat beside him, I pick up the white shell he had been playing with and hold it up to the sun, the water

glimmering on the smooth surface. "Do you know that if you put the larger ones by your ear, you can hear the ocean?"

His eyebrows pull in as he stares at me with a blank expression, and I gather he has no idea what I am saying. It had only been a few months since I had started learning Italian, so I decided to give it a go.

"*Il mio nome è Darcy.*" *Placing a hand on my chest, I extend the other, hoping I've pronounced my words correctly.*

"*Rafael,*" *he answers, and I smile as he shakes my hand.*

"*Perché sei da solo?*"

Why are you by yourself?

"*Sono stato da solo da quando sono nato.*"

I've been by myself since I was born.

His expression falls into sadness as he averts his eyes and continues to fiddle with the shells. My heart breaks for him a little, and I do the one thing I can think of that might cheer him up. Taking off my necklace, I place it in his hands.

Growing up in a strong Catholic family, I was forced to attend church, but the more I went, the more questions I had and when they went unanswered or answered with "you cannot question God," I stopped believing. Ever since then, this necklace meant close to nothing to me, but I hoped it'd give him some comfort knowing a stranger would gift him something personal of theirs.

He eyes the cross in his hand and looks up at me.

"*Quando ti senti solo, pensa a me. Siamo amici adesso, se vuoi.*"

When you get lonely, think of me. We're friends now, if you'd like that.

His smile appears again as I'm grabbed by my arm and pulled to stand.

"*Darcy! You don't wander off like that!*" *I can almost feel the anger in my father's voice as he eyes Rafael.*

. . .

My phone rings, and I immediately unlock it, only to be met with disappointment as I read the text from Clara.

CLARA

We are worried about you.

Almost twenty of her texts went unanswered, and I have no intention of answering her now and dealing with making a decision on whether I stay. Everything pulls me back to London, and I hate that I thought I got out.

After that day on the beach, I had thought about Rafael often, wondering where he might be or who he was becoming. I wondered about his family and if he had a warm bed to sleep on until one day I received a letter. I remember being fourteen and just entering my parents' world as they slowly allowed me to attend functions with the founding families. I often wondered how he had found my address, but the moment I tore into that letter and read his flawless English handwriting, I knew he was doing pretty well for himself.

Since that day, we exchanged letters almost every week, updating each other on our lives and spilling our darkest fears. We became like brother and sister, sharing our youth on opposite sides of the globe, and one day I learnt the truth about his family. It was by accident, but I still remember the day as if it had happened yesterday.

Tuesday afternoon after school, I raced out of the car to meet my mother on the stairs as she hurriedly ushered me into my room and shut the door. It was so out of character for her not to shower me with her affection that I wondered what had caused her to act this way, so I did what any teenager would do. I promised her I'd stay in my room and snuck out at the first opportune moment to head to my father's study, where voices filtered out of his door.

"We've kept this secret for nineteen years, we are not about to broadcast it to the Dixons." My father's voice is enough to frighten me but the way he just spoke sends a shiver down my spine.

"We need them on our side if we want to take down the Casellas," my uncle says. "And what better way to gain their trust than to let them in on a secret?"

"I said no. We keep this between us. No one else needs to know this, at least for now."

My heart falls down into my stomach when I hear him speak next. "Rafael has been spotted with the Petrucci family, any ideas on where this might go?"

"Fuck." I hear the distinctive sound of a lighter, and within seconds, the stench of tobacco seeps into my nose. "Keep an eye on him. We don't want to get involved in whatever happens with the families in Italy. We have enough to worry about with Dominic, we don't need him finding out that his wife has a living son from a Guerra."

My heart pounds inside my chest as I bolt back into my room and pick up the pen and paper I have lying on my desk. I scribble down the words as fast as I can think them, not worried that it doesn't make sense because I just need to get this down, even if I don't end up mailing it to him.

I dial Rafael's number again, desperate to get in contact with him and after a few rings, it hits his voicemail. "Raf, getting worried now, call me back."

Resting my head on the back of my couch, I stare up at the ceiling, wondering if I'll get any sleep tonight. The key in my hand feels like it's burning a hole through my skin as my heart pulls in my chest, and it's no doubt in the direction of wherever Nicholas is. I know we shared something, and I know whatever it was, it wasn't nothing. I love him and not just because I was expected to, but because I saw how his broken pieces fit perfectly with mine.

CHAPTER
FORTY-FOUR
Nicholas

I t's been tense the past week between Jackson, Asher, Ezra, and me. I wish I could say our bond is unbreakable, but I fear if secrets keep surfacing at the rate they are, we might just lose the brothers we grew up with. Rafael has been tight-lipped about his loyalty and whether he wants a claim to the throne, adding to the uncertainty in the air.

I watch as Ezra paces the office floor, deep in thought, no doubt about how the fuck we got here and how many more secrets will be uncovered when we find the Dixons.

"How the fuck did this happen? How did we not know about any of this?" He talks more to himself than me as I pinch the bridge of my nose, feeling a fucking migraine surfacing.

"We can keep asking, but we won't find the answers between us," I utter, wishing he would stop pacing like a fucking lunatic.

"Our first phase is simple," Rafael chimes in, flicking his lighter open. "We need to lure them into a trap."

"You think they'd fall for that after what happened six months ago?" I chuckle. "Fucking amateur."

"You have a better idea?" he asks, and Ezra looks at me expectantly.

"If it were up to me, I'd torch their shit, then them,

and be done with it." Shrugging, I light up a cigarette, uncaring that Ezra wouldn't want me to smoke in his office.

"Would it kill you to give advice we could actually take on?" Ezra asks. "They are one of the founding families."

"Sure, but so were the Brayfords. They're now buried six feet deep. Maybe it's time for only one family to be the sole ruler of London because history almost always repeats itself."

He considers my words when there's a knock on the door. Turning, he opens it, and Aries walks in, belly first, her small frame carrying my nephew.

She gives me a small smile and returns her attention to Ezra. "Your mother will be here soon," she warns, glancing at Rafael, then to me, and back to Ezra.

"You shouldn't be taking those stairs by yourself." Ezra's overprotective nature has multiplied by the hundreds since Aries had fallen pregnant, and although she protests, he ensures she's off her feet most of the time.

"I'm not a doll that you can keep boxed up on the shelf, Ezra," she whispers, placing a gentle hand on his jaw, and he leans into it.

"I'll be done in a bit. Let me help you down the stairs." They exit the room, leaving Rafael and me alone.

Given the circumstances in which we met, I don't know if we can fully trust him, but I like to give people the benefit of the doubt because I'd like the same courtesy shown to me.

"Are you ready to meet her?" I ask, and his piercing eyes meet mine. Uncertainty taints them as he purses his lips, almost like he's considering if there's a possibility to skip this step.

Flicking the lighter closed, he places it in his pocket. "If

I don't, I'll think about it for the rest of my life. So, it doesn't matter if I'm ready or not. What matters is what the outcome will bring."

"Are you always this fucking deep, man?" I blow a puff of smoke into the air, the nicotine calming my nerves.

He chuckles. "Are you always this uncaring?"

"Pretty much." I shrug, but it couldn't be further from the truth. I do care, more than most.

He smirks as Ezra's footsteps begin to get louder, and he appears at the door. "It's time." He steps into the room and motions for us to exit. "She's here."

Taking the stairs two at a time, I step beside my mother and watch Rafael walk down the stairs to stand in front of her. No one speaks, waiting for what her reaction will be. Then she lifts her hand and places it in the middle of his chest.

"*Mio figlio,*" she whispers as a tear rolls down her face. "*Tutti questi anni…*"

"The years that were stolen from us," he utters, bowing his head.

"I'm sorry." She sobs, clasping her hands together at her chest. "I'm so sorry for what happened."

I see Aries slide her hand into Ezra's beside me, and all I can think about is Darcy, about how she should be with me—with us—where she belongs.

"It's the way of our world, right?" He looks to Ezra, and he doesn't speak, letting Rafael have his moment with our mother.

"It doesn't have to be." Ezra shocks everyone in the room as all eyes turn to him. "I want to trust you, but I need to see your loyalty first."

Everyone's loyalty is tested, whether it be in the task of a murder, a robbery, or in this case, war. In the end, we all need to show that we're capable of keeping our promise to do everything in our power to ensure the founding families rise higher with each generation. When the peace pact was made and the founding families were formed, strict rules were put in place to ensure the agreement stood the test of time, but when greed takes hold, its force is unstoppable. Nothing in its path could ever come close to stopping it. I wouldn't be surprised if the hate between the families festered because of someone's greed, and now it'll be the cause of its downfall.

"I want no part of what you have here, Ezra. I will do you a favour and help you through this but when it's done, I leave." Rafael's tone is hard, making it clear that he wants nothing to do with us.

"You won't stay?" Mother asks, wiping a tear from her cheek.

Rafael swallows. "What's happened is in the past. My future is in Italy. One I have worked hard for with Dante Della Torre. This is just a side quest that I will complete in thanks for sparing Darcy's life."

The mention of her name ran daggers against my soul, and I can almost feel the scar the bullet left throbbing.

"We haven't yet solidified a plan on how we get to the Dixons," I mention, and Rafael leers.

"I think I have an idea." Sliding his phone out of his pocket, he dials and places it to his ear. "Any chance we can have a reunion?" He speaks into the phone, and Ezra and I share a glance. He smiles. "See you soon, *fratello*." He hangs up, his tall frame towering over my mother, and I see the resemblance.

"Wait for my call." He moves toward the door, and Ezra steps forward.

"No, I'm coming with you. You do nothing without my

approval." He looks back at Aries, and she nods, telling him she's fine, and they leave.

Aries comforts my mother as they take a seat on the lounge, and my heart breaks for her. Losing a son once would have been hard enough, but hearing him say he would not return mustn't have been what she wanted to hear. Taking a seat beside her, I pull her into me, and she sniffs.

"How did it happen, Mama?" I ask, curious of her past with Gabriele Guerra.

"I loved your father, Nico, I did, and you have to know that," she begins. "But before him, my heart belonged to Gabriele." She sobs, tears running down her face as Aries hands her a tissue. "Gabriele and I met at one of the founding fundraisers a long time ago before I met your father. Before I knew I was matched with Dominic."

"We were inseparable. We snuck out to see each other because we knew if my father found out, he would kill him. Then, when I was matched with Dominic, we shared one last night together. That night I knew I would never see him again, not in the way I wanted." Tears begin to glide down her cheek as she speaks. "I never once contacted him after that night because I knew what my fate would be if I did. Then when I found out I was pregnant with Rafael, your grandfather tried to keep it a secret and had me deliver under the cover of darkness in an unknown hospital with strangers. Then when they told me my baby was stillborn, it broke me in a way I never thought possible. I swore I would never bear children again, and somewhere between the hate of marrying your father, I began to love him."

"Love grows, huh?" I chuckle, repeating the words she once told me.

"You tell me, son." Placing a hand on my knee, she practically looks into my soul. "Did yours?"

She already knows the answer to her question, so I leave it without giving her the satisfaction of knowing she is right. It absolutely grew, it grew into something I would have never imagined on the night I married her. It grew into something toxic and dependent until I was able to see what she truly wanted. Even though I didn't want to give it to her, I did, because I can't bear the thought of being the reason behind her dissatisfaction with how her life turned out, even if it means I live mine in the agony of missing her every fucking day.

"What about all the dinners, the galas, the fucking founding family charities?" I ask, unsure of how she put herself through that every night, seeing her ex-lover in the same room as her husband.

"In our world, love isn't enough, son. Love is a small part of a bigger recipe for the succession of our line, it is never the main ingredient," she says solemnly. "I spent the first six months of my marriage wishing I was with someone else. Stolen glances, formidable longing, and the lonely nights I'd spend waiting and wishing he would come to the gate and whisk me away, but he didn't because he knew better, because in our world, love is never enough."

Placing my head in my hands, I take a breath and realise just how much our family has given up just to be where we are today—just to be on top.

History repeats itself, in a slightly different way.

"Have you spoken to Gabriele since?" I ask, unsure if I want to know the answer to the question I've just asked.

She shakes her head. "I loved your father. In all his messed-up ways and in all his glory. He treated me with the utmost respect, and although he'd never show his love amongst others, he showed me in abundance when we were alone."

I feel her hand on my back, and I close my eyes, thinking about the words my mother had just uttered. Dominic Casella and love do not belong in the same sentence, and in my eyes, I'm fucking glad he's buried six feet deep.

"I know he was not the best father to you boys, and I tried my best to get him to be, but his ambitions for this family far outweighed his need to be a better father to you two."

Standing abruptly, I stride out the door, slamming it behind me, not wanting to hear the rest because I cannot accept the love my mother had for my father.

A fucking monster.

CHAPTER FORTY-FIVE
Nicholas

nother useless day, clamouring between torture and searching for James Dixon. It feels like the more we look, the deeper into his hole he falls. Rafael had word from Dante that he had returned to London, but our search has us coming up empty almost every fucking time. The only luck we've seemed to have was that we found one of his guards in the middle of relocating one of their shipping containers. Although a small win, it turned out fruitless. He either truly didn't know anything or he was hell-bent on dying for the Dixons.

Slick sweat glides down my chest as the crowd roars, chanting my name. It's a regular occurrence now, in order just to feel. I've become obsessed with the rush, with the secret hope that one day I will get to feel her touch again. I never want to forget what it feels like or what her lips taste like, and that's why I fight. I fight to feel instead of searching to numb the pain.

I fucking welcome it.

It keeps me closer to her, closer to the one person on this earth who taught me that in order to heal, we need to feel. If I can't have her, maybe I can try to heal the broken parts of me I refused to acknowledge for so long, and maybe then she'll come back to me.

My jaw throbs as I hear a crack, the familiar pain radiating through to my temple, thrusting me back into the ring as my opponent huffs, struggling to catch his breath as beads of sweat form on his forehead. I force myself onto my feet to continue as blood seeps into my eye. Wiping it off with the back of my hand, I motion for him to attack, and he doesn't wait a second longer as he lunges toward me. With every ounce of energy I have left, I kick my leg up, my foot connecting with his temple, and he plummets to the ground with a thud as the bell rings, euphoria rushing over me at the sound of my triumph echoing through the thundering crowd.

I stare at myself in the mirror as I wipe the blood from my busted lip and notice Asher walk through the door.

"Fuck, Nicholas," he hisses as he takes in the bruises and cuts on my face.

"You should see the other guy," I say, and he rolls his eyes.

"I did," he deadpans. "He could've died."

"He should've thought about that before getting in the ring." I continue wiping the blood from my face. You don't get in the ring if you don't want to fight, even if that fight is with your own demons.

"You're not going to listen to me, are you?" he asks, pulling out his phone.

"When have I ever?"

"One day, you won't have me here to stop you," he warns.

"And until that day comes, I look forward to seeing you at every single fight."

Shaking his head, he stays quiet.

Finishing up, I get dressed, and we leave the club, making our way to the port where Ezra and Rafael await. Rolling to a stop, we exit the car and make our way to them through a sea of shipping containers.

"Why are we meeting here?" Asher asks.

"This secret is too big for anyone else's ears," Ezra answers as Jackson pulls up in his Aston Martin.

"Someone called for a party?" He tries to break the ice as he exits and makes his way to us, standing beside Ezra.

"So, I guess we're all tied together now?" Asher asks, and all eyes look to Ezra. I know he hasn't decided yet on how involved he wants Rafael to be, but I can see he doesn't want anything to change between us and the Guerras.

"We can't make this obvious," I state, knowing that once this secret is out, it'll cause havoc over the London followers. "We keep this between us. No one else needs to know."

"Like a sinful secret?" Rafael asks in an accusatory tone.

"All I'm saying is if people know, it'll cause problems."

"It's not foreign to me to be cast aside." He shrugs, and I can't be sure if he's being sarcastic or not.

"Where are we at with the Dixons?" Jackson changes the subject, and Ezra sighs.

"All our information leads to nothing." He runs a hand down his face, clearly frustrated. "These fuckers know how to hide, and whoever is helping them hide will die alongside them."

The skid of tyres fills the void in the air, and all heads turn to the sports car entering the port. We all reach for our guns, aiming in the direction of the Bugatti as it screeches to a stop in front of us. A man steps out, dressed in an expensive all-black suit, his fingers covered in rings and dark ink, as he extends a hand to Rafael.

"Been a while, Raf." He smiles, his bright teeth shining in the dim light, his dark hair almost camouflaged. The green of his eyes grows deeper as his gaze lands on Ezra, who has now lowered his weapons.

"Dante." He speaks as he holsters his guns. "We weren't expecting you in London."

"The Della Torres always return the favour, Casella," he responds.

Everyone's weapons are now hidden, the new question bouncing around in everyone's mind.

What the hell is Dante Della Torre doing in London and what made him leave his Island?

"It's good to see you." Ezra smirks, taking a step toward him and extending his hand.

Dante takes it, and they share a brief handshake. "I wish I could say the same, Ezra." His eyes find mine as he reaches into his breast pocket and takes a few steps over to me, handing me the envelope.

"We know where they're going." Dante confirms as I stare at the images before me.

My heart plummeting into my stomach as my throat works to swallow at the sight of multiple photos of Darcy in her house, taken from outside her home. Rage ignites within me as I throw the photos to the ground and grab Rafael by the collar.

"What happened to keeping her safe!?" I yell, getting in his face as I spit my words. "What happened to knowing her every fucking move!?"

His eyes land on the images on the ground, and I've never seen a man change as fast as he just did right in front of me, pure fear whirling inside his eyes.

"Blood or not, if something happens to her, I will fucking skin you alive." I push him, and he regains his balance, smoothing out his shirt. My boots knock on the concrete floor as I walk to my car in a hurry, determined to find her before they do.

"Nicholas!" Ezra calls after me, but all I hear is Darcy. She's in my head, in my heart, and everywhere besides in my fucking reality.

"Nicholas!" Asher grabs my arm, twisting me around and gripping my face. "We need to do this together, brother."

I focus on my breathing, to hear the reason behind Asher's plea, and I force myself to see how much we have riding on this going right.

"They are still in London, but they have plans to leave in a week," Dante explains, watching me for my next move.

Ezra paces toward me and places a hand on my shoulder. "Out of respect for you, brother, I want to know how you want this to go."

"I stand by what I said before. It's time for there to be *one* ruling family of London." I glance around at the men who have no doubt followed tradition their entire lives, and I struggle to see how they will bend their rules to do things my way, but Ezra surprises me.

"I'm with you," Ezra confirms.

Asher and Jackson nod, turning to face me, solidifying their intent on remaining loyal, and I look to Rafael, waiting for his answer.

He flicks his lighter, watching the flame dance in his hand, and as he looks up to meet my gaze, the reflection of the flames in his eyes. "Let them burn."

CHAPTER FORTY-SIX
Darcy

I've been checking my phone for the past two days, even for a message or something to let me know the two people who mean the most to me in life are okay, but each time I do, I remain disappointed. My mind is still in chaos, and the reality I thought I could have might not be possible for me after all.

I stare out the window as I watch the snow thaw on the branches of the trees under the bright sun, thick layers still covering the path. After wallowing in self-pity, I decided it was time.

Time to take back the control I had lost. After a quick goodbye, I left Dahlia with Oliver yesterday, making him promise me he would take care of her.

Grabbing my keys, I head out the door and take one last look around before I lock it behind me as I make my way to my car. Although I couldn't sleep last night, I'm thankful I chose to spend it putting chains on the wheels of my car, because in this snow, I'll need it.

Guilt claws its way into my heart again as I realise what I'm about to do, but I don't let it stop me as I place my seat belt on. My phone vibrates on the passenger seat, and I pick it up immediately to see Rafael's name appear.

"Raf!" I sigh in relief, bracing myself on the steering wheel. "Thank God! Why didn't you call?"

He pauses for a minute before he answers me. "I just needed to know you were okay."

"No, don't hang up."

"Stay where you are, Darcy," he warns, his tone harsh.

"What the fuck is going on?"

A loud knock on my window sends the breath from my lungs as I lurch back in my seat and look up to Clara, standing and waving apologetically. Rolling down the window, I hear a beep from my phone as Raf hangs up.

"I didn't mean to startle you, dear, but I was very worried when we didn't hear from you for a while. What's going on? she asks with concern.

"Sorry, Clara, I need to go."

The engine roars to life, and she steps back as I pull out of the driveway with one destination in mind.

Maybe the way to move forward is to confront your past head-on. Live it, breathe it, and survive it. I cannot be certain how the deceit or disloyalty began within our families, but I know one thing…it's time it all fucking ends. I'm sick to death of hiding, wanting to be free, but never truly taking that step. It's fine to want something, but when you don't take action, how can you truly work towards it?

Picking up my phone, I dial the one number I never thought I'd want to see again, and when he answers, a sickening feeling swirls around me, pulling me deeper into its core.

The plans I have are filled with risks, ones I know are not in my favour, but with every risk comes a reward if you are willing to pay the price. That price may cost you your life or the lives of the ones you love, but that's a gamble you need to be willing to take if you want to move on.

I speed down the highway toward the airport, trying to

make up for lost time, but how can I make up for the six months I've lived without him?

The days I spent mourning him?

How can I pretend like I was okay when the whole time I was fighting with myself to return to London to give myself over to them?

My tyres skid on the ice just a fraction as I take the exit, and within a few minutes, I see black SUVs pulling out to block my path.

What the fuck?

Slowing down, I come to a stop, leaving just enough of a gap between us as I remain in the car, unsure of what is about to happen. Two men step out of each vehicle dressed in black suits, and my heart jumps into my throat as they slide their hands behind them to reveal their guns. Without wasting time, I put the car in reverse and floor it, ducking as bullets fly through my windows, cracking and shattering them. The noise startles me as I swing the car around, my sweaty palms sliding on the steering wheel as the adrenaline pumps through my body, priming it for a fight.

NICHOLAS

What's the definition of insanity? Doing something over and over and expecting a different outcome, or living in a constant state of unhappiness because of your own choices? The more we think about the consequences of our actions, the more we choose ones that are safe and that keep us in our comfort zones.

In the years I spent choosing things that were easy because I knew the outcome and because I knew how it would make me feel, the better I got at ignoring my search for happiness that I thought I didn't deserve. Now, there isn't anyone or anything that could keep me from her, because she's it. She's the only source of happiness that I need and will ever want.

"Isn't it awkward?" Asher asks Jackson as I stare out the window of the car.

"Of course it's awkward, but it is what it is, and until we can work this shit out with the Dixons, it's going to have to wait," Jackson replies as Rafael flicks his lighter open and closed.

"That's really fucking irritating," I remark, watching him smirk.

"Tell someone who gives a shit," Rafael replies.

I watch as the car approaches the tarmac and see Ezra standing outside speaking to Gabriele, who has arrived before us. The driver pulls up beside them, and we all file out one by one. He's been in France for a prospect we've been eyeing and recently just touched down back in London. Upon learning of his first-born son who had been hidden from him, he wanted to come back and straighten things out with Ezra.

"Boys." Gabriele nods in our direction, and Jackson scoffs.

"Really? That's all you have to say?" Jackson shoves his father with both hands, rage evidently surfacing beneath his cool exterior. "After all these years, you never once thought to mention it?"

"Son..." Gabriele begins when Asher cuts in.

"Are you going to lie to us in front of the Casellas, Father?" His tone is one he usually reserves for me when he needs to get me to see reason.

"I didn't know," Gabriele replies.

Jackson scoffs, running a hand over his face, and

Gabriele's eyes meet Rafael's. For a minute, no one speaks, and the silence is thick.

"We can place blame on each other, but the real threat remains well known, and if we continue to play into their games, we will be the ones to give up London." I try to reason with them to see the bigger picture.

"My brother is right. The more we fight, the closer they get to taking the one thing we worked generations for, and I'm not ready to give it up without a fucking fight," Ezra says, placing a hand on Gabriele's shoulder. "Can I count on your continued loyalty, even through this?" he asks.

Gabriele nods, glancing over to Rafael, who looks completely disinterested in meeting his biological father. I guess it's understandable when he's been kept a secret all these years.

"I wasn't Dominic's closest ally, for reasons you already know, but I never once wavered in my loyalty to your family. Even when the love of my life was betrothed to him," Gabriele replies with unexpected emotion. I could never understand how he might feel, because if that were me and Darcy was taken from me, I'd do everything in my power to get her back to me, even if that meant forcibly taking her.

"I appreciate your candour." Ezra nods, waving to Henry to load the bags onto the plane. Bags that are filled with weaponry and ammunition that our men had packed earlier.

"I will be sending my men to be at your disposal when you need me to," Gabriele confirms as he pulls out his mobile.

I watch Rafael pull his phone out of his pocket to answer it, and his face instantly turns white.

"What?" I ask, taking a step toward him.

"Are they certain?" Rafael asks, holding his hand up to me, making my blood boil enough to want to break his fucking fingers. "Fuck!"

"What the hell is going on!?" I yell, losing my patience.

His eyes square with mine, and I don't need his words to confirm my greatest fucking fear.

"She's been spotted at the airport, exiting Heathrow."

Everyone scrambles to tear open the duffels we've packed and begin to load the machine guns with magazines as the silence lingers with the inevitable violence to come.

"How did she get back into the country without our fucking knowledge?" I ask Rafael as he stuffs a pistol into the back of his belt.

"I taught her well." He grins, making me want to crack him across the jaw. "She knew she was being followed, and I taught her how to lose a tail."

"Evidently not well enough," I fire back, and he raises his brows, gripping me with one hand by my neckline.

"If she didn't want to be found, she wouldn't have come back."

"She's planning something." I peel his hand off me.

"But what?" he asks, and at this moment, I couldn't be any more sure of where she is.

"I know exactly where to find her."

Tyres screech on the asphalt as we hasten our chase, my leg bobbing up and down, the pistol bouncing on my knee as I race through almost every single possibility in my head.

Why would she do this?

Why would she put herself in danger if she didn't want anything to do with this life?

"We're almost there," the driver says as we begin to enter the gates of Darcy's family home.

Multiple cars are already parked out the front, ones that don't belong to us, making the unease grow in the pit of my stomach. I grip the pistols tight in both hands as I wait for the car to stop moving. Glancing over at Rafael, I notice he looks just as tense as I feel, as does Ezra, who admires his gold pistols that shine in every way he holds them. I remind myself to stay calm and not react to whatever situation is happening inside, but all reason fades when I step out of the car and walk through the front door to see the Dixons surrounding Darcy in the middle of her family home.

"Nicholas?" she breathes, holding a gun to her head, and my heart lurches forward, pulling me to her when I'm stopped in my tracks by my brother.

Fuck, Darcy, what have you done?

"Why did you come?" she asks, and I gather she wishes I hadn't.

"Gentlemen." James's sinister smile takes over his entire face as he turns toward Ezra. "Come to see a live show?" he japes, and I swallow down the lump in my throat at the scene unfolding before me.

"This isn't about them," Darcy begins and that gains their attention again. "It's about me."

"She's doused this place in petrol," Rafael whispers to me as I take a deep breath and notice the familiar smell.

"Let's end this once and for all, shall we?" She raises the lighter in her hand and flicks it open.

"Darcy!" I take a step forward, and multiple guns point at me, stopping me from getting to her.

"You've all come here to get some sort of information you think will give you eternal reign over London, but like every other simple man in life, you've failed in that pursuit." She smiles, closing her eyes. "Because the only way I'll speak is when I'm dead."

"Darcy!" I yell. "Don't fucking do this," I warn, but she ignores me as she raises the lighter higher.

"You don't have the guts to burn this place down," James challenges her, and she opens her eyes to slide the gun behind her waist, then proceeds to pull out a yellow envelope that has been rolled up.

"That's where you're wrong, James." She holds out the envelope in one hand whilst lowering the lighter to it. "Because I will do anything it takes for my husband." That's when I notice the envelope she's holding is the divorce papers I left her. The flames lick at the edges, lighting it slowly, eating away at the paper until half of it is engulfed in flames, dancing to the edges of her fingertips.

"Fuck," I hear James utter, and the envelope drops to the floor. The flames light up the house in almost an instant, but the only person in my sight is her. I launch myself over the flames to get to her as she stands in the middle of the room with her eyes shut and arms wide open like she's giving in to her fate.

Over my dead fucking body.

My heart pounds with anger as bullets fly through the room, missing her by an inch. It's complete and utter chaos inside, the flames rising, taking down everything in their path.

Unforgiving, just like the woman I love.

The thud of a large piece of timber falling startles me, and I look over to where it landed, seeing James struggle underneath it. The house begins to fall apart, the flames eating away at the wood as I approach her.

CHAPTER FORTY-SEVEN
Darcy

A FEW MOMENTS EARLIER

The musty air hits me in the face the moment the front door swings open, and I'm transported back to a time I worked so hard to remember. Memories I trained my brain not to forget. It's when I step into my bedroom that I realise it's been years since I have been in this home. A home I once hated. One I thought had high walls and gilded cages, hiding the secrets within it. The events of the last few days play in my head, and a tear trickles down my cheek before I swat it away.

Well, Darcy, you got what you wanted.

I run my fingers along the crisp white walls which were once decorated with my family's portraits, but now are empty, just like me.

The faint scent of lavender creeps its way into my nose, and I notice a breeze carrying the scent through the open door. The familiar smell of my childhood—a time when so many things were much simpler. It's no secret that my family was not innocent...but I was.

Not anymore.

The things I've done are not forgivable. They cannot be forgotten, and there will come a time when I will need to accept that. But right now, all I want to do is remember the moments that I took for granted. The ones I imprinted in my brain, forcing myself to never forget.

The last few years of my life, I thought would never happen to me. I thought I was destined to live like any other person would. The slow life—a life of *normalcy*—but in the life we lead, in the roles we play, our lives are anything but *normal.*

Being back here feels wrong, but I needed to relive what I thought was the cage keeping me out of the real world, but in reality, it was a cage keeping out the nightmares waiting for me.

I grew up believing that one day I would know another world other than this one I'm currently living in, and now that it's within my reach, I hesitate to grasp it. I hesitate because of the things I once believed, the people I once trusted. I want nothing more than to be done with this place, but my bleeding heart wants something else.

It wants him.

In a way, he saved me.

If there was one thing I was sure about, it was the way he looked at me. The way he really saw *me.* Not just some girl who was groomed to be something she wasn't supposed to end up being, but a woman who wore her heart on her sleeve, wanting nothing more than to be loved like she deserved.

I don't regret what happened, just the way it did. I was naïve and stupid for thinking love would be enough to fight the world we live in, the darkness that ensnares us when we sleep, and the lies—the never-ending lies and secrets that surface anytime things would go remotely right.

The rain patters on the roof of my childhood home as I sit on my bed, thinking about all the lies I've told, the secrets I kept hidden for so long only for them to creep up in my dreams, threatening to lay waste to everything I worked so hard to keep. Forgiveness isn't easily given from those who live in our world, but there's one person in particular I know whose heart is as fragile as mine, even if he hates to admit it.

I had spent the six months living in a lie, which I forced myself to swallow because of all the things I had done and left unsaid. I lived a life I thought I wanted in a place far from here, but my heart remained in London with the man I swore I would never love. The same one who shares the same memories as me—the same life but in a different body. I never once considered us a possibility, not even when we were forced to marry, forced to be around each other even when we despised one another, but all that changed in such a short amount of time.

All of which changed *me*.

Leaving was easy, knowing that once I got here, I'd know what to do. Once you've accepted your fate, it becomes easier to live with it, and with the plan I have, there's only one way through it. The Dixons are dumb enough to be lured into my home because they know I'm alone and not under the protection of the Casellas anymore, but they have no idea what they are about to walk into.

Grabbing the jerry can, I begin to pour the petrol over every surface of my family home. On the vintage couches which haven't been touched in years, the sheer curtains my mother installed herself, and the chessboard that is still in its rightful place on the dining table. I'm ready to say goodbye to it all—to the life I once knew, to the life I've lived, and to the love I have in my heart now. I'm ready to give it all up if it means ending this age-old war between our families. It's time people knew peace, even if I'm not here to see it.

After being chased, I managed to lose them, and once I did, I made my way to the airport and got a one-way ticket to London. I knew I was being followed, but I didn't care because that's what I wanted. I wanted them to follow me here, to know exactly where I am, because once I have them all where I want them, I'm taking us all down together. No more feud, no more blood ties—I'm sick to death of it.

My phone rings, and I don't bother to check it, knowing it's either Nicholas or Rafael. Continuing my warpath, I douse the rugs in whatever's left in the can and open the front door, then take a seat in the middle of the room and wait.

Minutes pass, and the roar of engines fills my ears as they arrive, spilling out of their cars one by one, some approaching through the front and others filing out to the back.

"You made it. About time." I mock as James enters my living room.

"Well…well…well…you've changed," he says, running a finger over the top of the couch. "Maybe it's all that mountain air you've been breathing."

I raise my chin, tightening the hold over my gun.

"Do you know what you're doing, Darcy?" he asks with a smirk on his lips.

"Spare me," I scoff. "It's too late for a warning."

He nods, sliding his hands into his pockets. "I had a lot of respect for your family. The Brayfords were a force. One with a lot of prospects."

"Look where those prospects got them," I fire back.

"You're right, I guess maybe they were a little too ambitious." He shrugs.

"And you're following in their footsteps," I warn. "Why do you want to break the peace treaty?"

He sighs as the rest of his men walk into my home. "Things cannot stay like this forever, Darcy. Every once in a while, they have to change to keep up with the times."

"They'll never let you have it."

"The kingdom? Oh, I know, which is why I intend to *take* it."

I raise my gun, aiming at his chest as his men surround me, the petrol sloshing on the rugs with each step they take toward me.

"Do I need to force it out of you, or will you tell me willingly?" James asks as he pulls out a knife from his pocket. "Because I'd hate to mark that pretty face of yours."

"You've wasted your time coming here because you will not get anything out of me," I say with my head held high.

"Just months ago, you were begging me for a way out, for a way to be rid of Nicholas, what's changed?" he asks, and I swallow at his words, at how quickly everything changed when I got to know Nicholas. When he showed me who he truly was, underneath his careless, cold exterior.

"Something your minuscule brain would not be able to comprehend, I'm afraid."

My words make him visibly angry, and he reaches behind him and pulls out his gun, aiming it towards me. Another set of engines roar at the front, and all heads turn to watch *all* the Casella brothers exit their vehicles and make their way into my home. Their presence is heavy enough to raise the hairs on my neck. I place the barrel of my gun to my temple and take a deep breath, the air beginning to crystalise in my lungs the second Nicholas's eyes meet mine.

"Why did you come?" I whisper the words, forgetting we're not alone, and right now, I wish we were, because every part of me wants to fall apart in his arms, to apologise, but I don't. Instead, I force my gaze away from him and onto James.

The flames crackle hungrily, taking down every part of the home I once loved to hate. I hear Nicholas call my name in the distance as I close my eyes and wait for the flames to find me, for them to take me home, but they don't. Instead, I'm propelled across the room, Nicholas's body slamming into mine, falling on top of me as a bullet ricochets off an old grandfather clock in the corner of the room.

"You're going to be the death of me," he whispers before he takes my lips in a heated passion, his tongue forcing entry into my mouth with anarchy ensuing around us. Time stops as I hold him close to me, tasting him on my tongue and feeling him everywhere around me like no amount of time has passed.

He whisks me up and begins to pull me to the back door, but I stop and search for Rafael, my eyes darting around the room, flinching at the bullets being fired in the enclosed space.

"We can't wait! Come with me!" he yells over the noise, gripping my wrist and tugging me forward into him. "You're my first priority, do you fucking understand?"

I nod, unable to form words as I'm yanked outside

where multiple men await. Raising my gun, I pull the trigger, the bullet finding the man's chest as he barrels over, Nicholas shielding me as we make our way to his car. Looking back, I see Ezra closing the door and motioning for his men to retreat. We make it to the car, and once in, Nicholas floors it as I look back at my family home. Within a minute, the entire place explodes, shaking the ground beneath us as flames and smoke billow through the sky.

"What the fuck were you thinking!?" Nicholas's face goes red, the veins almost popping out of his throat as he yells. "Why would you do something so fucking irrational!?"

His fury brings out my own, the tears stinging my eyes as I speak. "I knew *exactly* what was about to happen! That's why I planned it this way!" I fire back, ignoring the anxious beating inside my chest.

"What? Throw yourself in the pit and then what? Did you expect to come out of that alive?" He eyes me, reading the answer I'm afraid to say aloud.

"Fuck Darcy! Do you have any idea what it would have done to me?"

"You left, Nicholas. You chose London!"

He swerves the car onto the highway, angrily gripping the steering wheel as we head south, and my mind races. "What about the others?" I ask, genuine worry clouding me.

"They have support from Dante and Gabriele," he snaps, focusing on the road, the night beginning to grow darker. The wheels rumble beneath us, and it's the only sound that breaks the otherwise ice-cold silence in the car.

We drive for what seems like hours until finally arriving at a house that sits slightly atop a hill. One with rustic charm and two large English oak trees adorning both sides.

The engine stills when Nicholas puts the car in park, and without a word, he steps out to walk around the car and open my door. I still feel the remnants of his anger when he curls his fingers around my wrist and tugs me into the home. Pulling out of his hold, I look around. The old character of the house is inviting and reminds me of the life I almost convinced myself I could have.

"Are you okay?" Nicholas's voice echoes through the house when he answers a phone call, my ears perking up, straining to hear the conversation. "It's going to take more than a few police to cover this up. Might need to get the lawyer off his ass."

"We're good," he says and hangs up, striding over to me.

"We need to lay low until this is dealt with."

"Ra—"

"Rafael is fine. He is with Ezra, cleaning up the mess *you* made." His words provoke me, and I unleash everything I've wanted to say for days.

"My mess!?" I grunt, pushing him with all my strength, all my rage bouncing around within me. "I wouldn't fucking be here if it wasn't for your family and your stupid fucking rules!"

"*My rules?*" he scoffs. "You think I wanted any of this to happen?"

I roll my eyes, turning to walk away when he whisks me back, my chest slamming into his front. Struggling in his hold, I do my best to get away, but his grip on me tightens.

"Stop," he warns, but I don't listen. The skin around my wrists burns under his control, and a scream rips through my throat until the tears finally surface.

"Why!? Why didn't you choose me!?" I shout, and when his hands loosen around my wrists, I break free from his hold to take a step back, feeling the weak fissures in my chest cave into large splits.

"I did choose you…" He speaks through furrowed brows. "I chose you before you chose me. I gave you the freedom you've wanted since you signed those fucking papers!" He beats his hand against his chest, roaring, "I chose you before I chose *me!*"

The words I wanted to say dissipate into nothing inside my head as I take him in, remembering a time I hated him with every ounce of energy I had. Now all I want is to be beside him until I take my dying breath. Even if it means staying in his world.

He takes a step toward me, closing the distance between us and lifts my chin with his index finger. "What you did tonight was reckless and irrational, and I never want to remember it. The possibility of losing you to death made me realise the phenomenal mistake I made when I left you."

I swallow back more tears at his confession, barely holding myself back from leaping into his arms.

"I desperately wanted to be the person who gave you what you desired all your life, even if it meant I couldn't be in it."

His declaration floors me, and I'm overpowered with emotion as tears now flow freely from my eyes.

"I don't care about my freedom anymore." I sob, our bodies colliding, his strong arms wrapping around my waist and holding me tight. My fingers glide through his hair as our mouths meet, our tongues tangling with the mixture of our lust and passion for each other. My body comes alive with the familiar sensations the roaming of his hands bring, and I melt into him, our kiss washing away the nights we spent without each other.

The thud of my back against the wall pushes out the air that's left inside my lungs, and I run my hands along his shoulders, down to his chest, gripping at his shirt and tugging it off. The cool air kisses my stomach as he lifts mine over my head and discards it on the floor, his eyes running over my body.

"You're so—"

"No time for that," I breathe, smashing my lips against his, leaping into his arms and wrapping my legs around his waist. I barely notice my surroundings as he carries me into a bedroom and throws me onto the bed, removing my pants along with my panties.

"I'm so fucking angry with you," he rumbles, climbing on top of me.

"Angry enough not to fuck me?" I ask with a smile.

"I'm not going to fuck you, *fenice*, I'm going to show you how much I've missed you," he says, lowering himself to spread my legs apart, his eyes fixed on mine.

I rest my head on the pillow, closing my eyes and waiting for the feeling I've been craving, but it doesn't come. Instead, I hear chains rattling against the bedpost, and when I look up, he's secured both my ankles to them. Before I can sit up, he pushes me back down and expertly cuffs my wrists above my head, anchoring them to the bedhead.

"I want you immobile for this next part." He slides off me, removing his pants, and I admire the man standing before me, strong, masculine, and *eager*. "Tell me, *fenice*, have I lived up to my promise?"

I look up at him, confused, until I remember the first time we were together. Our drenched clothes strewn on the hood of his car, nothing but the desire for one another in our eyes as we took what we wanted. What we worked so hard against wanting.

"Once I fuck you, the only thing you will crave is my touch, my mouth, and my cock." His words ring in my ears, and I nod, thinking back to all the times I wanted to touch myself, wishing it was him.

I tug on the chains, the leather feeling cool against my skin, and he smiles, watching me spread my legs and rock my hips.

"What are you waiting for?" I taunt.

He forces my knees further apart, spreading me wider, his tongue lowering onto my clit. Gasping, I buck my hips wanting to ride his face, to take the pleasure I've been craving from him for far too long, but he doesn't let me have it. Instead, he licks me agonisingly slow, sucking my clit into his mouth and grazing his teeth along it.

"I'm not about to let you have all the fun," he says, sliding his tongue into me.

My moans fill the room, my wrists tugging on the chains as my body tenses. I thought I remembered everything about his touch and the way he made me feel, but right now, the sensations that are coursing through me feel different in a way I cannot explain. Like our bonds were never broken, like the tie holding us together is a link impenetrable by any blade. We may have been brought into this world to hate each other, however, time has buried that hatred deeply alongside the rest of my family, and the only thing left behind is the pure and unfiltered devotion I feel for Nicholas.

His fingers glide into me as he sucks my clit into his mouth, and my nipples harden at the arousal he commands out of me.

"I want you to feel what I felt when I had to leave you,"

he whispers onto my pussy when I look down at him between my legs, his dark eyes centred with mine. "Bound by my own set of emotional chains of wanting you to be happy but never wanting to let you go."

"Nicholas…" I speak softly, wanting to wrap my arms around him.

His tongue continues on its warpath, devouring me until I'm a shaking mess. Beads of sweat pool between my breasts as I heave the oxygen into my lungs when he hovers over me, his mouth glistening, covered in my arousal.

Grinning, he lowers his lips to mine, and I taste myself on his tongue. The feeling in my hands begins to fade as pins and needles take over. "Loosen the chains." It's not a question I ask, but a demand I make because, as much as he wants me to see what he felt, he should know how I felt too. I watch him work to loosen the chains around my wrists first, then my ankles, the cuffs still attached to them.

"Where do you want me?" He smirks, pulling on the chains still attached to my wrists.

"Right here." I smile, pushing him down onto the mattress and coiling one of the chains around his neck. On instinct, he brings his hand to his throat to grasp the chains that cinch his skin, but I pull, tightening them further. "It's my turn to show you."

CHAPTER FORTY-EIGHT
Nicholas

My cock twitches when I feel the heat of her pussy on my crown, and as she lowers herself, she pulls on the chains, making me hiss.

"I felt your hands around my throat, denying me air, from the moment you stepped out of my life and left me with our memories." She lowers herself further, stretching around me. "It felt like that hand never left my neck, and even in the days you were with me, I knew you would eventually leave."

The skin on my throat burns the more she pulls, and I feel the air thinning in my windpipe, but the moment she takes me completely, I lose all the air in my lungs, feeling the sweet warmth of her pussy envelop all of me once again.

Gritting my teeth, I remove my hands from the chains, giving her full reign over me, showing her that I can take the pain she's willing to inflict, which only makes her angrier. Lifting myself up to a seated position, I wrap an arm around her, and she rolls her hips, causing my mind to reel with the pain and pleasure morphing into one inside me. The chains loosen a touch, allowing me to speak.

"Never. Again. *Fenice.*" I lick her lips, grinding into her, feeling my need for her grow with every second that passes.

"I promise to make you happy, even if it means breaking the code."

Her eyes widen, knowing the weight of my promise, and she tugs on the chains, the coil tightening around my throat again as she rolls her hips and tips her head back. Placing my hands on her hips, I follow her movements as she grinds on me, moving her glistening body back and forth, pulling the chains for her mouth to crash into mine, our breath escaping between our pleasured moans.

"Take it…" I whisper into her mouth, and she draws my bottom lip between her teeth, biting down until a bead of blood trickles down to my chin. "I give you every single fucking part of me. The light, the dark, the wrong, and the right. You can take it all, *fenice,* because without you, I roam the streets like a soul damned in limbo, desperately searching for its other half."

I bared my soul to her because it's all I have ever wanted to do. From the moment I saw the scars on her body, I knew we shared more than I wanted to admit. I knew we were more alike than I wanted us to be, but even then, nothing would have prepared me for how lost I would feel without her. Nothing could have saved my heart from the tattered edges of her betrayal or the soothing relief of the confession of her love.

"I will set fire to the entire kingdom if you ever leave again…" she says, taking her pleasure, lifting herself and slamming back down, a groan slipping from my throat as the sound of our skin slapping echoes through the room. "I will watch as everyone burns beneath the ruins of our love…" my arousal builds, her hips continuing to roll, buck, and slam into mine as she tightens the coil around my throat. "If that's what it takes to have you, I will do it without batting an eye, because you, Nicholas, are worth losing *everything*."

"Fuck," I hiss, the skin on my throat beginning to become raw as my dick hardens inside her. She slams her hips into mine, riding me, and I can barely hold on, barely breathe. Rolling her lips together, I watch as her breasts bounce, my tongue darting out to lick them when she forces them into my face. An animalistic need riots inside me, shaking the cage, so I let it free, taking her nipple between my teeth and biting.

"Good God..." she breathes, her moans growing louder as my tongue swirls to soothe the sting I left behind. I feel her buck one last time as she rides the wave of her pleasure, her pussy tightening around my thick, hard cock, and finally, it twitches inside her, filling her with my commitment and promise.

The cool night breeze drifts through the open window, filling the room with a slight chill as Darcy nuzzles closer into me. There has been nothing else on my mind but her. Ever since she lit that fucking flame inside my chest, all I have ever thought about was her. Didn't matter if I wanted to kill her or fuck her.

It was always *her*.

I meant what I said. I would leave this place, this fucking city, the kingdom, everything, if it meant she'd be happy. Ezra wouldn't be too happy about it and would definitely tell me I'm making a mistake, but I don't care.

For any of it.

She is what matters to me.

"What are you thinking about?" she asks, her beautiful emerald eyes looking up into mine. A smile tugs on the corner of my lips at her soft pink ones, and I realise in this moment, it's them I've missed the most.

"I give you my word, *fenice*, if this life isn't what you want, I will go with you wherever you decide."

Her brows pull in, concern beginning to etch its path into her eyes. "But what about—"

"I will leave it all behind." My fingers brush the skin on her arm and she bites her bottom lip. "For you."

If the Nicholas I knew had met the one I know now, I would call him a wanker. Dropping years—no, *generations* —of blood and wealth for an *enemy*. The old Nicholas would be beside himself but not me.

No.

A familiar feeling, one I felt so many years ago before my father beat it out of me, swirls inside my chest, makes its way up my shoulders, and forms a smile on my face.

Excitement.

For something new, something promising, and something I actually fucking want.

"Ezra's going to be pissed," she whispers, tracing my jaw with her finger.

"What's the worst he can do?" I shrug.

"Have you met him?"

I chuckle.

Ezra might be following in the footsteps of our father in some ways, but in others, he couldn't be further akin to Dominic. He cares for his family more than anyone else I have met and wants what's best for them. He would never judge me for wanting what I want, especially because he's been through it too.

The difference between us is that he was born to be the fucking king.

Born to lead.

Me?

I was born to struggle to make sense of life because what I wanted wasn't wealth, it wasn't blood, and it sure as fuck wasn't to be a prince. On the night Dominic beat me to a pulp, he said a Casella should never aspire for anything trivial, but to me, my dreams were pertinent to my sanity, and he crushed them with everything he had, leaving me a broken shell in his wake.

"Did I ever tell you I wanted to be a firefighter?" I ask, knowing I never once shared this piece of information with anyone before.

She stares at me, and for a moment I freeze, wondering what she's going to say, wondering if sharing this with her would change her view of me.

"I can see that." She smiles, placing a small peck on my lips. "But what about the fire between us?" she asks, climbing on top of me.

Twisting, I flip and pin her back onto the bed as I hover over her. "There's not enough water on Earth to extinguish that."

Trepidation slowly descends on me as I pour wine into a glass, watching the liquid slowly rise inside it. I've never once opened up to Ezra or anyone else about what I had felt or wanted in my life, and now that I plan to take what I want unapologetically, I still want the support of my family.

I want to be able to live a life outside of this and still be able to see them, talk to them, and be there for them if they ever need me. The one thing I care about right now is approaching this topic the only way I know how.

Directly.

Placing the glass on the table in front of Asher, I take my seat across from Darcy and look around the dining table. Late last night, I got a text from Ezra saying he wanted to take Aries away from London, so I thought it'd be a good chance to invite them all over and get this fucking thing over with.

"You look like shit." Asher grabs a Danish from the basket in the middle of the table and takes a bite.

Rafael's laugh is throaty, like his voice when he replies, "Have you taken a look in the mirror lately?"

"Every day, actually. I like to practice my killing voice."

"What the fuck is a killing voice?" Darcy asks.

"You know the one Ezra does when he plays with them like toys?"

Ezra's eyes jolt to Asher, and his laughter subsides. I also don't miss the way Aries places her hand on his arm.

"He's…passionate," she says, smiling.

"Ezra…" I stand, all eyes now in my direction. "A word?" My chest pounds so loudly, I want to silence it with a pillow. We make our way to the expansive yard out the back, and he stops me in my tracks.

"I know what you're going to say, and you're fucking dreaming if you think I'll let you have it." He slides his hands into the pockets of his slacks and waits for my response.

I knew he wouldn't let it happen without a fight, so I'm lucky I came prepared for one.

"It's not up to you."

"Like fuck it isn't, Nicholas. You're my brother, a Casella, and we stick together."

"I can't fucking do this anymore, Ezra." I sigh, pulling out a cigarette, placing it between my lips, and lighting it. The cathartic act provides me with a brief sense of relief from the conversation I'm initiating.

"I need you here."

"No, you don't. You have Rafael, you have Jackson and Asher. You don't need me. Not anymore."

He shakes his head, dropping his gaze to the ground, considering my words.

"You and I both know I wasn't meant for this life. It's not what I want. It's *never* been what I wanted."

He pauses, and for a moment, I think he might fight me further.

"Do you remember the day Dominic burned down the tree house in our country home?" he asks, bringing me back to the moment I knew my life would always be miserable with him in it.

"Vaguely." Sarcasm oozes from my lips, and he smiles, knowing I recall it like it happened yesterday. Dominic woke up one morning and decided that day was our last day to be children, to enjoy the things most children enjoy, and so he torched it.

With everything inside.

"I won't ever forget how crushed you looked."

I shrug. "It was one of the least terrible things Dominic had done."

He sighs, running a hand over his face, then placing it on my shoulder, his black eyes finding mine. "I *never* want to see you in pain again." His voice is low, insinuating my manic-depressive episodes of bingeing whatever drug was closest to me, and in this moment, I truly appreciate all he's done for me.

"Ezra—"

"You don't need my permission, because your mind is already made up." It's the first time in a long time that I've seen my brother smile. Not the crazy one he shows off when he kills—no, the sincere smile I knew from when we were young, kicking soccer balls and chasing girls.

I clench my jaw, fighting the emotions pooling inside my eyes as I remove the cigarette from my mouth, and he pulls me in for a hug, slamming his chest into mine, gripping my back with one hand. I nearly succumb to tears when he speaks again.

"This isn't goodbye. Our bond will remain unbreakable, Nicholas, no amount of distance could change that."

Without another glance my way, he walks back inside, leaving me with all new hope for mine and Darcy's future and a sense of loss, knowing that things will change in our family and depending on where we end up, distance may become part of our reality.

CHAPTER FORTY-NINE
Darcy

Forks and knives clatter around the dining table and muffled voices surround me, but my eyes are glued to Ezra and Nicholas standing out back. I can't make out what they're saying, but I know the conversation is important because Asher, Jackson, and Rafael remain at the table.

Aries shuffles in her seat, her hand resting on her large belly as she takes a sip from her cup of tea.

"Are you okay? Do you need something?" I ask her, and she winces.

"Yeah. Can you get this baby out of me?" she huffs, and I give her a sympathetic smile. "Doctor says it shouldn't be long now, but it feels like I've been pregnant for three years."

"That's what you get for marrying a Casella," Asher jests, and she throws her knife at him. "Hey, hey…chill."

"You're lucky it's a butter knife." She raises her eyebrows, daring him to say anything else.

I glance over to Rafael, who's now sitting back in his chair, pushing around a half-eaten Danish on his plate with a fork. We haven't had a chance to speak, and I wonder if he hates me because of the secrets I've kept from him.

It's as though he feels my gaze on him, so he looks at me and smiles, and it makes me wonder what it's like for him to find his family and be around them when he grew up with no one. To know that all this time, he was a product of pure love between two people who were destined to share a life apart.

"Can we talk?" I ask him, and he nods, standing to move to the other room.

I follow him, leaving the rest at the dining table. He stops and turns around to face me, but I can't meet his gaze because I feel ashamed. Embarrassed that I hid this from someone I love so dearly.

"I don't blame you for any of it, Darcy." His gruff voice breaks the silence, and I look up into his ocean eyes. "You did what you had to do."

"That shouldn't be an excuse as to why I didn't tell you about Gabriele."

He shrugs, completely unfazed. "It doesn't matter to me."

"Why?"

"Because I lived all my life without these people. I don't need them to survive."

His curt words send a pang of sympathy straight into my chest. I feel sorry for him. Sorry that he didn't get to experience life with his family.

"What you did—"

"I know. It was stupid, and I wasn't thinking." Sighing, I cross my arms, itching for this uncomfortable feeling to go away. I never feel like this in his presence, and I hate that I do now.

"Your death wouldn't have solved anything, you know that, don't you?"

"The Dixons wanted *me* because of what I knew. If that secret were to fall into their hands or others, it could have caused outrage amongst their loyal followers, and you know this," I explain.

"What I'm trying to say is that whatever happens between the founding families should not result in you dying a martyr. What you did was the opposite of everything I taught you."

I scoff. "Give me a fucking break, Raf. I don't need a scolding from you."

Before I can turn away, he grabs me by my wrist, and I stop to look up at him. Something flickers in his eyes, and I can't be too sure if it was uncertainty or anger.

He takes a breath before he speaks. "I'll always look out for you. Being a Casella or a Guerra doesn't change anything between us."

Slipping my hand into his, I smile, remembering the deepest parts of ourselves we shared with each other. The feelings we poured onto the pages for the other to read. Despite only knowing each other from afar for a long time, it only strengthened the understanding and mutual respect that grew between us, surpassing any geographical barriers.

"What happened back at the house?" I ask because Nicholas hasn't shared anything with me yet, and I doubt he knows either.

"James escaped through a broken window, before we could get to him."

Anxiety gathers into a ball inside me. "So he's—"

"Alive." He finishes my sentence for me.

"Now what?"

Two sets of footsteps enter the room, and I slowly take my hand from Raf's to turn.

"We've located him and a few of his men north of London," Ezra answers. "Tomorrow night, we will be ending this." He turns to face Nicholas. "Are you up for one last hurrah, brother?"

A smirk curls on the corner of Nicholas's mouth and he nods. "Until death."

The night flew past in a blink, filled with chatter and laughter, and if anyone else was watching, they would not believe all the events that transpired between the few people here tonight. After our chat, Rafael mentioned that after they handled James, he would go back to Italy with Dante. I knew he wouldn't stay here.

Why would he?

There's nothing tying him to London, and as he's said so himself, blood ties aren't strong enough to generate that much of a pull, even if he shares the blood of two of the most prestigious families in London.

"Don't be late," Ezra calls out to Nicholas as he escorts Aries and helps her into the passenger seat.

Asher clasps a hand on Nicholas's shoulder and smiles at me, then looks at him. "You finally fucking did it…"

Nicholas bites back a smile and gives Asher what can only be described as a "bro hug."

"Don't forget about me amongst all your disgusting happiness." He grins and begins walking to his car.

"I'll see you tomorrow, you wanker." Nicholas chuckles, closing the door and turning to me. "Finally." His hands are on me, running over my breasts, down to the button on my jeans as he kisses me.

"Wait…" I tug his hands off me slowly, and he looks up at me, confused.

"What?"

"What did you talk about with Ezra?" The suspense is killing me, and I just need to know.

He groans. "I promise to tell you if you let me lick every fucking inch of you." He picks me up, and I instinctively wrap my legs around his waist. His tongue invades my mouth, pushing, taking his pleasure from mine, and I moan, the vibrations of my voice lingering on his lips.

"I can't wait to have you all to myself..." he whispers between kissing me. "Every. Fucking. Day."

Sliding out of his hold, I take a step back and remove my shirt, flinging it to the ground, and he watches me intently, waiting on my next move.

"I think I want to play a little..." I tease, slowly removing my bra and letting it slide off my arms and to the floor.

Groaning, he takes his bottom lip between his teeth, making me want to suck it free. "Haven't you played with my heart enough, *fenice*?" He smiles, taking a step toward me.

Flashbacks of that night race through my mind, and I feel my face fall. Would it always be like this? Forever stuck in the guilt of the pain I caused him?

"Hey, hey...where did you go?" He closes the gap between us and cups my face into his hands, his worried eyes finding mine.

"I'm so sorry, Nicholas," I say with sincerity, and his brows pull together at my apology. "I will never forget the way you looked at me that night."

"Shhh, hey, I said that as a joke." He trails his hand down to mine and places it flat on his chest, covering mine, until I feel the beating beneath it. "Shit happened between us that we both are not proud of, but I wouldn't ever dream of changing it."

"Why?"

"Living in the absence of you each night reminded me of just how much you taught me to feel. Without you, I'd be stuck on the path of death, but you brought it to me and showed me just how much I did not want to die." He places a gentle kiss on my forehead before tangling his fingers through my hair and tugging, causing my neck to crane and his eyes to blaze through mine. "When I felt that bullet, all I saw and felt was you."

I swallow down the guilt at his admission and take his lips with mine, the familiar fire burning between us. Only this time it's passion instead of blind hatred.

"Nicholas…" I breathe through our kisses as his hand glides down to my pants, unbuttoning my jeans.

"Don't say it," he warns.

"But—"

"I don't need to hear it, *fenice*, because I've felt it the moment I saw you in that emerald dress in my apartment." His hand slides into my panties, and I feel his fingers glide into me as I grip onto his shoulders to stabilise myself.

"We hardly knew each other."

"The heart rarely listens to the mind." He plunges his fingers deeper, and I struggle to stay upright, clinging to him as my toes curl with desire. "Now it's your turn to let go of everything you know, because once we make it out, I'm going to show you a world you've only dreamed about."

His hands work fast to remove my pants, along with my panties until I'm standing naked in front of him. Without losing a second, he lifts me, taking us both out to the back. The brisk breeze hits my bare back, and it annoys me that he's fully clothed, so I begin pulling at his shirt.

"Why am I always naked when you're not?" I whisper through our tongue-twisting kisses, and the rumble of his husky chuckle makes my pussy clench.

"Hungry for it, *fenice?*" He smirks, lowering me onto the side of the hot tub and removing his shirt, the light of the moon skating over his bare chest, accentuating all the perfect divots of his muscles. My eyes are glued to him as he removes his clothes, finally standing before me, his pierced cock hard and ready. My stomach flips, wanting him inside me and wanting to taste him at the same time, so I slide into the hot tub and lean back, my head hanging upside down.

"Starving." I grin, watching the glimmer in his eyes as he steps forward, placing his muscular legs on either side of my head.

"Should we have a safe word?" he asks but doesn't wait for me to answer, and I feel the tip of his cock on my lips. Opening my mouth, he slides himself inside, groaning with every inch he gives me. Gliding my hand down into the water, I slide my fingers into myself and moan around him.

"Fuck," he hisses, driving himself further into my throat. I stick out my tongue, inviting him further, and he accepts my offer, thrusting himself deeper. "You look devastatingly powerful," he rasps, groaning with another thrust.

Pulling himself out, I watch as a string of saliva connects my mouth to his cock. He pumps himself, gathering my saliva, smearing it over my mouth and down my neck as he reaches over me and down to my pussy, forcing my hand away.

I moan when his fingers enter me, rocking my hips, I

greedily thirst for my own pleasure as his cock twitches in front of me. Cradling his balls into my hand, I push his cock into my mouth as I swirl my tongue along his crown, feeling his cock harden.

"If you keep doing that, I'm going to come," he warns, ripping himself from my mouth and swiftly getting into the water with me.

"Isn't that the point?" I ask sarcastically, wiping the excess saliva from my mouth, and he gives me a sly smile, pushing me to my front and forcing me to brace myself with both hands on the edge.

A rush of adrenaline flows through me at the feel of his lips behind my ear. "Not until you come on my cock."

He stretches me inch by inch, the veins on his arms protruding as he grips the edge of the hot tub, pushing his cock deeper into my pussy. Our movements are slow at first, working up to the fire building slowly as he glides his hand between my legs and begins to drive me insane with his fingers over my clit. Chuckling, he slams into me, my body jerking forward. "I quite like it when you lose control."

My moans fill the night air as I lay my chest onto the side of the tub, and he drives in deeper, taking his pleasure. "Harder," I whisper, and he complies, removing his hand from my clit and twisting his fingers into my hair, tugging my head back.

"Do you miss it?" he asks in a breath. "The way I fucked you before?"

"Yes…" I barely recognise my voice, the heat beginning to billow through me, taking over all of my senses.

"Ask me for what you want, *fenice*."

He makes me work for it, but I don't mind because I

like this push-and-pull game that we play. In one moment, he can be in control, and the next, the roles are reversed.

"I need you to fuck me like you still hate me."

Without a minute wasted, he thrusts into me harder, the sting in my skull growing as he rams into me, his other hand curling around my breast and pinching my nipple. I gasp at the pain, and he pulls me into him, my back arched, my neck craned.

"You didn't warn me that this would become addicting…" he begins as he wraps his hand around my neck, squeezing. "The sensation of pain with pleasure."

"Once an addict, always an addict," I tease, earning me a snarl as his hand grips tighter, his movements becoming angrier. I feel myself reach the edge, one I'm not afraid to jump from and yield—letting myself go around him once again.

"For you, I will remain addicted to feeling if it means I get to keep you." His release follows mine, but he doesn't let me go. He keeps me there until he's emptied himself into me completely.

CHAPTER FIFTY
Nicholas

When do you get to call yourself a survivor? Because that's what it seems people are calling it these days after surviving something like alcohol, drugs, or abuse. For me, it never truly sat right to call myself a survivor because I never truly survived, I just existed. Existed in a world hell-bent on moulding me into something I wasn't. I don't hate who I am, and I'm certainly not ashamed of what I've done.

Not anymore.

It takes too much pressure and unnecessary guilt to carry on your shoulders every fucking day, so there is one thing I will agree with.

Acceptance is key to growth.

You cannot grow until you accept your past, and that's what I've been learning to do.

I was an addict.

I was an alcoholic.

I was abused.

I'm no longer ashamed of it because this is me.

"So, have you decided what you're going to do after this?" Asher asks me as Rafael loads bullets into his handguns.

"Not sure." I shrug, but the truth is, I do know. I know

I want to get as far away from London as I possibly can. I want nothing to do with it anymore.

"Probably focus on making it up to his wife with how he mistreated her, I assume?" Jackson says, lifting the corner of his mouth, holding back a smile.

"She's the one who shot me." I defend my actions, and Rafael scoffs like he has something to say.

"Enough." Ezra slams a machine gun on the desk, sending objects clattering to the ground. "We are here to finish this fucking war."

All eyes are on him as he speaks.

"For too long we have lived in a way we thought might bring peace amongst the founding families, not realising that greed would be the cause of our downfall. It ends tonight." He looks to Rafael, who cracks his neck from side to side. "We are now tethered together by blood, and I will not have it broken by those gutless fucks thirsty for power."

"They die tonight," Rafael snarls, standing and cocking his gun.

"I have one request." Their eyes shift to me as I stand and slide the gun into my holster. "James is mine."

Darkness envelops us, casting shadows over any possibility of positive thoughts as our men gather behind us. The house is small, in the middle of acreage that was probably used as a farm many years ago.

The drive up to Cambridge took fucking forever. Sitting in a van with five other men who had nothing but revenge and blood on their minds was taxing. Ever since I decided I wanted to live a life outside the confines of the founding families, I cannot lie and say I didn't think about the feeling you get when you take a life. The finiteness of the moment, the power, everything that comes with watching the light diminish from their eyes.

Will I miss it?

Will I crave it one day randomly in the life I'm about to lead?

Will a part of me regret leaving all this behind?

Leaving all I *know* behind?

It's fine to want a different life, to fantasize about it even, but it's different to pursue it and make it become your reality.

These heavy thoughts weigh down on my chest, and I wonder if it'll be enough. The silence, the peace, and the all-consuming love I feel for Darcy.

I'm wrenched from my thoughts as a light flicks off in one of the rooms of the house, and Ezra snaps the magazine into his machine gun next to me.

"They've got backup." Rafael's voice echoes through my earpiece, and a shiver rolls down my spine at the impending violence. "Looks like Enzo's men."

"I fucking hate him," Asher whispers from my left as he eyes the property, bursting with the need to sprint to it.

Dante wasn't meant to be here tonight, but he insisted on being part of this takedown for Rafael. It seems as though their bond is what a brother's bond should look like. Granted, I know nothing about him, but I can sense he feels protective of him, as does Rafael.

"Whenever you're ready, King." He speaks, and Ezra grins, gripping the gun harder in his hands.

"Fall in on three." He sneaks closer through the grass, inching his way to the house. "One."

I wait, feeling my heart nearly shatter my ribcage, a reminder to keep breathing.

"Two."

I swallow down the rest of the nerves and hold my handguns in each hand, preparing myself.

"Three."

Under the darkness, silhouettes of bodies sprint to the house in silence as do I, following closely behind Asher. We don't know if they see us coming, but we don't care either because it ends tonight.

"Oh fuck!" one of the men at his post yells as he fumbles to reach for his gun, resulting in his blood being plastered on the wall behind him, and this is when the chaos unfolds.

Gunfire reverberates through the vacant air as a rush floods through my veins. The house is filled with men, some loitering and others by their posts. Ezra barges through the doors one by one, unloading an entire magazine in under thirty seconds, sending bodies dropping to the floor.

I see Enzo flee through the back door, and without a thought, I follow him, chasing him through the dark. "You better fucking run!" I call out after him, and he fires a few shots back at me, all of them missing me by an inch. Asher follows me, running closely behind, taking shots of his own, but the darkness hinders his ability to aim perfectly.

Enzo's laughter echoes around us, making the fury inside me boil. I stop, holding a hand out to Asher, and he halts as we turn our heads, searching the land around us for a sign of Enzo. There's tall grass on our left and cornfields on our right. He could've easily slipped through either side.

"Fuck this." Asher sprints into the cornfield, and I curse at him for not thinking. This must be what he felt each time he begged for me to see reason, and I don't like it. I fucking hate it.

"Asher!" I call out behind him, following him into the cornfield, catching glimpses of him through the greenery. It feels like forever passes, and I see a small opening, leading back to the house, so I follow it, but I'm stopped in my tracks when I see Asher's gun by my boot. When I look up, he's kneeling before Enzo, blood gushing from a wound on his head and his nose, flowing freely down his chin. He looks over at me, and in that moment, I blink just as the sound of gunfire echoes around me, followed by silence. Asher's body falls limp to the ground as I raise my guns and fire in Enzo's direction, but I'm too late. His men have arrived, and in a flash, he's gone.

Fuck, fuck, fuck, fuck.

"No, no, no, no." I run and drop to my knees, sliding on the wet mud to get to him. "I swear if you die, I will never fucking forgive you." My voice comes out croaky as I fight back the emotions. Lifting his head, I wipe the blood from his face and notice Ezra, Jackson, Rafael, and Dante emerge from the house. "Breathe, Asher, just fucking breathe through it."

"A-Asher?" Jackson sprints to us, his hands flying to his head, assessing the scene before him. "Fuck." He falls to his knees, taking Asher into his arms. He cradles his head, tears rushing down his cheeks as he sobs. "ASHER!"

His eyes begin to droop, and the rage inside me turns to grief when he closes his eyes, taking one last breath. My hands dig into the dirt, bracing myself, beginning to mourn the loss of someone who was a part of me my entire life. A pain I thought I'd only experience when we were old and senile makes me nauseous as I try to focus on my breath. I feel a hand on my shoulder, and when I look up, Ezra's lips thin, his expression turning sombre.

"James," I force out through the tightening of my throat, and he nods.

"Burning with several bullets in his skull as we speak." He motions to the house, the flames eating up the wood, sparks spurting into the black night, and more than ever, I thirst for revenge.

Flicking the cigarette in my hand, I lift it and take a drag, blowing the smoke into the air. It wasn't supposed to happen this way, and it certainly wasn't meant to be him. The air smells stale, with ravens vocalizing above the resting place of my dearest friend, the moon's light cascading over the freshly carved stone.

Here lies Asher Frederick Guerra, beloved son, brother, and friend.

I can't bring myself to read the rest because he was meant to live his life, to see the world, have children, and grow old, watching them conquer the world he would've planted at their feet. I grit my teeth, the ache behind my chest growing stronger with each wave of grief that plagues me.

"I'm sorry," Darcy whispers from beside me, resting her head on the side of my shoulder.

I can't find my words because they don't fucking exist. No words could sum up the feeling of his absence, and I know what he would say. He would tell me to move on, to forget the pain, and to be smart about my next moves, and to focus on my life, but I can't even bring myself to think about it. Not once did I think I'd live in a world without him by my side, and now that I stare at his headstone, it becomes clearer to me.

"We don't have to leave." She consoles me, and I love her more for it. For knowing what I'm thinking without me having to say it.

"We will, eventually." I flick my cigarette to the ground and smother the burning tip. "I just need to know if you'll stay." I lower my gaze to her lips, and the corner of her mouth curves into a small smile.

"I'm with you, whether we're at war or at peace." She turns me to face her, the green of her eyes darkening in the night. "But right now, you need to speak with your brothers." She motions me forward, her hand in mine, as we enter the old church.

Ezra sits in the front pew, phone in hand, as Jackson and Rafael speak in a hushed tone, visibly planning our next moves. Rafael nods at something Jackson says, and Dante stands facing the crucifix. He places his necklace on his lips and looks back up at Jesus hanging on the cross.

Jackson and Rafael notice me entering the church with Darcy, which gathers the others' attention, and Ezra stands to walk to me. I've never been a religious person, not back in my teen years when it was forced upon me, and not now. Not when things as dark as death, blood, and revenge consume our world.

"Do we know where Enzo is, or has he fallen into a fucking hole again?" I ask Rafael, and he slides his hands into his pockets.

"It'll be harder to find him this time, but we're already in motion," he answers, not a sliver of emotion to be seen on his face, making me pause and really assess him.

"Do you even fucking care?" I seethe, and Jackson steps between us.

"It's not the time to fight." He places his hand on my chest, and I try not to take out my frustration on him.

"I may not have known Asher as well as you, but I do care," Rafael insists, pushing Jackson out of his way so he can see me. "I care because I swore I would help this family, and although I didn't know him, I will seek the penalty for his death from Enzo."

Clenching my jaw, I pause before I nod, not wanting to create animosity between the few people I care about.

"My question is, will you be joining us, brother?" Rafael asks, extending a hand to me as Ezra, Dante, and Jackson watch me with apprehension, but there's no reason for them to hesitate because I'm willing to do whatever it takes to see Asher's death avenged.

"An eye for an eye until the whole world is fucking blind."

EPILOGUE
Darcy

TWO YEARS LATER

The sun beams through the open windows as I lay there, reminding me of a time when I had wondered if a moment like this would come. If I would ever experience this with Nicholas, and I'm beyond grateful I stayed to help him through the healing, because now we get to enjoy everything we missed.

My fingers trace the wings of the phoenix tattoo on his back as I stare out the sleek, crisp white window.

"It's beautiful," I whisper more to myself, watching the clouds move in the sky and hearing the sound of water spraying and splashing against the shore. I didn't know this was what I wanted until I had it. The love I thought I didn't deserve from the man I once hated.

My fingers run over the scar on his back, and I smile. Long ago, I only felt sick with guilt whenever I would see or feel the scars I had inflicted on him, but now, it reminds me of how we fell for each other.

So irrevocably hard.

So unapologetically.

I thought love was give and take, but for us, love is fire and that fire is what keeps us returning to each other every single day.

Nicholas stirs beneath my touch and turns to face me, pulling me into his embrace, our naked skin brushing against each other.

"I don't think I'll ever get used to this." He smiles, placing a gentle kiss on my lips.

"Get used to what?" I giggle when he buries his face into my neck.

"Waking up to you basking in the glorious sunlight…" He kisses my neck, trailing down slowly to my chest. "The promise of having you by my side tomorrow…" Kiss. "And the next day…" Kiss. "And the next."

"But we're so far from home," I say, and he raises his eyes to mine.

Smiling, he gives me a wink. "That's the beauty of it, *fenice*."

His knee separates my legs as he sticks two fingers into his mouth, swirling his tongue around them, and I wonder if *I'll* ever get used to this sight. Him on top of me, making me feel things only he's been able to make me feel.

I gasp when he trails his wet fingers down my pussy and slides them into me. Bucking my hips, I try to push them deeper, and he chuckles, pressing his thumb on my clit.

"I love when you get greedy," he rasps, licking my lips and thrusting into me with his fingers, my arousal now covering them.

My breath shakes and my nipples harden as he takes my mouth with a feverish passion. Running my hands along his back, I explore the ridges of his muscles, the same ones I once loved to hate, but now all I can think of is running my tongue along the dark ink over his body. Breaking the kiss, he flips us so he's on his back and I'm on top. I watch him reach for something behind him, and he smiles when my eyes widen.

"What are those?"

"Nipple clamps." He grins wickedly, holding them in his hands. "Thought you might enjoy a little bit of pain with your pleasure."

Grabbing them, I place each clamp on my nipples, feeling a slight initial sting at the contact. The chain attached to them dangles, and I moan when he gives it a little tug.

"This is going to be fun." He slips out a leather band—something that looks like a collar with a thick chain attached to it—making my heart race. "Want to be my pet, *fenice*?"

I smile, and he places the collar around my throat, buckling it behind my neck. Bracing myself on either side of his head, he yanks the chain, jerking me closer, my face now an inch from his.

"Do you want to be a good girl or my dirty little toy?" he whispers against my lips, and I almost forget to breathe.

I answer him with my actions when I slide my hand down his body, fisting his hard cock, spreading his precum over the crown. "I'll be whatever you want me to be."

He groans, releasing the taught chain, and I slide down to take his cock into my mouth, licking up his shaft, gently fondling his balls in my other hand, and he curses.

"Fuck, I love watching you like this." His cock twitches in my hand, and I smile. The power I feel when he can't hold himself back is unlike any other I've felt.

"Tell me how you want to use me," I say before I take him into the back of my throat and out again, my saliva now coating half his cock.

"Deeper," he commands, pulling on the chain around

my neck, forcing me downward as he thrusts into my throat. "I want to hear you choke."

And I do exactly that. I open my mouth wider and take him deeper, still so many inches of his cock remaining. I push myself to go further, and I choke when his piercing touches the back of my throat. My wet choking, along with the sound of me heaving for air, fills the room, and he chuckles. The one sound that turns me on more than anything is his deep, throaty chuckle.

"That's a good girl."

I moan at the praise he's giving me and pump the lower half of his cock as I work my mouth on the top, then take him into my throat and stick out my tongue.

"Get up." He yanks on the chain, causing the leather to rub against my skin as he rises with me, forcing me face-first against the wall. I try to push off the wall but he holds me there, threading the chain between my legs and rubbing it against my clit.

"What makes you think I'll listen to you?" I play, knowing what I'm asking for, and like a good husband, he gives it to me.

"Playing *that* game, are we?" He holds the chain taut, and I cry out as the pressure on my clit grows. "Do you want to come, *fenice?*" he asks in a low voice, and I squeeze my eyes shut, trying to ignore the arousal building in my body because I want to win at whatever game it is we're playing.

"No," I breathe, willing my hips to remain in place, but it seems they have a mind of their own as I slide my pussy back and forth on the chain, feeling the cool metal rub against my clit. The clamps around my nipples tug, and I groan, moving my hips faster.

"Say my name, Darcy." His body is now against my

back, his breath beside my ear, and I push back against him, rubbing myself along his cock.

"Make me," I whisper, and he fists my hair, pulling my head back, making the pressure on my clit grow with every second that passes.

"You want to be my dirty little toy, do you?" I don't answer him, and he growls, pulling my hair tighter. "I asked you a question."

Smack.

The skin on my ass stings as a moan escapes me, my clit rolling on the chain pressing against it. "Yes," I whisper, breathless. "I want you to use me."

The tip of his cock prods against my pussy, and I gasp when he enters me slowly, stretching around his thickness. Bracing myself against the wall, I push back, taking more of him, but it's not enough. He senses my desperation and begins thrusting into me, filling me with almost every inch of him.

My breathing grows heavy, the clamps on my nipples bumping against the wall, causing the teeth on the clamps to tug on the raw skin. Biting my bottom lip, I stifle a moan when the chain of the collar dangles loosely in front of me and Nicholas's fingers pry my jaw open.

"I want to hear it, *fenice*." His ability to be rough with me draws an animalistic need from deep within, and I almost salivate as I reminisce about him taking my ass on his motorbike.

"And I said, *make me.*" I reiterate my words from earlier, making him angrier or hornier. I can't tell which when he slides out of me completely, and I whimper at the loss of his body on mine, but it isn't long before I feel his fingers fiddle with the buckle behind my neck.

Ripping off the collar, he closes his hand around my

throat, turning me to face him. His eyes are wild, filled with lust and desire.

"You might regret that…" He spits onto his hand and strokes his cock whilst holding me captive with the other around my throat. "Because when I'm done, you're going to be kneeling in a mess of your own cum."

I smile in defiance, and he smirks, sliding his fingers down and into me.

"You think I'm joking?"

I don't respond, and he begins fucking me with his fingers hooked inside me, and I curl my toes, the pressure inside me rumbling, just begging to be released.

Fuck.

He moves quicker, and with one press of his thumb over my clit, I cry out his name, shuddering with every pulse that shoots to my pussy. I think I get a moment to breathe until he takes his fingers out and tastes them.

"Kneel," he orders, and I do, one knee before the other, watching him stand above me, stroking his length.

"Do you like it better when I'm your good girl or your dirty little toy?" I grin, watching him lose his mind at the sight of me like this, the veins in his forearm and neck pulsing as hot streams of his cum coat my chest.

One crucial lesson grief has taught me is that it never stops hurting, no matter how much time has passed.

Still, to this day, I'm plagued with memories of my best friend, my brother, who walked through life by my side, never once straying from his loyalty to me. Picking up my slack and catching my vomit at times, he'd always been there, and I wish I didn't regret the way I took him for granted. The way I dismissed him each and every time he would beg me not to use, to see reason, and to live my fucking life.

Some days it hurts less when I think about all the good times we shared with each other, and other days I want to drown myself in the bottom of a bottle just to avoid feeling.

No matter how many years it's been, a reformed addict will always have this part to them.

Desperate, weak, and depressed.

The only light I see is her...my wife. She's been the only one able to pull me out of this hole, once when I was so determined to end it and again when I lost Asher. I did terrible things during the last two years, all of which were deserved by my counterparts, but I'm not proud of it. I thought I wanted a world where we could move on from things like revenge, but as it turns out, revenge is what makes our world spin.

London is now a memory in the back of my mind. I visit when I need a reminder of who I am and where I've come from. Most importantly, it's what keeps me grounded here, knowing that part of me is still accessible if I need it. The murderer and the prince, readily available if the time should ever arise.

Sweat trickles down my back at the beaming heat of the sun as I gulp down the coldest water I could find. All this time spent here and I still struggle with the heat.

"That was a rough day if I'd ever had one." Gilly wipes the remnants of the black smoke from his cheek and guzzles down some water.

"Fuck, you'd think this would get easier." Vick chuckles, removing his uniform.

When I came here asking for a job, they almost immediately took me in. Only, I had to complete a thirteen-week course on intensive practical tests and theory sessions. I don't know what I thought it would be like to be one of them, but I know how much they sacrifice, and the people who work at this station are probably the most selfless of men.

"Nicholas, you did well, mate." Gilly slaps a hand on my shoulder, smiling.

It had been weeks since the fires started, taking some homes and threatening wildlife, so that meant we were on duty. It was my job to save people for once, instead of taking their lives, but no matter how many lives I save, it won't ever come close to being absolved from those I took.

"It was a cunt of a day." I smile back at him, and he chuckles.

"You've only been here a short time, but you're already sounding like one of us."

It's hard not to feel at home here, amongst other people who want anything but violence. The days are mostly the same: wake up, give Darcy a kiss, and head to the station, then come home and have sweet, hot sex with my fiery wife.

After the short drive home, I head into the expansive kitchen and catch the scent of one of her freshly baked red velvet cupcakes. It's become one of my favourites. The pan is still warm, meaning she must have taken them out of the oven not long ago. Lifting one to my nose, I take a whiff, and saliva pools in my mouth, but before I can take a bite, her green eyes pierce into mine.

"Don't even think about it," she growls, snatching it from my hand and placing it back on the tray. "I get paid for these."

I groan, swallowing the saliva in my mouth. "I can pay you."

A smile creeps onto her face, and I can tell she wants to hide it. "No, Nicholas. How many times have I told you this is a business, and you can't just come home to eat all the things I bake for my customers?"

Even in her pink apron smothered with chocolate, she looks fucking divine.

"Have you forgotten who I am?" I pull her into me, and she pushes against my chest.

"You're going to get soot all over me."

I ignore her protest and press my lips to hers, smearing blackness over her pristine skin. "You used to be okay with the dirty look." I chuckle, watching her eyes glimmer. "In fact, you used to love it."

Her resistance stops, and she threads her fingers through my hair, taking my lips with hers, my cock hardening beneath my pants when she smiles at her victory. Pausing, we stare at each other, both of us wanting to ask the other the one question that's been on our minds since we arrived but neither having the courage to, so I finally bite the bullet.

"Are you happy, *fenice?*"

She doesn't answer me for a minute and takes a breath, making my heart race in my chest.

"If this isn't—"

"I'm living the life I always wanted," she whispers. "With the man I love beside me. That's all I need to be happy, Nicholas, but are you?"

I let go of my breath, relief flooding over me as I lift her, placing her on the counter and spreading her legs. "Every single day I get to spend between these thighs is a high I'll never give up."

Thank You!

Thank you so much for reading!

The third book in this series is currently underway.

Rafael and Nera's story is still being written
but keep an eye out on my socials for more information
on main tropes, blurb and cover reveal.

Although it is the third book, it will be an interconnected
stand-alone in the Casella brothers' series.

Have you read Ezra's book yet?

'The Casella King' is available now!

EZRA

They call me King, but it's just the mask I wear to conceal the true evil behind it. If I wasn't born into this life, I'm afraid there would be nothing on earth that could satiate my thirst. Not for the thrill that comes from killing a man, no. That doesn't last long. Nothing could fill the void where I store countless bodies and souls, only to thirst for something more. To feel something other than emptiness.

It's my turn to continue the Casella bloodline, and I will do it my way. Striking a deal with her was the first part of my plan to get my family off my back, but she doesn't know that I plan to keep her. Even if she begs for me to let her go, I will make her see just how much she belongs in my world.

ARIES

I thought the only evil in my life would be my drunk father, but it turns out, there is something darker that lies in wait for me. Meeting Ezra was the easiest part of my story, it's everything that came after that was difficult. He is everything they say he is, and more, but there is something about the way he looks at me, the way he only sees me that terrifies me.

They say everyone has their own demons they wrestle with daily, but Ezra doesn't. He embraces them and treats them like his friends. What scares me the most is how the darkness within me awakens every time he's near, like his abyss snuffs out the light within me. It spreads into my veins, consuming me, until I no longer know who I am without him.

About The Author

Welcome to my corner of heaven, where the villains and heroes drop to their knees before strong women. My books will have you clenching your thighs and reaching for the bedside table for your best friend.

If I'm not writing, you can find me chasing my favourite bands in concert, or curled up with a glass of red, reading a filthy book.

To be the first to find out about upcoming titles, you can sign up for my newsletter at
https://www.cbfreyauthor.com/subscribe

Thank you for supporting independently published authors.

Join C.B. Frey's Morally Grey's reader group:
https://www.facebook.com/groups/1501524207371036/

Find C.B. Frey on social media:
Facebook: https://www.facebook.com/profile.php?id=
100094454168503
Instagram: https://www.instagram.com/c.b.freyauthor/
TikTok: https://www.tiktok.com/@c.b.freyauthor

Acknowledgments

Firstly, I want to thank my friends in this industry who have guided me, supported me, and continue to be the bedrock of my sanity. I appreciate you sharing your knowledge with me and welcoming me into the world of self-publishing. I don't take your advice lightly and I hope other self-published authors have the same support you all give to me.

To my husband, who continues to stand by me no matter what. I appreciate the journey we've been on together and look forward to the next with you right beside me. I hope our son gets your work ethic and honesty in life.

To my friends who continue to support me, those who attended my very first book signing this year, and those who cheer for me every step of the way. I love you so much for it.

To my cover designers, I appreciate all the effort and work it takes to put a good cover together and I thank you for putting up with my one million and one changes. Same goes to EJ from Quirky Circe. I know I'm annoying, but I appreciate you never telling me so.

Finally, to my editor, who continues to teach me each time she edits. You are amazing, and I thank you for prettying my words and making them make sense. I know the manuscript always looks like a hot mess when it arrives in your inbox, so I appreciate the time it takes to edit.

I am beyond grateful to have such a supportive team around me, always cheering me on to follow my dreams and desires no matter what they may be. I feel so very grateful to have had the opportunity to tell this story and look forward to where this will take me in the future.